I KNEW
YOU WERE
TROUBLE

Paige Toon

I KNEW YOU WERE TROUBLE

SIMON & SCHUSTER

First published in Great Britain in 2015 by Simon & Schuster UK Ltd
A CBS COMPANY

1 3 5 7 9 10 8 6 4 2

Simon & Schuster UK Ltd
1st Floor, 222 Gray's Inn Road
London WC1X 8HB

www.simonandschuster.co.uk

Simon & Schuster Australia, Sydney
Simon & Schuster India, New Delhi

A CIP catalogue record for this book
is available from the British Library.

PB ISBN 978-1-4711-1880-7
eBook ISBN 978-1-4711-1881-4

Typeset in Goudy by M Rules
Printed and bound by CPI Group (UK) Ltd, Croydon, CR0 4YY

MIX
Paper from
responsible sources
FSC® C020471

Simon & Schuster UK Ltd are committed to sourcing paper
that is made from wood grown in sustainable forests and supports the Forest
Stewardship Council, the leading international forest certification organisation.
Our books displaying the FSC logo are printed on FSC certified paper.

For my former English teacher, Chris England,
and the students at Altwood School.
Thanks for the memories.

Hello!

Before you get started on *I Knew You Were Trouble*, I just want to say a big thank you for buying it – I really hope you enjoy reading it as much as I enjoyed writing it!

If this is the first book of mine you've picked up, then you may not know how much I love hearing from my readers, so please drop me a line to say hi on **Twitter @PaigeToonAuthor, www.facebook.com/PaigeToonAuthor** or **Wattpad.com/PaigeToonAuthor** – I'm dying to hear what you think about Jessie and her journey so far.

I also wanted to mention that last year I launched a unique, free book club called *The Hidden Paige*. Think of it as DVD extras but for books – featuring extra content, free stories, news and competitions, all delivered directly to you in one handy email.

There's more information about *The Hidden Paige* at the end of this book, along with an exclusive Jessie-related short story that you will have missed out on if you're not already a member. But to avoid that happening again, do sign up at **paigetoon.com**!

Now, without further ado, here's *I Knew You Were Trouble*…

Lots of love,
Paige
Toon x

Prologue

'Stop looking so worried.'

'It's just… I don't know, Jessie, you've got a bodyguard for a reason.'

I scowl out of the window at the scenery flashing past. 'Yeah, and it's ridiculous,' I mutter under my breath.

Four months ago, I didn't even know that I *had* a dad, let alone that he's a famous rock star. It was all fun and games in the beginning when my identity was still a secret, but now it's out there that I'm Johnny Jefferson's daughter and everything's gone one stop too far on the crazy train.

He doesn't say anything and, when I look back at him, his jaw is rigid with tension. My eyes travel along the length of his long, lean arms until they rest on his tanned hands gripping the steering wheel. I'm suddenly tempted to unclick my seatbelt and climb closer so I can press my lips to his warm neck, but I know that would be pushing my luck. He's come over all protective these days.

He glances in the rear-view mirror and his frown deepens.

'What is it?' I ask, my thoughts still on kissing him.

'I don't know,' he murmurs. 'That white van has been behind us for a while.'

I swivel in my seat and look through the back window, but I can't make out anyone in the driver's seat. 'You're being paranoid,' I say, brushing him off, and then he's swerving off the main road into a smaller one.

'Whoa!' I gasp, trying to stay upright. The van flies straight past us on the main road. 'See?' I exclaim. 'Nothing to worry about. Jeez! Pull over.'

He doesn't bother indicating as he crunches to a stop at the entrance to a private driveway. I flash him a dark look and wrench open the door, hopping out onto the gravel.

'Oi,' he calls. 'Where do you think you're going?'

'I need some air,' I state, slamming the door shut.

A moment later he joins me. I glare up at him.

'Come on, maybe we should go to your dad's place,' he says gently.

I stare at him, incredulous. I can't believe he's saying that to me. 'No!' I raise my voice. 'I'm sick of feeling like a prisoner! I just want some alone time with my boyfriend – is that too much to ask?'

'Hey,' he says softly, sliding his arms round my waist and pulling me against his firm chest. To my surprise, I discover I'm fighting back tears.

It's all been too much. I want my anonymity back. I'm fed up of getting harassed by the press and being followed around by a bodyguard every minute of every damn day. I'm sick of it all. I just want to be left alone. So today I made a run for it. I'm free! And now he's telling me to go back? No bloody way.

'Kiss me,' I demand, tilting my face up to him.

He touches his lips to mine, but withdraws all too quickly. 'We're parked in somebody's driveway,' he says uncertainly.

I start to laugh, but the sound is verging on manic, the laugh of a crazy person that's been locked up for too long.

I take a few steps backwards, away from him. He snatches my hand and pulls me towards him and this time he kisses me like he means it. The sun, surprisingly warm for October, beats down on our heads as his hands circle my waist and then he pushes me back against the car door and traps me with his body. We kiss like it's our last, and it is so, so sweet. I draw a sharp breath as he wrenches his lips away from mine and stares past me, over the car roof. His whole body tenses.

'The van,' he says in a low, urgent voice.

Before I can roll my eyes, I hear it, like thunder, hurtling towards us. And then it screeches to a stop and my heart stops with it because I *know* we're in danger.

'RUN!' I scream, shoving him away from me. 'RUN!'

Six weeks earlier

Chapter 1

I stare contemplatively at the girl in the mirror. She looks the same as her reflection of a couple of months ago. She has the same light-blonde hair, tied back into an untidy braid, the same green eyes, outlined with black mascara, and the same school uniform cut daringly high. But she's not the same girl. She is anything but.

Before the summer holidays, that girl there was Jessie Pickerill: an orphan of six months. But *I'm* Jessie Jefferson, daughter of a global megastar. The only thing is, hardly anybody knows it.

My ears prick up at the sound of my rock-star dad's name being mentioned on the radio.

'Johnny Jefferson's world tour sold out in minutes on Friday. Which lucky people among you managed to get tickets?'

I smile to myself. *I'll have ringside seats!* Of course, the tour isn't until next year – ages away – so I'll have to put it out of my mind for now. But the thought of hanging out backstage with

Barney and Phoenix, my two little half-brothers, makes me want to spontaneously combust on the spot.

'Are you nearly ready?' Stu, my stepdad, calls up the stairs.

'Coming!' I call back, my stomach instantly swamped with nerves.

If Mum were here, she'd hug me tightly and then crack some joke to make me laugh. But she's not here, and I don't want to cry today, so I try to put her out of my mind.

It's my first day of school in Year Eleven, but I'm unusually apprehensive. My friend Natalie has moved on to sixth-form college, and my ex-best friend Libby is now living in her new bestie Amanda's pockets. I have no idea where I stand with Tom, the boy I had a crush on before the summer holidays. We were meant to go on a date, but I haven't been in touch with him since I got home from America. I've been so busy and, I don't know, maybe I've missed that particular train. I guess I'll find out soon enough.

For a moment, Jack's blue-grey eyes stare back at me from inside my mind and the image is so tangible, I want to reach out and push his black hair away from his face.

I'm still certain he'd break my heart if I gave him the chance. But God, I fancied him. Unfortunately I still do.

'We're going to be late!' Stu calls.

'I'm coming!' I shout back again, grabbing my bag and pushing all thoughts of LA bad-boy rock-stars-in-the-making out of my mind.

Just one more year to get through, I remind myself as I jog down the stairs, and then I'm free to do what I want. Free to move to America if I want to. Free to tell the world that *I'm* Johnny's long-lost, fifteen-year-old daughter.

4

No one would believe it if they could see me now.

I pull the front door shut and climb into Stu's little white Fiat, looking back at our shabby 1970s townhouse.

As disguises go, mine rocks, I think with a smirk.

Everything may feel different, but it all looks weirdly the same.

'Have a good day,' Stu says, raising one eyebrow at me from behind his black, horn-rimmed glasses as he wanders off to the staffroom.

'You too,' I call after him, hesitating uncertainly in the corridor as he disappears out of sight. On impulse, I decide to go to the bathroom, where I play Candy Crush on my phone until I hear the nearby courtyard start to fill with people. I wish Stu didn't have to come into school so early. He's a Maths teacher here, so he doesn't really have a choice. Libby would sometimes get in early to hang out with me, but those days are well and truly gone.

I sigh and switch off my phone, stuffing it into my bag as I hear someone enter the cubicle next to mine. I flush the loo and go to wash my hands, jolting when I see Amanda leaning up against the wall.

'Oh! Hello!' I say.

'Hi, Jessie,' she replies, her voice lacking the warmth she reserves for my former best friend. A split second later she switches her attention to the locked cubicle. 'Get a move on, Libs!' she calls good-naturedly. 'We're going to miss out on our table.'

An uneasy feeling rolls over me. Of *course* they'll be sitting together this year. I wash my hands quickly and leave the bathroom just as I hear Libby ask, 'Was that Jessie?'

*

The morning drags by. I end up sitting next to Louise, the new girl, in Science. Libby and Amanda sit at a table behind us. Libby gave me a little wave and mouthed, 'You OK?' as Amanda hurried her past me, but I don't know how she expected me to reply. It's not like I can talk to her about Johnny in front of everyone. She knows about him – she's been sworn to secrecy – but we haven't caught up properly since I've been home. I've spent most of my spare time with the Jeffersons. We all had to rush back to the UK together because Johnny's dad had a heart attack – luckily he's going to be fine. I got to meet him last week and he seems a real character. I'd like to get to know him better.

On top of that, shortly after I returned from LA, my grandmother passed away. I barely knew her – she hadn't been close to my mum or me, and she'd been in a home for years, suffering from senile dementia. But I was her last living relative, and she was my last blood connection to Mum, so I found it understandably difficult to organise everything and then attend her funeral. Stu helped and came with me, thankfully.

Anyway, with everything that's been going on, I haven't had a chance to see much of anyone.

After English, I spend break in the library on my own, before finding myself beside Louise again for History and Maths.

When the lunch bell rings, Amanda makes a big show of gathering all her stuff together and talking overexcitedly to Libby about going to eat their lunch on the playing field. I take my time and, after a moment, I become aware that Louise is doing the same. If I felt apprehensive about school today, I can't imagine how she must feel.

'Want to come to the cafeteria with me?' I ask her impulsively.

'Sure,' she replies, a little too quickly.

We follow Amanda and Libby out. Amanda has hooked her arm through Libby's and is whispering something conspiratorial into her ear. Her OTT behaviour makes me want to gag. *Libby is lapping it up*, I think meanly. Suddenly Libby looks over her shoulder at me and smiles.

'You coming to eat on the field?' she asks, pulling Amanda to a stop.

'We're going to the cafeteria.' I indicate Louise.

She nods. 'See you later maybe?'

'Not if I see you first,' I joke, but don't quite pull off my attempt at humour. Libby smiles at me awkwardly as Amanda steers her downstairs.

Disheartened, I traipse after her, turning to the new girl as we walk. 'Where have you moved from?'

'Portsmouth,' Louise replies, looking awkward.

She's about my height and has bleached blonde hair with dark roots cut into a choppy, short style. There's a tiny hole in the side of her nose that I'm guessing is from a piercing she's removed for school. I like her look.

'My dad got a job here,' she elaborates with a shrug. 'He's a doctor.'

'Cool.' She's just answered my next question. I try to come up with something else to ask her. 'Bit rubbish having to start a new school in your last year of GCSEs,' I say, as we reach the bottom of the stairs.

'It sure is,' she replies flatly.

Now I'm lost for words.

The smell from the cafeteria engulfs us before we reach it and we go to stand in the queue.

7

It's then that I see him: Tom Ryder, a few metres ahead of me. He's in sixth form now and looks even better out of school uniform. He's wearing denim jeans and grey Converse trainers with a faded yellow T-shirt, and his brown hair is streaked with highlights from the summer sun. As he turns to say something to his mate, Chris, I see his profile: straight nose, long eyelashes, bronzed skin...

I jolt when I realise that Louise is talking to me.

'Sorry, what?'

'Who's that?' she asks me, her lips curling upwards at the corners.

'Who?'

'Him.' She nods at Tom.

'Oh.' I shrug. 'Just, you know, Tom Ryder.'

She smirks at me knowingly.

I frown at her. 'Is that what you asked me?' I'm sure that wasn't the question she came out with when I was busy swooning.

'No, I was wondering if the food here is any good, but this subject is far more interesting.'

I blush and, to my mortification, Tom chooses that exact same moment to catch my eye.

'Hey,' he says.

'Hi,' I mumble, looking down as the burning sensation on my face intensifies. When I look up again, he's being served.

A few moments later he passes by with his lunch, but he doesn't say anything, just raises his eyebrows at me and gives me a small, uncomfortable smile. He's walking too quickly for me to strike up a belated conversation and my embarrassment transforms into disappointment. That wasn't at all how I expected our first meeting after the summer holidays to go.

A few minutes later I'm sitting at a table with Louise, deep in thought.

'Want to talk about it?' she asks, dunking a potato wedge into some ketchup and popping it into her mouth. 'You can trust me,' she adds. 'It's not like I'm going to tell anyone. You're the only person who's said more than two words—'

'I wish I had more to say,' I cut in, as an image of Amanda and Libby with their arms linked comes to mind. I could do with someone to confide in. 'Basically, we were supposed to go to the cinema during the holidays, but I went away and haven't had time to text him since I've been back.'

'You haven't had time to *text?*'

'I've been really busy.' I shrug defensively, not wanting to go into details.

'Wow,' she says, deadpan.

'It's not like he's texted me, either.'

And, from the look on his face as he walked past earlier, I doubt he ever will. I can tell by Louise's expression that she's thinking the same thing.

'Hey, chick.' Johnny's warm voice spills down the line early that evening. I still can't get used to calling him Dad. 'How was your first day back?'

'It was OK,' I reply non-committally.

'That good?'

'It was fine. What have you been up to?' I ask, changing the subject.

'Meg's been catching up with a friend of hers today, so I've had the boys to myself. We went to the park. Fed the ducks.'

Meg is Johnny's wife. When we first met, she and I had a few

9

issues, but she seems to be over her initial mistrust of me now. I hope so. I really want us to get on.

'Sounds nice,' I say, wishing I could have gone with them.

'It wasn't that nice. Barney slipped over in the mud and nearly fell into the river. Sam almost had a heart attack.' He chuckles.

Sam – Samuel – is one of Johnny's bodyguards from America, and came with the family on this trip to the UK. Barney, age four, is older brother to Phoenix, who recently turned one. They're so, so cute.

'I can just imagine,' I say, my voice still tinged with sadness.

'You alright?' Johnny asks with concern. 'You seem down.'

'Oh, you know, first day back and all. I miss you guys.'

'You'll see us this weekend,' he reminds me.

As if I could forget. I'm going to stay at their massive mansion in Henley. I can't wait.

'So what have you got planned for the rest of the week? School, school and more school?'

'I've got a birthday party on Friday night,' I tell him.

'Whose?'

'A friend of a friend,' I reply.

'Which friend?'

'Natalie. Her friend's name is Liam.'

'How old is he?'

'He's just turned eighteen.' Jeez, what's with all the questions?

'Isn't that crowd a little old for you to be hanging out with?' he asks.

'Are you taking the piss?!' Rock star or not, dads can be *preeettty* irritating.

'Just behave yourself,' he adds.

OK, that's one step too far. This is coming from a former womanising drink and drug addict! 'As if *you* can tell *me* to behave!'

'That's exactly why I *can* tell you,' he says coolly. 'I've been there, done that. I know where it gets you.'

'I get enough of this shit from Stu,' I complain.

'That's why I like your stepdad,' Johnny says cheerfully. 'Oh, and watch your mouth,' he snaps as an afterthought.

Stu was initially a little stand-offish with Johnny – I'm not sure he's quite forgiven him for the way he treated my mum.

I'm not sure *I've* quite forgiven him, I think with a pang. Mum died eight months ago, at the beginning of this year, and her death is still so raw. I'm getting better at not thinking about it every minute of every day, but sometimes it still hits me out of the blue.

She was killed in a freak accident on my fifteenth birthday. She'd been rushing around, trying to get everything ready for my party, and she'd finally hurried out of the house to buy my birthday cake. I waited and waited for her to return, getting increasingly pissed off with how long she was taking. Eventually that annoyance turned to dread.

All of my fears were founded. The police turned up to say that she had been walking along the pavement when a loose fourth-storey windowpane had crashed down on her, killing her instantly. I broke, then, and I'll never be fixed.

Mum had kept the secret of my real father's identity from me my whole life. A few months after her death, I began to resent the fact that I would never know the truth. Poor Stu didn't know what to do with me – I was being a total bitch. I had no idea that he knew who my biological father was and, when he finally made the decision to come clean, I didn't believe him.

I still remember the exact moment that I found out.

'*Please tell me*,' I'd begged him. '*I need to know. It's why I've been so… angry… I can't move on, I can't say goodbye to her. Not really. I'm so hurt and upset that she kept this from me.* Please…'

In the end, he came right out with it: '*His name is Johnny Jefferson.*'

That wasn't the moment, by the way. Like I said, I didn't believe him at first because Johnny is a household name, like über-successful. As if *he* could be my father!

But Stu explained that Mum was a groupie of Johnny's first band, Fence, before they became megastars. He said that she followed the band everywhere and was completely obsessed with Johnny, their lead singer. This seemed more plausible because Mum was such a rock chick.

I warned Stu that if he was lying to me I'd walk out of the door and he'd never see me again. Then – and *this* is the moment – he swore on my mother's grave that he was telling the truth.

I believed him, then. He wouldn't lie about that. I felt dizzy with shock, like my world had broken away from its axis and started to roll downhill.

That was just over two months ago, and my world is still out of control.

When I went to LA for the summer, Johnny himself told me what had happened between him and my mother, and it wasn't pretty. He said they hooked up after one of his concerts and had a bit of a thing going for a while, but, when Mum started to want commitment, he pushed her away. He even scored with another girl right in front of her. Bastard.

She never told him about me. By the time she found out she was pregnant, he was off on a world tour and stories about him and his groupies kept hitting the headlines. She realised she was just one of many. It broke her heart, and Stu was around to pick up the pieces.

So no, I don't think my stepdad has fully forgiven Johnny for his behaviour in the past, even if my dad is a changed man now, thanks to Meg and the boys.

The sound of a wailing child pierces my ears, bringing me back to the present.

'*You OK, buddy?*' Johnny shouts to his son over the cries.

'You gotta go?' I interrupt.

'Yep, sorry, Jess. Barney's banged his head on the table.'

'Ouch. Give him a hug from his big sister.' *Half-*sister, but no need to be technical about it.

'I will. Take care,' he says warmly. 'And be careful at the party!'

'Yeah, yeah,' I reply, but he's already gone.

By the time Friday rolls around, I've taken to calling Louise 'Lou', I've filled her in on the history between Libby and me, and she even knows that my mum died earlier this year, although I didn't give her many details. She's alright, actually. I like her. And it's a relief to have a new friend to take away the sting of Libby and Amanda's twosome.

'Any plans for tonight?' Lou asks when we're sitting on the field at lunchtime.

'House party,' I reply, distracted by Tom and his mates playing football. I didn't see him at all yesterday. It was raining so we spent our breaks in the cafeteria. He was probably in the sixth-form chill-out area. The *inner sanctum*…

'It's at Natalie's friend's house,' I elaborate. I've told Lou about Natalie, too. 'What about you?'

'Nothing. Well, I said I'd call Chloe after dinner.'

Chloe is Lou's best mate from Portsmouth. I'm not the only one who's pining for a friend. The difference is, Lou's circumstances were thrust upon her. I can only blame myself for the end of my friendship with Libby. I was hurting so much after Mum's death that I wanted to dull the pain, not add to it by talking it through all the time. And Libby's family is so perfect that being around them just reminded me of what I'd lost. I take a deep breath, trying not to dwell on Mum. I don't want to lose it at school.

'Why don't you come to the party, too?' I suggest.

'Thanks, but I don't want to gatecrash.'

'Nat won't care.' At least I don't think she will.

'OK, maybe,' she says.

I jolt as I see Tom glance our way, then someone kicks the ball at him and he's off again.

'Is he going?' Lou asks me, noticing who has my attention.

'I don't know.' I drag my eyes away to see Libby coming our way with Amanda in tow.

'Can we join you?' Libby asks, with a wavering smile.

'Of course,' I reply, pleased, ignoring the sour look on Amanda's face as she reluctantly follows suit and sits down next to Libby on the grass.

'How's your first week been?' Libby smiles at Lou.

'Not bad,' Lou replies.

I listen to their polite chat, trying to figure out why Libby is bothering. It's clear she's Amanda's now. In fact, she's so deep in her new friend's pockets that I'm surprised Amanda hasn't stamped MINE, MINE, MINE all over her.

Maybe she's missing me, a small voice inside me whispers. My instinct is to quash it, but I'm not sure that I want to.

I look towards the playing field again and, at that very moment, Tom locks eyes with me. A shiver goes down my spine as he smiles. I shyly return the gesture, then make a concerted effort to join in the conversation around me, but I still feel nervy for ages afterwards.

After final bell has rung, Lou and I walk out of the classroom together.

'So do you want to come tonight or what?' I ask her, slinging my backpack over my shoulder as we burst out of the double doors into the afternoon sunshine.

'Thanks, but I think I'll give it a miss.'

'You sure?' We walk across the cobbled courtyard.

'Yes, but thanks. Next time?'

'OK.'

At least I offered.

Up ahead, I see Tom exit the sixth-form block alone, pausing for a moment to wait for someone.

'Why don't you go and talk to him?' Lou suggests, as my footsteps falter.

'No, I couldn't.'

'Why not?'

'Things are too weird.' I shake my head decisively and glance up at Stu's corner office.

'He's looking at you!' Lou whispers urgently, making me do exactly what you're not supposed to do in this situation: shoot my head round and meet his stare straight on. Oops. It's now completely obvious that he's the subject of our discussion. Before I can look away again, he grins.

Lou giggles, I shush her and then his mate Chris walks out of the door behind him. Tom nods in our direction and they amble over to us.

'Alright?' I say casually, praying my face doesn't imitate a beetroot this time.

'Alright,' Tom replies. 'Hey.' He nods at Lou, and I introduce them.

'Are you going to Liam's eighteenth tonight?' I ask.

Tom frowns. 'Who's Liam?'

Disappointment surges through me. I'll take that as a no, then. 'He goes to college with Natalie,' I explain.

'You know Liam,' Chris chips in, elbowing Tom. 'He's Isla's sister's... What's her name?'

'Lauren,' Tom offers.

'Yeah, Lauren's ex.'

I stopped trying to follow the connection at the mention of Isla – Tom's ex-girlfriend. And I switched off when Tom implied he wasn't going...

'Oh,' Tom says slowly. 'Yeah, I know the guy. Is it at his house?' he asks me.

'I think so. I think anyone's invited,' I add lamely, hoping that's actually the case.

'You going?' Chris asks Lou.

'Maybe.' She shifts on her feet and, to my surprise, blushes. Does she like Chris?!

16

'Might see you there, then,' Tom says, bringing my attention back to him. I suddenly perk up again.

'Sure.' I nod casually and indicate for Lou to join me as we walk away. 'So are you coming after all?' I whisper.

'Maybe,' she replies, her colour deepening. 'I'll ask my dad.'

Chapter 2

'At long bloody last!' Natalie exclaims, as she engulfs me in a hug in her doorway.

'I'm only ten minutes late.' My voice is muffled by her shoulder.

She laughs and pulls away. 'No, I mean, about time we had a big night out. It's been how long? Let's make up for it now!'

We walk to the party. Stu dropped me at Nat's, but not without warning me to be good. 'You're as bad as Johnny,' I mumbled. He found this comment annoyingly funny.

'You look amazing. I love your dress!' Natalie gushes.

'Thanks.' It's a black and mint minidress that Johnny bought for me in LA, but I keep that information to myself. 'You too.'

She's wearing a black skirt with an H&M top that I recognise. It's pale blue, like her eyes, and contrasts well with her dyed-black hair.

'How's school?'

'It's OK,' I reply. Better today, thanks to Libby's effort. And the fact that I managed to speak to Tom without making a total fool of myself. 'But I wish you were still there,' I add. 'How's college?'

'Great,' she replies, flashing me an apologetic grin. 'Sorry. One more year and you'll be there, too.'

Or I'll be in LA. I've got no idea how my life is going to pan out in the next twelve months, or how I want it to.

I've already filled Natalie in on my time in America because she came over last week, so we spend the walk chatting about boys, namely Tom and Liam, the latter of whom is Natalie's current crush.

We pick up Lou on the way to the party and, when Liam answers the door to the three of us, I can see what Nat sees in him. He's a tall, skinny emo-boy with messy black hair, a lip piercing and a small tattoo of a thorny red rose on his right forearm. Totally and utterly her type.

'You got it done!' Natalie exclaims, grabbing his wrist and admiring his ink.

'Yesterday.' He laughs. It does look a bit raw, but still cool.

'Happy birthday,' Natalie says, proffering a bottle of vodka.

'Cheers.' He takes it from her as he shows us in. 'Drinks are in the kitchen.'

He disappears into the first room on his left, where Thirty Seconds to Mars is pounding out of the stereo. Natalie leads the way into the kitchen, flashing me a 'what-do-you-think?' kind of look.

'Hot,' I mouth, which pleases her greatly.

We grab a few drinks and head outside. After a while, my phone buzzes. My heart jumps when I see it's a text from Agnes, Jack's sister:

> Hey, you, bored out of my brains in Geography. Map of
> UK reminded me of you. How's life? Miss you.

I met Agnes in LA through Jack, but she's kept in touch ever since.

Unlike her brother…

I emailed Jack shortly after I got back from America, but he hasn't even bothered to reply. I really wish I hadn't now.

I text Agnes back:

> I miss you too. At a party. Nothing like Lottie's…

I smirk as I press Send. Lottie is Charlotte Tremway, a famous teen actress and the star of *Little Miss Mulholland*, one of my favourite TV shows.

It's going to be weird watching her on the small screen now that I know her. There are a lot of people here who would go nuts if they knew I'd been to a couple of her infamous parties.

Another text from Agnes comes in:

> I'm so jealous. Crap, teach seen phone. Gotta go.

I giggle and stuff my phone back into my bag, shrugging off Natalie's inquisitive glance. It's a weird feeling: my two worlds colliding in one small moment.

About an hour later I'm squeezed onto a three-seat sofa with five other people as the music pounds out of the stereo and straight into my left eardrum. I'm pretty tipsy now – it doesn't take much – and I'm having fun, despite the fact that Tom still hasn't turned up.

Liam is on the decks and he's just put on 'I'm Not Gonna Teach Your Boyfriend How to Dance With You' by Black Kids.

I love this song, even though it reminds me of Jack. I helped him DJ at Agnes's sixteenth birthday party in LA. Was that only a few weeks ago?

Before I can think about it, I'm squeezing out of my Natalie/Lou sandwich and pushing through the crowded living room to get to the DJ decks. Liam gives me a confused sideways look, but nods when I indicate his record collection. I dance along to the music as I rifle through his vinyl, smiling as I come to The Wombats. He looks amused when I point to 'Tokyo', then shrugs and takes the record from me. Jack's going to see The Wombats in LA this month, and for a moment I'm right back there with him...

He's leaning against the wall with his guitar in his hands, his legs stretched out and crossed in front of him. He plays a jaunty little tune and then he begins to sing, and I laugh out loud when I realise that the song is 'Live While We're Young' by One Direction. He doesn't know all the words, but he makes some up and it's so funny. I'd been teasing him by saying that he'd copied the POW! tattoo he has on his forearm from Zayn's ZAP! one, and Jack had bet me that he'd got his done first. (He had.) He gives his guitar one last strum and grins up at me, his black hair all sexy and dishevelled, and his blue-grey eyes twinkling as my heart flips over and over.

I want to hate him – he messed around with me while he was still seeing Eve, the lead singer of his band – but I can't.

I wonder if he's still seeing her. There's no way I'm going to ask Agnes. I try to put Jack out of my mind, but suddenly I'm standing in his games room, staring up into his eyes, the feeling of his warm, firm chest pressed against mine. And then his fingers are in my hair, his palm cupping my jaw, and his lips on mine.

I flush at the memory of our first kiss, and then I glance at the doorway and see Tom standing there, staring straight at me. Brazenly, I maintain eye contact and, almost instantly, butterflies take flight in my stomach. Talk about confusing.

'Er, *hello?*'

I jolt at the sound of Natalie's voice. I didn't even notice her approaching.

'Oh, hi!' I exclaim with a grin until I see her expression. My face falls. 'You OK?'

She leans in so only I can hear her. 'I'm *fine*. How are *you?*' Her question is laced with meaning and, up close, I can see her eyes dart pointedly towards Liam.

Oh, shit. Does she think I'm flirting with him? How stupid am I?

'Let's go get a drink,' I say, hopping out from behind the decks and taking her by the arm. 'Drink?' I shout at Lou as I pass. She nods and gets to her feet. Tom is no longer in the doorway, but my focus is on Natalie, anyway.

'I'm sorry,' I say, as soon as we're in the kitchen. 'I didn't mean to tread on your toes. It's just… that set reminded me of Jack. Black Kids… The Wombats… I wasn't thinking.'

'It's fine.' She brushes me off, but I can see that I've got to her.

I would never – ever! – hit on one of my friend's crushes. Doesn't she know me better than that? The answer, I find myself admitting, is no. She doesn't know me very well at all. We've only been friends for a few months.

'What's up?' Lou asks, catching up with us.

'Nothing,' Natalie and I reply at the same time, as we simultaneously crack open bottles of cider. Johnny and Stu never told me not to drink.

At that moment, Chris and Tom walk into the kitchen.

'Hey,' Tom says to me.

'Hi,' I reply with a smile.

'Didn't know you could DJ.'

'I can't really. I was just checking out Liam's record collection.' I change the subject. 'We were just about to go outside for a bit. Coming?'

'Sure.' He grabs a couple of beer bottles, passing one to Chris, and together we walk out to the garden, my pulse racing a tiny bit faster.

Dougie and Em, Nat's college friends, are smoking on the lawn, so we all sit with them, Tom next to me. I decline a cigarette while most of my friends light up.

'You quit?' Tom asks me with interest.

'Kind of. Don't feel like one at the moment.'

Johnny put me off when I went to stay with him in LA. One pep talk from my rock-star dad worked better than dozens from my geeky stepdad. I say that with affection. I love Stu to bits – he's the only father figure I've had for most of my life – but he doesn't know shit when it comes to misbehaving.

'Cool,' Tom says. Unlike Jack, he doesn't smoke. One–nil to Tom.

I listen as everyone chats around us. The grass is damp and the night air is cool, but it's a welcome relief after the stifling heat of the living room. I look up to see a clear night sky, the starlight muted by orange streetlights lining the road beyond the house.

'How was America?' Tom asks.

'Great,' I reply, tensing slightly.

'You went to stay with a friend of your mum's?'

That's the story I'd told him before I left. It was sort of true, but I wish I could be honest. Maybe I still can, in a way.

'Actually,' I keep my voice low, 'I went to stay with my dad. My real dad.'

He looks taken aback. 'Wow. How did that happen?'

I sidestep his question, unable to fully explain. 'I wanted to tell you before I went, but I didn't know what would happen.'

'But how did you find out who he was?' he asks.

I obviously didn't sidestep far enough.

'Turns out Stu had known about him all along,' I reveal.

'Not a criminal, then?' He gives me a poignant look. We had a bit of a heart-to-heart last term about how I'd feel if I found out my real dad was a lowlife. It was actually Tom who gave me the idea to ask Stu about him.

'No.' I smile. 'He's just an ordinary guy,' I add, before I can stop myself.

My first lie.

'How was Ibiza?' I turn the tables. I know he went with his mates.

He grins. The kitchen lights are reflected in his eyes, making them glint in the darkness. 'It was a laugh. Messy,' he adds.

We sit and chat, and after a while I feel myself loosening up. I'd almost forgotten how easy Tom is to talk to.

'Where did you go in America?' he asks me.

'LA,' I reply.

'Nice. Hot?'

'Very. My dad has a swimming pool so I spent most of my summer in it.'

'I can tell by your tan,' he says, and we instinctively press our forearms together to compare. My skin tingles at the contact and I laugh, pulling away. 'So what's the story? Who is he?' he asks, and for a split second I think he's talking about Jack, but then I realise he's continuing the conversation about my dad. God. I really have to sort my head out.

'It's complicated. But oh, did I tell you he has two sons? I have half-brothers!'

'No way!'

'All my life, I thought I was an only child. They're so cute.'

'What are their names?'

I stumble, not wanting to give the game away. 'I call them Bee and Little Bird.' This makes me cringe – half with embarrassment, half because I've just lied again. But I do call Barney 'B' sometimes, and I've often thought Phoenix looks like a little bird when he's eating. And a phoenix *is* a type of bird…

'Hey, what about *your* dad?' I switch the focus and instantly regret it when the smile slips from his face.

He shrugs. 'I never hear from him.'

'I'm sorry,' I say quietly.

Poor Tom. His dad left his mum last year. Ran off to America with a woman he'd been having a three-year affair with. So bad.

'Where in America is he?' I ask.

'San Francisco.'

'You won't call him? Try to see him?' My tone is tentative.

'Not any time soon,' he replies, his lips downturned.

'How's your mum?'

'She's OK. Lonely, you know?'

I nod, and my thoughts flit towards Stu. At some point, he'll get a new girlfriend, but the thought of him replacing my mum makes me feel like someone is squeezing my chest hard.

'What?' Tom snaps, whipping his head towards Chris. I'd forgotten he and the others were there. Chris must've nudged him. Tom looks up and I follow his gaze to see his ex-girlfriend, Isla, standing a few metres away from us. He broke up with her before the summer, and she does not look happy.

'Can I talk to you?' she mouths. Turns out I can lip-read.

I glance at Tom to see his face harden, then he nods, and my stomach plummets as he gets to his feet.

'Back in a bit,' he says.

I try not to look bothered about him stepping over my friends to reach his beautiful ex-girlfriend. I try not to pay attention as I watch Isla lead him somewhere private. I try not to think about what she's saying to him. Because whatever my feelings are – or were – for Jack, I'm here, now, with Tom. And I don't want that to end.

Once Tom told me that he and Isla were over for good; that he 'never goes back'. I hope that's true. Tall, slim and very pretty, with long dark hair piled up into a big, tousled bun on the top of her head, Isla doesn't look like the sort of girl many guys would walk away from.

'Let's go inside,' Natalie prompts, as I pull up handfuls of grass to keep my mind busy.

I nod quickly and get to my feet, dusting myself off. Somehow I manage not to look back as I follow her.

The living room is even busier than before, My Chemical Romance blaring out of the speakers now.

I notice that Chris is walking close behind Lou. She turns to say something to him and he smiles down at her.

Natalie pulls me into the crowd to dance, but I'm distracted. I wish I could numb the anxious burning feeling in my stomach. Maybe alcohol will help. I take a large gulp of my cider. Suddenly Liam appears, looking all sweaty and wasted. He wraps his arm round Natalie's neck and grins at me.

'Having fun?' he shouts, looking straight at me.

'Yeah, cool party!' Natalie shouts back. I just nod.

'I haven't seen you at college?' Liam says, again staring at me.

Natalie goes from looking like the cat that got the cream to thoroughly put out in one swift moment.

'I still go to school,' I reply uncomfortably.

'Really?' Liam asks, letting Natalie go and taking a step closer. 'How old are you?'

'Fifteen.' I shrug, shifting on my feet.

'Shit!' he exclaims. 'You look much older, man. Hey, you want to do some shots?'

He lifts up the bottle of vodka that Natalie gave him earlier. It's half empty.

'No thanks,' I reply.

'I will!' Natalie exclaims, barely looking back at me as she drags Liam off the makeshift dance floor.

I nip to the toilet and, when I return to the living room, I see with a jolt that Tom is standing with Chris and Lou.

'Hey!' He smiles at me as I approach.

'Hi.' I don't want to ask him about Isla, but sometimes my mouth has a mind of its own. 'How's Isla?'

'She's alright,' he replies, looking a bit miserable.

'Are you and she…' I have to lean into his ear to shout this over the music.

'What?' He pulls away and glances at me with surprise. 'No.

No.' He shakes his head to reiterate his point, then he leans towards me and his breath is warm against my ear as he speaks. 'She wants to get back together.'

'Oh.' I straighten up and nod, but he pulls me back to him, his hand on my arm.

'It won't happen. It's over,' he says, sending a shiver rocketing down my spine.

His hand is searing my arm and, when he withdraws to look at me, my heart skips and skitters against my ribcage. There's so much meaning in those last two words.

'Why didn't we ever go to see that movie?' he asks with a frown.

'This summer was a bit crazy,' I reply with a small shrug of regret. 'But I'd still like to.'

'Me too,' he says.

Another shiver. He hasn't taken his eyes away from mine.

'I don't think Joseph Strike's film is on any more,' I say with a cheeky grin.

He rolls his eyes good-naturedly. 'I forgot you fancied him. I'm not sure I want to sit next to you drooling over some actor's pecs, anyway.'

I laugh and tuck my hair behind my ears.

'Want to see something else?' he asks, his gaze dropping to my mouth.

'I'd love to,' I reply, feeling an internal warmth that this time I'm certain is not alcohol-induced. 'When?'

'What are you doing tomorrow night?'

I'm going to see Johnny at his UK home, but I can't tell him that. 'I can't tomorrow. But what about Sunday?' I ask quickly.

'Yeah.' He nods. A moment later he looks past me. 'I think Chris likes your new friend.'

I glance over my shoulder to see Lou standing on her tiptoes as she says something into Chris's ear.

'I think the feeling's mutual,' I reply with a smile. 'Shall we ask them if they want to come?'

'Sure,' he replies with a nod.

I don't know what makes me look to my right, but, when I do, I see Isla surrounded by her friends, and they look like a pack of wolves out for blood. Specifically: *my* blood. Suddenly I'm being yanked away from Tom, away from the living room and out into the corridor. I stare in surprise at the thief trying to steal my hand from my arm and come face to face with Natalie.

'What the—' I start to say, then notice her expression. 'What's wrong?' I ask with concern. She looks upset.

'What a wanker,' she spits.

For a split second, I think she's talking about Tom, but then I realise she means Liam. 'What did he do?'

'He's just a twat. I don't want to be here any more. Are you coming or not?'

'Where do you want to go?' I ask.

'Home. Come with me?' She sounds like she's pleading, which is rare for Natalie.

I nod tersely. 'Of course.'

The relief on her face is palpable.

'Are you OK?' Lou asks, appearing by our side.

'We're leaving,' Natalie snaps.

Lou's expression freezes. 'Oh.'

'You can stay,' I suggest, feeling sorry for her.

'No.' She shakes her head. 'I'd better come with you.'

I wouldn't want to stay at a party without my friends, either, even if I was interested in a boy.

'I'm just going to say goodbye to Tom,' I tell them.

'I'll meet you outside,' Natalie replies, stomping towards the door and yanking it open. I hear it slam, even over the noise of the music. I flash Lou a wary glance and we walk together back to the living room. Tom and Chris are in a huddle by the back wall.

'We've gotta go!' I shout.

Tom frowns. 'Really? Why?'

'Nat's not well,' I reply. 'But Sunday?' I cast a meaningful look in Chris's direction and Tom nods, turning to him and Lou.

'Do you guys want to come with Jessie and me to the movies on Sunday night?'

Lou's eyes light up and I feel better as they both say yes. Tom smiles down at me. 'I'll text you.'

'OK.' I nod and, as sparks fly between us, I sense he wants to kiss me. Surely it's only a matter of time, I think with a thrill, as I turn away from him. Jack and LA suddenly feel like a hazy dream.

Once more, Isla and her friends watch me as I leave the room, and I try not to care. I've got a date with Tom Ryder!

Chapter 3

'Hey, girl,' Johnny says warmly, opening the door wide and wrapping one tanned, tattooed arm round my neck. He pulls me in for a squeeze, but my face barely touches his neck before he releases me again. His hugs never last long enough.

'Hi,' I reply, my face burning a little. I always feel shy when I see him after a break. It's only been a week, but I still don't know him that well really.

'Stu,' he says with a friendly nod, leaning past me to shake my stepdad's hand. 'Time for a cuppa?'

Stu's going to visit his parents today, so I'm staying here alone tonight.

'Sure,' Stu replies. He still seems a little awkward. I don't know if he'll ever feel totally at ease in front of my rock-star father.

Before we've even stepped over the threshold, the little ball of energy that is my half-brother Barney appears in the hallway.

'Jessie!' he shouts. 'Come and see my Lego station!'

I laugh as he drags me towards the playroom at the back of the house. It's actually a bit of a relief to get away from Stu. He complained that I stank of booze and fags this morning and I hadn't even been smoking. As for the drinking… Jeez, give a girl a break. I can't be an angel *all* of the time.

Johnny and Meg's UK base is a seven-bedroomed Georgian mansion in Henley. When they moved back to LA, they thought about selling or renting it out, but in the end it stayed empty for when they visit. I guess it's not like they can't afford a spare home or ten…

'Hey, you,' Meg laughingly says when Barney and I burst into the playroom – a large, airy room stocked with toys, comfy sofas and bookshelves crammed with brightly-jacketed books. She's sitting on the carpet in the bay window with Phoenix, my one-year-old half-brother. They're surrounded by Playmobil emergency vehicles.

Meg gets up to give me a hug. At five foot eight, she's taller than me by a couple of inches and she's slim and pretty with straight, shoulder-length blonde hair and brown eyes. She seems genuinely happy to see me, which makes me feel kind of gooey inside.

Phoenix's face lights up at the sight of me. He babbles something incomprehensible as he gets to his sturdy little feet and waddles over.

'Hi, cutie,' I say, breaking away from Meg to pick him up and give his cuddly body a squeeze.

'Look, Jessie, look!' Barney interrupts, tugging on my hand. 'The cars go in here.' He starts to prattle on about Lego so I put Phoenix back down, flash Meg a grin and give the eldest of my two small half-siblings my full attention.

Meg leaves us to say hi to Stu, but returns after a few minutes with the temptation of chocolate-chip cookies, the one thing that is guaranteed to get my little brothers' feet running in the direction of the kitchen.

'How are you? Good week?' Meg asks with a smile, as the boys tear off down the corridor.

'It was OK,' I reply. 'How was yours? Johnny said you were catching up with a friend this week?'

'Bess.' She smiles. 'You'll have to meet her one of these days.'

'Is she a good friend?' She must be if Meg is willing to reveal my identity to her. So far, she's been keen to keep it hush-hush.

'The best,' she replies. This makes me think of Libby and my heart hurts. 'How's school been?'

'Oh, you know.' I shrug.

'Missing Natalie?' she asks. 'And maybe even Libby?'

'A bit,' I admit, a little taken aback. I told her about Natalie moving up to college and Libby finding a new friend in Amanda, but I guess I didn't think she'd remember. I still have a small chip on my shoulder that I'm not welcome here, but I really need to get over that. She's been nothing but nice to me for weeks.

'Come have a cup of tea before Stu leaves. We'll have plenty of time to chat later.'

'OK.' I nod and follow her to the living room.

Johnny and Stu are sitting on oversized brown leather sofas. They stop talking when we enter the room and Stu clears his throat.

'Not gossiping about me again, are you?' I ask wryly.

'I hear you had a big night last night,' Johnny replies, equally wryly.

'It wasn't that big,' I scoff, slumping down next to him and sinking into the comfy cushions. 'And despite what he'll tell you,' I say, giving Stu a pointed look, 'I wasn't smoking.'

'Your room certainly smelled like you were when I woke you up this morning,' he says.

'I had a couple of drinks, but that's all. Jesus, it's not like I wasn't offered cigarettes, but I said no! I wish I'd said yes if I'm going to get stick for it anyway,' I snap.

'OK, OK.' Stu puts his hands up in defeat. 'I believe you. Sorry.'

'You should be,' I reply crossly.

Stu looks hurt and that makes me feel bad.

'Where are the boys?' Johnny asks Meg, changing the subject.

'Eddie's got them in the kitchen,' she replies. Their American cook often travels with them.

Speak of the devil, Eddie walks into the room with a tray. 'Hi, Jessie!' he says brightly, placing it on a beautifully carved wooden coffee table.

The style of this house couldn't be more different to the Los Angeles pad, which is modern and sparsely furnished, with floor-to-ceiling glass featuring views over an infinity pool and the city beyond. Their American home is allegedly more to Johnny's taste, but I think Meg prefers it here, where a combination of modern and classic art hangs on the flocked wallpaper walls and the rooms are chock-full of antiques.

Stuart leaves shortly afterwards.

'You're too hard on him,' Johnny says when Stu's little white Fiat has driven out of the driveway and the heavy wooden gates have clunked shut behind him.

'I know,' I mutter, feeling a twinge of guilt. 'But he never believes anything I say.'

'Maybe you haven't given him enough reason to.' Johnny turns to me, his brilliant green eyes piercing mine. 'Time will sort it out,' he adds kindly, closing the front door.

I don't respond, but I still feel bad as we head back to the living room.

'So I didn't get a chance to tell you this, but my dad's coming to stay today as well.'

'Really?' My face breaks into a grin as I sit on the other sofa next to the empty space vacated by my stepfather. I wasn't bothered about sitting next to Stu when he was here, but I feel a bizarre sense of loyalty now that he's gone. 'How's he feeling?' I ask.

'Much better this week,' Johnny replies.

Johnny's dad had to stay in hospital for a few days after his heart attack and since then a nurse has been caring for him at home. Johnny took me to meet him for the first time about ten days ago. He still seemed pretty fragile, then, so I'm glad he's well enough to visit now. From what I gather, my grandfather got married to a younger woman a few years ago, but now they're divorced, and there isn't anyone special in his life. He was a full-blown womaniser when Johnny was younger, and I don't think age has changed him much. Johnny went to live with him after losing his mum to cancer at the age of thirteen. Unfortunately we have our mothers' untimely deaths in common.

'What are you thinking about?' Johnny asks me with a frown, seeing the expression on my face.

'My mum. Don't worry about it.'

He nods, his gaze drifting sombrely to the coffee table.

'So what time will he be arriving?' I ask. I don't know what to call my biological grandfather. Barney calls him Gramps, but that feels so familiar. I suppose I could call him by his first name, Brian, like Meg does, but at the moment he's just 'Johnny's dad'.

'Sam's gone to get him,' Johnny says. 'They should be back around lunchtime.'

'Cool.' I smile. 'It'll be good to spend some more time with him.'

'You know, you could always go to visit him once we're back in LA,' Johnny points out. 'You don't need us to be around for you two to catch up.'

My heart lifts at the idea, but stutters when I compute what he's saying. 'When are you going back?'

'End of the week,' he says gently. 'Meg wants to be back in time for Barney to start school.'

'Hasn't he missed the start of the school term already?' I ask with confusion.

'Private school. Starts back later,' Johnny explains, his eyebrows knitting together. We're both thinking the same thing: *I* don't go to private school. Not that I want to, but he doesn't know that.

'I've gotta get back as well,' he adds uncomfortably. 'Work to do. But we'll be here again soon and then, of course, you're coming to visit us at Christmas.'

That feels like ages away.

'I can't wait!' I try to sound upbeat. 'And I'd love to visit your dad while you're gone.'

'I know he'd like that, too.' Johnny smiles. 'He thinks you're – what did he say? – "sparky".'

'Oh.' I'm not sure if that's a good thing or not.

Johnny laughs. 'It's a compliment, believe me.'

I smile.

My phone buzzing against my thigh distracts me. My heart flips when I see a text from Tom.

Still good for tomorrow? What shall we go and see?

'What's his name?' Johnny asks.

'What?' I splutter, my eyes shooting up to meet his. 'How do you know it's from a boy?!'

'I know that look,' he replies nonchalantly. 'So?'

'So what?'

'What's his name?' he persists.

'Tom,' I reply begrudgingly.

'And is Tom your boyfriend or do you just want him to be your boyfriend?'

'What are you, my dad now?'

'Yeah, I am, actually,' he replies with a twinkle in his eye.

I chuckle. It's still so weird to have *Johnny Jefferson* giving me fatherly lectures. 'He's not my boyfriend. We're just going to the movies tomorrow night.'

'Aah. So you *do* want him to be your boyfriend,' he says.

'Might do.' I purse my lips and look down at my phone screen.

'And are you going to reply to him?' he inquires.

'Later,' I tell him with a grin, wriggling to shove my phone back into my pocket.

Johnny smirks, but his smile soon turns genuine. 'I'm glad you want to catch up with Dad. It'd give me peace of mind to know you're doing that,' he adds.

'I'm happy to.'

I hope Brian's going to be OK. I'm afraid of losing him now that I've found him so unwittingly. I feel a sudden pang of loss for Mum's mum, the grandmother that I never had a relationship with, and Johnny's mum, the grandmother I never even knew I had.

'Do you have any photos of your mum?' I ask Johnny.

'Course,' he says. 'You want to see them?'

'Yes, please.'

He leaves the room and comes back a minute or so later with a brown, leather-bound photo album. He sits down beside me and rests the weighty book on my lap, leaning over my shoulder as I open it up.

'Aw, is that you?' I coo, peering at the picture of a little boy with bright blond hair and green eyes. He looks just like Barney.

'Yeah.' He smiles and nods down at the photo. 'And that's Mum.'

The woman in the picture looks young – probably only mid-twenties – and she's slim with tousled blonde hair. She's wearing a colourful print dress and is smiling happily at whoever's taking the picture.

'She's beautiful,' I say.

'Yeah,' he agrees quietly.

I remember that her name is Ursula. I scrutinise the next picture in the album, one of Johnny and his mum standing in the middle of a small garden bursting with flowers.

'She looks happy.' I glance up at him.

'She was, for the most part. Or, if she wasn't, she put on a good act,' he says. 'Meg made this album for me,' he explains, as I continue to turn the pages. 'I used to keep all of my photos in a shoebox,' he adds.

'That was nice of her.' I smile.

'Will you show me some pictures of Candy sometime?' he asks.

'Really?' I wouldn't have thought he'd want to be reminded of what he'd done to her. And I haven't looked at my albums for ages. It hurts too much.

'When you're ready,' he says gently, and his understanding makes my eyes prick with tears.

I nod because I don't trust myself to speak. I turn back to the album and lean into him a bit more.

The energy of the house changes the moment Brian walks through the front door. He looks like an ageing musician, with slightly too long, greying, light-brown hair. His skin is tanned, but I heard Johnny saying to Meg how pale he looks, so I'm guessing he's usually bordering on leathery. There were dark circles under his eyes when I last saw him – they're less apparent now, but he looks thin. Thin and wiry, though still oddly good-looking. And I can't believe I'm saying that about an ancient.

'Jessie, Jessie, Jessie,' he says, once he's fought off the affections of his other grandchildren and managed to make it more than a metre or so into the hall. Samuel walks past us with Brian's overnight bag. 'Hey, girl,' Samuel says to me, clapping me on the shoulder with one of his big hands.

'Hi, Samuel,' I reply warmly.

He bends down to pick up my own bag. 'I'll take these up,' he says.

'She's in the Orange Room,' Meg calls after him.

'Got it.' Samuel sets off up the stairs.

Johnny and Meg always seem to name their guest bedrooms

after colours. In LA, I stayed in the White Room. It was properly amazing.

'How's it going, kiddo?' Brian asks me.

'I'm good,' I reply with a smile. 'How are you?'

'Never better,' he exclaims. I notice Johnny cast Meg a look. She purses her lips at Brian's flippancy. He nearly died.

We spend the next couple of hours hanging out in the garden, playing croquet of all things. Meg wins two games in a row, cheering in a purposefully over-the-top fashion until Johnny grabs her and throws her over his shoulder, pretending to be annoyed. She squeals until he puts her back on her feet.

'What are we doing tonight?' Brian asks when they've calmed down.

'Eddie's got a roast planned,' Meg answers, slapping Johnny playfully.

'No offence to Eddie, but can't we go out?' Brian asks. 'I've been cooped up at home for weeks.'

Her face falls. 'I don't know if that's such a good—'

'Come on, Meggie,' Brian interrupts her jovially. 'Do this old man a favour. Isn't there a nice restaurant on the river where we could sit and watch the world go by? I've been bored out of my brains and I'm finally feeling perky again.'

'Sure, Dad, we can go out,' Johnny interjects casually, wrapping his arm round Meg's neck.

'Johnny…' Her voice trails off.

He glances down at her. 'What's the problem, babe?'

Her eyes dart towards me, and it finally dawns on me that she's not worried about Brian's health: she's worried about my cover being blown.

'It'll be fine,' Johnny says in a low voice, flashing me an

apologetic smile. 'I'll let Eddie know.' He claps me on the back as he begins to walk towards the house. 'You need to get ready?' he asks.

'I might change,' I reply.

'Cool.'

I don't dare look back at Meg as I follow him inside.

I get ready quickly, swapping my shorts for a pair of blue jeans. It's a sunny day, but it might get cold later. I choose a cream lace top and touch up my make-up, then head out of my room, stuffing my phone into my handbag. I still haven't replied to Tom. I need to check out what films are on first. I feel jumpy at the thought of sitting next to him in the dark.

'You want me to make a booking?' I hear Meg ask when I'm halfway down the stairs. She and Johnny are waiting at the bottom, a few metres away from Samuel, who appears to be standing sentry just inside the front door. He normally spends his time in the guardhouse by the gates, so I'm guessing he's driving us.

'No, don't call ahead,' Johnny decides. 'Let's go incognito.'

'Sir,' Samuel says. It sounds like a warning.

'S'alright, Sam, you can wait in the car.'

'Johnny…' Meg says.

'It'll be fine,' Johnny reassures her, glancing at me as I reach them. 'Dad?' he calls down the hall. Brian is with the boys in the playroom. 'You ready?'

'Coming!' Brian calls back.

Johnny grabs a baseball cap from one of the coat hooks and pulls it on.

'That's doesn't help,' Meg comments wryly.

'Fffff-udge it,' he says, stopping short of swearing. He rips the cap off and tosses it on the hallstand as Brian appears with his grandsons in tow. 'Let's go,' Johnny says.

As we walk out into the warm air, I notice that he's wearing a long-sleeved T-shirt, and I'm guessing he's trying to keep his telltale tattoos hidden. I'm pretty sure that his attempts to disguise his identity will be futile, though. His celebrity aura radiates from him like expensive aftershave. You barely have to glance at him to know that he's famous.

We should look like any other family. But Johnny doesn't look like any other dad. He's a little over six foot tall, with chin-length dark-blond hair. He has stubble at the moment, but he's often clean-shaven, and his eyes are an intense green, not unlike my own, or so I've been told.

The waitress leads us out onto a terrace overlooking the River Thames. The people at the next table start whispering before I've even pulled out my chair.

'Maybe I'm the one who should have gone in disguise,' I murmur when I see two teenage girls gawking at me from a couple of tables away.

'Put these on, just in case anyone starts taking pictures,' Meg says in a low voice, handing me the sunnies from her handbag.

'It's OK, I've got my own,' I reply, pulling them out and sliding them onto my nose.

Luckily it's sunny, otherwise I'd look like a right twat.

I notice Brian frowning at Meg. 'What's the big deal?' he finally asks. 'So what if they find out who she is?'

'She'll be harassed,' Meg explains irritably.

'*I* don't get harassed,' he says with a casual shrug. 'And I'm his father.'

42

'Yeah, you do, Dad,' Johnny chips in wearily.

'Not as much as I'd like,' Brian replies with a cheeky grin.

Johnny raises his eyes to the sky.

'Alright, girls?' Brian says to the two middle-aged women drinking glasses of white wine at the next table. They titter their replies.

I order a lemonade and lime and plaster a smile on my face, but I can't relax.

Later that night, when I'm on my way back to my bedroom from the guest bathroom, I hear hushed but irate-sounding voices coming from the downstairs living room. Last time I heard Johnny and Meg arguing, it was about me. I'm guessing nothing's changed. My heart sinks as I pause at the top of the stairs to listen.

'It was a bad idea,' I can just make out Meg saying. 'I know what it's like. Being well-known is *hard*. I'd take anonymity any day of the week.' Pause. 'Don't look at me like that,' she continues. 'You know I wouldn't change my life with you for a second. But Jessie is only fifteen.'

'The boys cope well enough with it,' I hear Johnny reply in his deep voice.

'They were born into it,' Meg replies reasonably. 'They don't know any different. But I remember what it was like to be fifteen. Going on dates, meeting boys…'

'Do I really need to hear this?' he asks.

'Oh, shut up,' she snaps good-naturedly. 'The point is, being ordinary is underrated. Jessie deserves to have a bit of normality before her whole life is turned upside down.'

'Alright, kiddo?' Brian says, making me jump. He's peering up at me from the bottom of the stairs. He proffers the glass of water he's holding. 'You want one?' he asks.

'Er, no, it's OK, thanks, er…'

'Call me Gramps,' he says, starting up the stairs.

I try to smile at him, but my face is frozen.

He cocks his ear towards the living-room door, then tuts. 'Don't worry about it,' he says, as he arrives at the top of the stairs, panting slightly. He puts his hand on my arm and guides me back towards my room. 'It'll all come out in the wash. Night, kiddo.'

'Night, er—'

'Gramps,' he confirms with a grin.

'Gramps,' I say, finally able to offer him a shaky smile.

I return to my room and sit disconsolately on my bed.

Johnny warned me that my life would change once my identity's out in the open. He told me I'd have to have a bodyguard accompanying me to school, out on dates, *everywhere*, and I wouldn't be able to live in my house any more because it wouldn't be easy to secure it against intruders. I can't really believe that such precautions are necessary, but I suppose that whenever you see the Beckhams, or Brangelina and their brood, there's always a horde of bodyguards with them. Johnny knows both families, and is easily as famous as they are.

This is all so crazy. The thought of having to move house makes a lump swell in my throat. You wouldn't have thought I'd be so attached to such a crappy pile of bricks, but I am. It was Mum's home. I can still feel her in it. I'm not leaving, even if it is 'unsafe'.

A big part of me wants everyone to know that I'm Johnny's daughter, but, at this moment, I hope that Meg's fears are unfounded. I'm not quite ready to be stared at yet.

I pull back the covers and climb into bed, then remember Tom's text. I quickly look up the film times on the iPhone Johnny gave me back in LA before replying. Lou can make it, and Tom texts me back to say that Chris can, too, so we arrange to meet in the foyer at six o'clock. His last text reads:

Night x

He signed off with a kiss. I wonder if he'll kiss me for real tomorrow. Feeling all jittery, I slide further down under my bedcovers and try to think about him instead of the niggling feeling in the pit of my stomach. I'm not sure if I feel uneasy about the possibility of my identity being blown, or the fact that I'm going on a date with Tom instead of Jack.

Chapter 4

'Go on, just say it,' I hear Johnny snap the following morning.

'I'm not saying anything,' Meg replies unhappily. They're in the kitchen and I'm about to round the corner.

'Go on, it's easy,' he says. '"I told you so."'

'Don't get shitty with me, Johnny,' Meg replies sharply.

'What is it?' I ask worriedly, walking into the room in time to see Johnny drag his hand across his mouth in a despairing gesture.

They both start at the sight of me. The kids are nowhere to be seen, but I knew that already as they don't swear in front of them.

Johnny casts Meg a wary look, but before he can answer I lean past him and pick up the iPad on the table.

I'm suddenly short of breath. The headline on the website for a local newspaper screams out at me:

Is Jefferson's secret daughter a local?

My heart skips a beat and I hear Johnny sigh heavily. He resignedly walks over to me and puts his hand on my back as I stare at the article.

There are three grainy pictures of me sitting at the restaurant table last night with Johnny and his family. One is of me grinning as I help to feed Phoenix, another is of me straightening my ponytail, and the last features Johnny and I smiling across the table at each other.

Words and sentences swim in front of my face:

Blonde like her father…

Had an English accent…

Didn't remove her sunglasses…

Staying with the Jeffersons…

Already part of the family…

Who is she?

If you have any information, contact…

I gasp, staring up at Johnny in shock as I read this last part. My eyes dart towards Meg.

'It's OK,' she says calmly. 'You were wearing sunnies.'

'Thank God you told me to,' I murmur.

'Why weren't we informed this was going to break?' Johnny is really worked up.

'It's just the website for a local rag,' Meg says. 'They think they can get away with anything.'

'They'll be running it in the paper tomorrow,' he says. 'And then the nationals will pick up on it, if they haven't already.'

'I'll do what I can,' Meg replies.

'That's not your job any more. Why hasn't Annie been in touch?' he snaps. Annie is his personal assistant in America.

'It's the middle of the night in LA,' Meg says reasonably.

47

'She should have come with us!'

Meg sighs, seemingly lost for words. She used to be Johnny's PA – that's how they met. She still helps him out, and obviously thought she could handle his business affairs while they were in England, rather than uproot Annie for the sake of a few weeks.

The phone rings. Flashing Johnny a bleak look, Meg answers. 'Hi, Stu,' she says, her shoulders sagging as she glances at me. I notice that she's still wearing her pyjamas. She must've rolled out of bed to this news. 'You got my text?'

I feel a wave of homesickness at the thought that my stepdad is on the other end of the line, worrying about me.

'Yes, she's right here. We were a bit slow on the uptake, I'm afraid, but I'm about to call Wendel.' That's Johnny's solicitor. I met him when Stu first told me Johnny was my dad. 'Can I put Jessie on the line?'

She hands me the phone, flashes me a small smile of sympathy and leaves the room, presumably to head to the office and call Wendel.

Johnny stays in the kitchen, despondently pulling out a stool and sitting down, resting his jaw on his palm as he stares down at the iPad.

'Hi,' I say.

'Hey.' Stu's warm voice comes travelling down the line. 'You OK?'

'Not really,' I admit, wishing he were here in person.

'Don't worry about this too much,' Stu says gently. 'Your cover hasn't been blown yet.'

'Yeah, but it will be, won't it?' I say flatly, feeling Johnny's piercing gaze directed at me.

'You never know,' Stu replies, trying to reassure me. 'If you keep up appearances, keep doing what you normally do, you might be alright for a bit longer. You'll just have to be more careful, that's all. When's Johnny going back to LA?'

'End of the week,' I reply in a monotone.

'That soon? Well, that might be a good thing,' he says calmly. 'Let things settle down a bit.'

'Mmm. Maybe.' I glance up to see that Johnny is still looking at me strangely. He holds his hand out for the phone. I nod at him.

'Johnny wants to talk to you,' I tell Stu.

'OK,' he replies. 'I'm setting off after lunch so I should be with you mid-afternoon.'

'OK,' I say again. 'See you then.'

I hand the phone to Johnny and slide the iPad back over, half skimming the article and half listening to Johnny's one-way conversation.

'I think it might be better if Sam brings her home,' he says. Johnny's the only one who calls Samuel 'Sam'. 'There could be paps outside the gate.' I feel startled at the thought of photographers with long-lens cameras hiding outside the property, trying to catch a glimpse of me. 'He'll be able to lose them,' Johnny continues, leaving the obvious out: that Stu won't. I picture Stu appearing at the house in his little white Fiat, and me driving back out with him in the front seat, with reporters tailing us the whole way home. Cover blown one hundred per cent.

I'm nervous at the prospect of leaving the house, even with Samuel. But I'm sure he knows what he's doing. He's used to dealing with stuff like this.

Johnny wraps up his conversation with my stepdad and ends the call, turning to look at me.

'I'm sorry,' he says. 'I should've listened to Meg.'

I stare at him with surprise. I wasn't expecting an apology. I shake my head, wanting to make him feel better. 'It's OK,' I say quickly, putting on a bright smile. 'They still don't know who I am. And anyway, like Meg said, it's only a website for a local paper. If she can stop this from going to print—'

'She won't be able to,' he says jadedly.

'Well, Wendel, then. If Wendel can stop—'

'The press are Rottweilers, Jess. The nationals are going to be pissed that a local paper's got this. They'll be going all out to get the scoop on your identity.'

'But don't we have any control over it? Won't they protect my anonymity because I'm still young, still at school?' I'm getting properly freaked out now.

'Not now this is out there,' he says, tapping the iPad. '*Now* your identity is anyone's game. I know how it works. They won't quit until they know everything.'

I chew on my bottom lip, nerves swirling unpleasantly around my stomach. I feel sick.

'I just want you to be prepared,' he says gently, covering my hand with his. His touch centres me for a moment, until he says, 'Everything's going to change.'

'Look, whatever happens, happens,' I reply suddenly, taking my hand away and pulling myself together. 'But for now I'm just going to do what Stu said. Carry on as normal, keep doing what I'm doing. If Samuel can get me home safely without anyone following us, I'll be fine. And at least I can still go on my date tonight,' I add with a goofy grin.

Johnny doesn't smile back at me. 'I don't like it,' he says, shaking his head.

'I'm going, Johnny,' I reply firmly, trying to stare him down, but giving up after a few seconds because he's obviously had more practice at this game. 'I'm going,' I mumble.

Stu calls us later to let us know he's home and waiting, so I go out to the garden to say goodbye to the boys and Brian. I'm still freaked out by the idea of a paparazzo's long lens directed at me from behind the trees, but Meg assured me that we're safe within the grounds of Johnny's home. It's illegal for the paps to sneakily photograph people on their own property.

'You off already?' Brian asks me with a frown.

I nod downheartedly. 'When are you leaving?'

He shrugs. 'Might stay on a few days. Keep these cheeky scamps company.' He ruffles Barney's hair. His grandsons are playing in the sandpit.

I bend down and pick up Phoenix, not caring that all of the sand sticking to his legs will soon be transferred directly to me. I kiss one of his squashy baby cheeks and then nuzzle his neck until he giggles and wriggles out of my grasp. I place him back amid his diggers and crouch down next to Barney.

'Bye, B,' I say, tears pricking my eyes as I rub his back.

'Bye-bye,' he replies chirpily, grinning up at me and then turning back to his toys. Not satisfied with that farewell, I pull him into my arms, feeling like he's literally tugging on my heartstrings with his tiny hands. I only get a quick squeeze before he pulls away and plants a sloppy, wet kiss on my lips, then he tears off across the lawn, roaring like an aeroplane. I watch him go sadly. I've seen so much of him and Phoenix over the last three months, but I don't think he understands that he's not going to see me for a long time. We won't risk another catch-up before they leave the UK, so today is goodbye.

I wonder if they'll miss me.

I straighten up and meet Brian's eyes.

'See you soon,' he says, grasping my arm with his bony fingers.

'You take care, Gramps,' I find myself saying. 'Maybe I'll come to see you in a week or two?'

'That'd be great,' he replies with a smile.

I wasn't expecting a grandfather to be part of the deal when I set out to meet my biological father, but now that I have him I don't want to lose him.

Meg and Johnny are waiting in the hall when I go back inside. Samuel has taken my bag out to the car.

'I'm so sorry about this,' Meg says sadly, giving me a hug.

'It's not your fault.' I look over her shoulder and see Johnny's gaze relocate to the floor. 'And it's not yours, either,' I tell him, detaching myself from Meg. 'It was bound to happen sooner or later.' I feel surprisingly brave. I suppose it's because this doesn't seem real. Maybe it won't until the news is well and truly out there.

'I'll call you tomorrow,' he says.

'OK.' I give a tight smile and nod, steeling myself for goodbye.

He pulls me into his arms and I press my cheek against his chest, staring with blurry, teary vision at the black ink trailing out from under his sleeve. I know for certain that I won't see him for ages and, if days can create distance, what will weeks do?

'Be good on your date tonight.' He breaks away, smiling down at me.

'I'm always good,' I reply, cracking a cheeky grin.

He rolls his eyes good-naturedly at Meg.

'Her father's daughter,' Meg says with wry amusement.

I consider that a compliment, but I'm not convinced it was meant as one.

As Samuel and I drive out through the gates, three men with cameras dart in front of the car, snapping away furiously. Even though my window is blacked-out, I sink with alarm into my seat. This is too weird.

The journey home takes much longer than usual, but eventually Samuel loses the cars tailing us and we're zooming along the country roads in the direction of Maidenhead.

'We're good now, girl. I'll have you back with Stu in no time,' Samuel reassures me when I look over my shoulder for about the fifteenth time.

I try to strike up a conversation to help me relax, but he's a big man of few words. I remember a time in LA when he made me laugh with silly jokes. I don't feel like laughing now.

'Are you going back to LA with the Jeffersons?' I ask him.

'That's the plan.'

'Do you miss it?'

'Nah,' he replies. 'I go where they go.'

'Do you have a family, Samuel?' I find myself asking.

'Nope. Just me, girl.'

'I guess that makes it easier to pack up and leave,' I murmur, looking out of the window.

Samuel doesn't reply. I wonder if he ever gets lonely, but I don't ask.

Twenty minutes later we're driving through Maidenhead town centre – just up the road from where I live.

'Better be ready to run,' Samuel warns. 'I'll bring your bags.

You get yourself inside.' He calls Stu to let him know we're nearby and soon afterwards we pull up in front of my house.

'Go!' Samuel commands.

I jump out of the car and run to the front door, which opens a split second before I reach it. A moment later my bags are in the hall and Stu is shutting the door on Samuel's departing back. I hear the Mercedes engine as Samuel drives away.

'Whoa.' My breath comes out in a rush.

'Are you OK?' Stu asks with concern.

'That was a bit hairy.' I feel rattled.

'What do you mean? What happened?'

We sit down and I tell him all about the waiting photographers and the high-speed journey we had, trying to escape them. Stu looks shaken by the time I've finished.

'It's OK, don't worry about it,' I say.

He sighs and runs his hands through his dark hair, messing it up, then takes off his horn-rimmed glasses and slowly polishes them on his T-shirt. He pops them back onto his nose and looks at me.

'Well, I guess I'd better get on with dinner,' he says finally.

'Don't forget I'm going out tonight,' I point out.

'Jessie—' he starts.

'No way. I am not cancelling my date. It's with Tom Ryder, for crying out loud! And remember you told me to act normally. I'm a pretty good actress, you know.'

'I *know* you are,' he states unhappily.

'What's that supposed to mean?' I'm still feeling pretty fraught.

'Forget it, Jess. You'll be going out no matter what I say.' He gets to his feet.

At least he's got that straight.

'I'm going to go and get ready,' I say.

'What time are you meeting Tom?' he calls after me.

'Six o'clock. We're going to get a bite to eat after the movies.'

'I'll drive you to the cinema.'

'It's only down the ro—'

'I'll drive you,' he says firmly. 'And you can call me for a lift.'

'OK,' I agree. Don't sweat the small stuff, I guess.

Chapter 5

All's quiet on our close when Stu and I leave the house later that evening. The jitters I'm feeling about my date join the ones already swirling around my stomach. I hope no one I know has recognised me from the photos and alerted the press. But if anyone from the papers is watching me they're well hidden. I resolve to try to enjoy tonight.

'Hi!' Lou says brightly when she opens the door. Stu offered to pick her up, too. 'Bye, Dad!' she calls.

'Don't be late!' I hear a gruff voice reply from a room off the hall.

She rolls her eyes at me, then pulls the door shut behind her. Lou's parents are divorced. I know it's awful of me, but when I found out I couldn't help feeling a little relieved that her family wasn't perfect, either.

'You look nice,' she says brightly.

'Thanks. You too.' We exchange smiles.

We had a little texting session about an hour ago and have

both stuck to our plan to dress in jeans with smart tops and heels. I'm wearing electric-blue slingbacks and a sheer-black long-sleeved top.

'Are you nervous?' she asks quietly. 'I am.'

I laugh. 'I am a bit. But you've got nothing to be nervous about. Chris really fancies you.'

'Well, Tom *definitely* fancies *you*.'

'Can you two keep it down?' Stu moans from the front seat.

Lou and I giggle, but ride the rest of the way in silence.

We're almost ten minutes late by the time we arrive, but Tom and Chris are nowhere to be seen. Lou spots them playing on a Formula One simulator. They're sitting side by side behind their respective steering wheels, deep in concentration.

'Boo!' I shout, poking my face between their heads.

They both jump in fright and then swear at me and nearly crash their cars.

Lou and I crack up laughing while they try to finish the game.

'Ha!' Tom says to Chris, holding up one finger in his face to signal he came first. '*You* didn't help,' he says, pointing said finger at me as he climbs out of his seat. He raises an eyebrow in amusement and walks a couple of steps towards me. My heart skitters as he stops and stares down at me with his dark-brown eyes. I smirk up at him.

'Yeah, yeah,' Chris says, shaking his head with mock disgust as he joins us. 'You can tell someone's getting his driving licence soon.'

'I'd better be, after spending half my life practising on my uncle's farm.'

'When's your birthday?' I ask, as we set off towards the foyer.

'Wednesday.'

He nods at the confectionery stand. 'We've already got the tickets, but do you want popcorn?'

'Definitely!' I reply. 'I'll get it.'

'No, no, it's alright,' he says, digging into his back pocket for his wallet. Chris does the same.

'If you bought the tickets, we'll buy the popcorn,' Lou reiterates firmly, and they reluctantly put their wallets away.

'Shall we share?' I ask Tom, as we go to stand in line.

'Sure.'

'Sweet or salted or both?'

'Both?' He screws his nose up.

'It's the best, I promise.'

He grins. 'OK. I trust you.'

His words, although flippant, do nothing to tame my butterflies. We don't really speak as we approach the front of the queue, but I can hear Lou and Chris chatting and I feel slightly self-conscious at the lull in our conversation.

Out of the corner of my eye, I see Tom rake his hand through his brown hair. His toned arms are the colour of honey, and he's wearing casual black trousers and an army-green T-shirt with black graphics on the front.

He is so gorgeous.

We stand off to the side once we've got our popcorn and drinks, waiting for Chris and Lou. I can see her laughing and him grinning across at her. They've really hit it off. I try to think of something to say to Tom.

'So your uncle has—'

'What did you do—'

We both speak at the same time. He laughs awkwardly and

grabs a couple of kernels of popcorn from the large bucket I'm holding. 'You first.'

'So your uncle has a farm?' I ask.

'Yeah,' he says between munches. 'In Suffolk.'

'Can you honestly drive?'

'Mmm.' He nods. 'He taught me to drive a tractor when I was thirteen. A car's pretty easy in comparison.'

'That's so cool! When are you going to take your test?'

'In three weeks, but don't tell anyone,' he says with a cheeky smile.

'Why not?' I didn't have him down as the shy type.

'I don't want the pressure of everyone knowing.'

'I won't tell anyone.' I can't help but feel pleased that I'm not 'everyone'.

'It's just as well I trust you, isn't it?' He grins down at me. 'And you were right about the popcorn.'

I laugh. 'Told you! You'll never have it any other way now.'

We barely notice when Lou and Chris approach.

'Ready?' Chris asks.

Tom nods and leads the way in, passing the tickets to the girl on the door.

We file into a row of seats – Chris first, then Lou, then me, and Tom on the aisle. The trailers are already playing and, as we sit down, Lou flashes me a smile in the darkness. I grin back at her and slide down in my seat. To my left, Tom does the same. I offer him some popcorn and he takes a handful, then leans his head close to mine.

'What did you do last night?' he asks, as the trailers continue to screen.

'Went out for dinner with my dad,' I tell him. I'm not going to lie if I don't have to. And I'm hoping to be able to tell him the truth eventually.

He glances at me. 'Mr Taylor?'

'No, my real dad. He's over here at the moment.'

'Oh, wow. What's he like?'

'He's great,' I reveal with a shrug. 'I'll tell you later,' I add in a quiet voice, nodding at the big screen. The film's about to start.

He keeps his head tilted towards mine, and I'm so aware of him sitting right next to me that I find it hard to follow the thriller that we're watching. His knee jigs up and down occasionally and I'm distracted by his hand resting on his thigh. His fingers brush against mine as we finish the popcorn and I feel on edge as I put the empty bucket on the floor.

When I sit back in my seat, my arm rubs against his and the contact gives me goosebumps. I instinctively put distance between us, then want to kick myself because what I want is *more* contact, not less. I stare down at his hand and rest my own on my leg, willing him to take it. I can smell his aftershave or deodorant, whatever it is, and it's distracting. I cast him a sideways look and he glances back at me, his dark eyes shining from the light of the screen. We return our attention to the film, but the restless winged creatures inside my stomach show no signs of calming down.

I shift slightly so our forearms are only just touching and I resist the urge to pull away. I'm so aware of the small contact that I'm barely breathing. His arm radiates heat. A torturously amazing couple of minutes pass, and then he moves. My heart free-falls for a split second until his arm crosses mine and he takes my hand.

It's the most innocent gesture of all, yet I feel like my heart is going to peter out. I smile at him shyly, then try to concentrate on the film. But it's completely futile. All I can think about is Tom.

When he starts to stroke his thumb across my wrist, it occurs to me that if I feel this way about hand-holding, how am I going to cope if he kisses me?!

When he kisses me…

Before I know it, the credits are rolling. Tom gives my hand a squeeze and lets me go. I flash him a tentative smile and then straighten up and turn to our friends.

We decide to go for a pizza and the four of us spend the next two hours laughing and chatting about everything from the film and school to the summer holidays and how Lou's finding her move.

'Better since I met Jessie and you guys,' she says, which makes me feel warm inside.

After dinner, Chris and Lou decide to catch a taxi from the train station and Tom offers to walk me home. I know Stu told me to call him for a lift, but he's overreacting – we only live ten minutes away. And anyway I want some alone time with Tom…

'I'm so stuffed,' he groans, putting his hand on his flat stomach.

'Me too.'

'You didn't eat much,' he points out.

'I wasn't hungry after all that popcorn!'

'At least you didn't force any more weird food combinations on me.'

I elbow him. 'You said you *liked* the sweet and salted.'

'I like you.'

My stomach goes haywire. I cast him a sideways look and find him smiling down at me. He reaches over and takes my hand as we walk.

'Do you remember this?' he asks, coming to a stop on the railway bridge. He stares down at the dark space where the tracks are.

'Yes,' I reply quietly.

Before the summer holidays, he walked me home from the train station and I stood right here with him, talking about my real dad and where he could be.

'You were the one who gave me the idea to ask Stu about him,' I tell Tom. 'If it hadn't been for you, I might not know my dad now.'

'I'm glad I could help,' he says, smiling. 'So what's he like?'

'He's really cool. And his wife is nice. I was a bit worried about how she felt about me at first, but I think she's getting used to me.'

'Do you know why your mum didn't tell you about him?' Tom asks.

I look away. 'I guess she didn't want to lose me, but I'll never totally understand. It's not like I can ask her.'

My voice trails off and he turns to face me, hooking his forefingers through my belt loops and tugging me a step closer.

I know in a heartbeat that this is it: he's going to kiss me.

A car zooms round the corner, the headlights temporarily blinding us. I giggle, but he's unfazed by the rude interruption. The next thing I know, his lips are on mine.

He kisses me slowly, but soon deepens the kiss, parting my lips with his tongue. I feel giddy as I kiss him back, and then another car zooms round the corner and its driver honks at us. We laugh against each other's mouths and break away. He kisses me again gently.

'I wasn't sure you liked me,' he says.

'What?!' I exclaim. 'What made you think that?'

'Well, you know, when I walked you home that time we spoke about your dad – we talked about going to see the film, then you went really quiet on me.'

'Only because I asked Stu about him the very next day,' I explain, placing my hands on his waist. 'I was completely distracted. I'd spent practically my whole life wondering about him and suddenly I knew who he was.'

'And then the next time,' he says with a small shrug, staring down at me meaningfully.

I rack my brains to remember the last conversation we had before the summer holidays. We talked about going to see a movie when I got back from… Oh. That's right. I told him I was going to LA to stay with 'a friend of my mum's'.

'Sorry, I should have told you I was going to stay with my real dad,' I apologise. 'But it was all a bit weird. I *wanted* to tell you…' I try to reassure him, but I can't give anything away yet. 'It was complicated because he had a family of his own and none of them knew I existed. They made me do a paternity test.'

'Did they?' He looks shocked.

'It wasn't a big deal.' I brush it off.

I take his hand again and we carry on walking up the hill at a leisurely pace. I don't live far from here, and I'm not ready for this to be over.

'It's just…' he starts, still seeming uncertain. 'I thought about you a bit over the holidays.' He laughs lightly, but it doesn't cover up his awkwardness. 'You didn't text me when you got home.'

I'm slightly taken aback. His confidence is wavering before

my very eyes. I want to reassure him, but what can I say? Yes, I was busy with my grandmother's funeral and seeing Johnny and co, but I wasn't so busy that I couldn't send a simple text.

The truth is, of course, that my head was still so full of Jack. I didn't know where to start, or how to pick things up again with Tom. But I can't explain that.

'The last couple of weeks of the holidays were a bit of a blur,' I say. He doesn't meet my eyes, looking straight ahead as we walk. So I tell him about the funeral.

'Oh, I'm sorry.' He's immediately sympathetic, and I feel so guilty for distracting him from the other side of the story.

'It's OK. I'm just sad that I barely knew her,' I say. 'But she pretty much disowned my mum when she fell pregnant with me.'

'Jeez,' he murmurs.

'And also my dad ended up coming back to the UK with his family, so I was with them quite a bit.'

'I see,' he says, nodding as we reach the close where I live.

I hope that's enough of an explanation. I squeeze his hand and pull him to a stop. He looks down at me. He's so lovely. I like him so much – both his confident side and this less secure side that he's *letting* me see now.

I want to tell him everything about Johnny, but it's too soon to open up. I don't know where this thing with Tom is going, but I need to be patient, just in case it all goes wrong and he somehow blows my cover.

I feel a trickle of fear at the thought of the press blowing it first. Tom would find out from the papers before he finds out from me and that would be awful. But now is definitely *not* the time to spill.

'Thanks for tonight,' I say, glancing at my house to see the lights in the living room are still on. Stu's up, probably waiting for my call. Oops.

'See you tomorrow?'

'You will,' he says, and I notice he's still regarding me a little warily. He knows something's missing from my story.

Jack.

But no, that's *over*, I tell myself with steely resolve. He had his chance. Now I'm here with Tom.

I stand on my tiptoes and press my lips to his. He cups my face in his hands and kisses me back, and the giddy feeling returns. He breaks away, keeping our faces close together. I let out a little sigh. He's such an amazing kisser.

'See you tomorrow,' he murmurs, kissing me one more time quickly before letting me go and turning away. I walk backwards a few steps, watching as *Tom Ryder* lopes away from my house, glancing back to flash me a grin.

I dizzily open up the front door and walk into the hall, jumping as Stu appears in the living-room door.

'I told you to call!' he says accusingly the moment the door closes behind me.

'Tom walked me home,' I say, annoyed with him for bringing me back down to earth with a bump.

'We had a deal!' he says.

'What's the *big* deal?'

'Don't you be clever with me, Jessie. I let you go out tonight and—'

'As if you could stop me,' I scoff.

'Oh, so we're there again, are we?' he says angrily. 'I thought you might've grown up in LA.'

'Seriously, Stu, you're completely overreacting. I walked home from the cinema *down the road*! I'm supposed to be doing normal things, right?'

'Not any more,' he says, a new flatness to his tone.

'What's happened?' I ask, suddenly scared.

'The story's running in the national papers tomorrow, Jessie.'

All hopes that Meg might have got the story pulled vanish.

'Apparently they've got other shots of you,' Stu continues. 'I don't know how recognisable you'll be in them, but at some point someone will realise it's you and tell the press.'

My heart sinks.

'You need to prepare yourself,' he says. 'Johnny's been talking to me about moving to a more secure house.'

'I'm not moving!' I yell, fury and fear twisting my gut.

'I don't want to move, either,' he says, and through my red mist I can see the tears glistening in his eyes. But I don't wait to see if they'll spill over, shoving past him and hurrying up the stairs.

Instead of turning into my bedroom, I go into the spare room, just stopping short of slamming the door behind me.

And then she's there with me.

Mum.

This is the room where we keep all of her belongings – neither of us has been able to bring ourselves to throw anything out yet, so we just shoved it all in here.

Tears track down my cheeks as I breathe in the scent of her perfume. Piles and piles of folded-up clothes have been taken straight out of her drawers and laid on the bed. Her dressing gown is folded up on the pillow and I reach for it, feeling the silky satin against my fingers. I put it to my nose and inhale, imagining her arms folding round me. In my mind, she holds me tight to her chest and I squeeze my eyes shut, then start to sob silently.

I fall asleep there, among her things. I don't want to be anywhere else.

Chapter 6

The following morning I'm so distracted reading the newspaper stories about me that I barely feel nervous about seeing Tom at school.

The story from the local newspaper website has made the front page of the print version, and the sight of the headline about me being a local girl scares the life out of me. It'll be all too easy for someone I know to recognise me.

In the national papers, though, the story isn't front page. In fact, a couple of the papers only mention it in passing in a tiny column, but one of the tabloids has done a whole spread about me, including photos of the time I went with the Jeffersons to the theme park on Santa Monica beach. The shots are crystal clear, but I'm wearing my sunnies again, so it's still not easy to make out my face.

It occurs to me that more people in LA know who I am than they do in Maidenhead. I grew up here, but I was in LA with Agnes and all of her friends when the news first broke about

Johnny having a secret teenage daughter. There was one girl, Lissa, who was especially bitchy towards me. What's to stop her or any of the others from telling the press my name? I'd have the paps on my doorstep within hours.

I wonder if I'll hear from Agnes when she wakes up in LA and discovers that the news about me is hotting up. I wonder if I'll hear from Jack, I think, with a guilty rush.

Has he thought about me at all since I left? We said we'd stay in contact, but he couldn't even be bothered to reply to my casual, chatty email. I won't be sending another. Especially not now I'm with Tom.

A strange muddle of emotions passes through me. Butterflies at the thought of seeing Tom this morning, and a weird aching feeling at the thought of not seeing Jack again. I try to ignore the latter and focus on the former.

Stu and I get to school a little later than usual after spending ages scouring the newspapers. My eyes dart around, looking at the students already arriving. Have any of them seen the papers this morning? It's the local paper I'm most worried about, the one screaming about me being from around here.

There are a few 'Alright, sir's directed at Stu, but no one gives me so much as a second glance as we wander into school past the cafeteria.

It's so weird. I'm all jumpy, acutely aware of everyone around me, but for my classmates it's business as usual.

'Try to put it out of your mind for now,' Stu whispers, as he goes up the stairs to his office.

I nod tensely, feeling especially vulnerable once he's gone.

I walk past the sixth-form block, glancing in to see if Tom has arrived, but it's deserted. I only have a few minutes to spare, but I decide to spend them locked inside a cubicle, away from everyone. I'm about to walk into the toilets when the sound of my name being called makes me jump out of my skin. I see Lou hurrying across the cobbled courtyard. She grabs my elbow and steers me into the toilets as my heart pitter-patters inside my chest.

'Spill!' she says.

I don't know what to say. Does she know about Johnny?!

'Did anything happen?' she asks eagerly.

I breathe a sigh of relief. She's just talking about Tom! I nod slightly, pursing my lips.

'Did you kiss?' she asks in a loud whisper.

Again, I nod, relaxing slightly.

She squeaks with excitement and a belated bubble of happiness bursts inside my chest. I've barely thought about the fact that *I kissed Tom Ryder last night*! Warmth continues to fill my stomach as I ask for the lowdown on Chris. He kissed her in the taxi and they exchanged numbers. They're going out again this weekend.

It's so nice to have a proper friend at school again, now that Natalie's gone. In fact, she hasn't even texted me this weekend I realise, before shoving the thought away. As for Libby…

The bell rings so Lou and I hurry out of the toilets towards our tutor room. I notice Libby in the courtyard, her ginger hair standing out in the crowd. She's talking to Amanda, but, when she sees me, her face freezes and her eyes widen. She knows my secret is on shaky ground.

Amanda shoots her head round to see who has Libby's attention and her brow furrows with confusion as she spies me.

70

She turns back to Libby and my former best friend adjusts her face into a more natural expression. I give her a small smile as Lou and I pass by, still arm in arm. Libby barely nods, but I can tell that she's worried about me. I have an overwhelming urge to be alone with her so I can talk openly about Johnny. And so I can pretend things are like they used to be.

Libby slips me a note during assembly and I jump at the contact. I'd been completely distracted, watching the door for Tom.

Come to mine after school? Hope you're OK.

I give her a grateful nod, my nose prickling because I suddenly miss her desperately.

I turn back to the front, just in time to see Tom walk casually into the hall, next to Chris. Scanning the room, he locks eyes with me and his lips tilt up at the corners. My stomach flutters uncontrollably and I barely think about anything else for the whole assembly.

Tom's waiting for me when I walk out of the hall, leaning up against the wall with his arms folded. He gives me a cheeky grin.

'Hello,' I say, mirroring his expression. Lou breaks away from me to talk to Chris, and I'm vaguely aware of Libby and Amanda glancing over their shoulders at us as they walk past.

'Where are you headed now?' he asks.

'ICT.' A circus full of tiny jugglers start to do their thing in my stomach.

He pushes off from the wall and I realise with glee that he's planning on walking me to class.

'You got home OK?' I ask, kicking us off with a nice, safe topic as we set off across the courtyard.

'Yeah. Good night?'

There's a question mark at the end of his sentence, but I'm surprised he doesn't know my answer.

'Really good,' I reply, cocking my head to one side and looking up at him.

'Good film, wasn't it?' he says slightly awkwardly, as we come to a stop at the bottom of the steps to my classroom. There are a lot of 'goods' being thrown around.

'I wasn't paying it much attention,' I admit with a smirk.

'Weren't you?' He's smirking, too.

I shake my head slightly and smile. 'No.'

He looks at my lips and a thrill darts through me. His eyes rise to meet mine. 'See you at break?'

'Yeah.' I nod and we turn away from each other.

He thought about kissing me, then. I wonder when he next will.

ICT flies by, largely thanks to the notes that Lou and I keep passing back and forth about Tom and Chris. Libby flashes me a few confused looks, and it strikes me that Lou and I are acting a bit like she and Amanda were behaving last week. I'll admit it gives me a little boost to wonder if she's missing how close we used to be.

Lou and I hang around the courtyard at break, sitting on the brick wall near the library. It's cooler today, but our black blazers are still soaking up the sun, warming our skin.

I don't know where Tom and Chris are. I'm resisting the temptation to go and peek into the sixth-form common room.

Three of our classmates walk past, and one of them, Nina, halts in her tracks and stares back at me with wide-open eyes and a humungous grin on her face.

'Oh my God, it's you!' she squeals, and my face freezes as I see the phone in her hand. She bounces on the spot with delight and points at me. 'It's Jessie! Jessie is Johnny Jefferson's secret daughter!'

I almost die, right there.

And then she cracks up, literally hoots with laughter. She passes the phone to her friends and they all peer at it, then at me, before laughing, too.

'Oh my God, you look just like her!' Michelle splutters.

It becomes suddenly apparent that, while they might think I *look* like Johnny's daughter, they don't for a second suspect that I actually am.

'Bugger off,' I say with annoyance. This only makes them laugh more.

'What's funny?' Tom asks, appearing at my side.

'Nothing,' I mutter, as Lou grabs the phone from Michelle.

'Hey!' Michelle shouts, trying to get it back. Lou holds it away from her and scrutinises the image on the screen.

'Wow,' she says sarcastically. 'They're both blonde. You'd give Sherlock a run for his money.' She passes the phone back to Nina, who rolls her eyes and stalks away, cronies in tow.

'What was that about?' Tom asks with confusion.

'Nothing,' I say, but I can't stop Lou from elaborating.

'They think Jessie looks like Johnny Jefferson's secret daughter,' she explains.

'Do they?' he says. 'That's random.'

I shrug. 'Oh, well, shall we—'

'Apparently she's from around here,' Lou continues.

'Shall we go sit on the field?' I suggest, putting an end to their conversation.

Tom checks his watch, but, before he can speak, the end-of-break bell rings.

'Lunchtime?' I suggest.

'I said I'd play football,' Tom replies, as we set off towards class. 'Come to watch?'

'Nah, I'm not going to sit on the sidelines like one of your groupies.' I giggle at the look on his face. 'I'll see you later?'

'After school?' he asks.

'I'm going to Libby's,' I tell him, glancing across the courtyard at that moment to catch Libby's eye. I wonder if she saw the exchange with Nina and co.

'OK, then,' Tom replies, and I can't tell if he's disappointed.

'See you later, though?' I say.

'Sure.' He nods and we go our separate ways.

Chapter 7

'How are you?' Libby asks me, as soon as she's closed the door to her bedroom. We barely spoke on the short walk here, and then we had to go through ten minutes of pleasantries with Marilyn, Libby's mum, before we could escape upstairs. Libby is positively bursting at the seams to get the lowdown on what's been happening.

'I'm OK,' I tell her tentatively. 'A bit worried that my cover's about to be blown. Johnny reckons it's only a matter of time.'

Libby's face flushes at the mention of my famous father.

'Gosh,' she squeaks. 'What will you do?'

I shrug, trying to seem nonchalant and convince myself as much as her that I'm not totally freaked out. 'I don't know. Johnny keeps threatening twenty-four-seven bodyguards and stuff, but… I don't know. I guess we'll cross that bridge when we come to it.'

'Wow,' she says, looking a little shell-shocked.

I fill her in on my stay with the Jeffersons, but we've barely even touched the tip of the iceberg when the doorbell rings.

'You and Louise seem to be getting along well,' Libby continues, assuming her mum will answer the door.

'She's great,' I say with a grin.

'Have you told her about, you know, your dad?'

Her voice sounds strained.

'No,' I say, and her face visibly relaxes. Is she jealous? 'Not yet,' I add, and she tenses up again.

'Do you think you can trust her?' she asks.

'I think so, yeah.' As I say it, I reckon it's true.

'You barely know her,' she points out, her jaw twitching.

'Libby!' Marilyn calls up the stairs. 'Amanda's here!'

'Oh!' Libby says with surprise. I instantly feel flat. 'Can you tell her to come up?' Libby shouts, nearly deafening me. 'Probably wondered where I went after school,' she says, as we hear Amanda's footsteps on the stairs.

Alone time with Libby over, then.

'Hi!' Amanda gushes, pushing the door open. Her face falls as she realises her bestie has company – with her previous bestie, no less. 'Oh. I didn't realise you were here,' she says, looking none too pleased to see me sitting at the end of Libby's bed.

'Jessie came over after school,' Libby tells her with a smile. 'I thought you had your piano lesson today?'

'It was cancelled.' Amanda looks put out.

'Bit of a last-minute thing, wasn't it, Jessie?' Libby says apologetically.

'Yeah,' I mumble. Libby's room is small enough at the best of times. Now it's positively teeny.

'Hey, I might shoot off,' I find myself saying.

'You don't have to go,' Libby says quickly.

'I don't have to stay,' Amanda chips in, somewhat grumpily.

'Don't be silly!' Libby exclaims, looking totally caught in the middle. 'Come on, let's just go to the living room where there's more room.'

The three of us file awkwardly out of her room and down the stairs without saying another word. I really, really don't want to be here any more. Stu is working late at school. I wonder if I can catch him before he leaves. Or maybe I could go and see Natalie…

'Actually, Libby,' I say, getting out my phone as we reach the landing. 'Don't be offended, but I haven't spoken to Natalie since Friday. I might drop by and see her.'

'Oh,' she says, looking at her feet.

'Thanks for the chat.' I touch her arm and try to inject some warmth into my voice as I start towards the front door. Libby follows me, but Amanda, thankfully, stays put.

'I'm sorry,' Libby whispers, as I open the door. Her face has gone red again.

'Don't worry about it,' I reply, forcing a smile. 'I'll see you tomorrow.'

When Libby closes the door on my departing back, I feel flatter than ever. I open up my Contacts and call Natalie.

'Hello?' she says.

'Hi, stranger!'

'Hi.' She sounds distinctly unenthusiastic.

'Are you OK?' I ask with surprise.

'Yeah, I'm fine.'

'Are you at home?'

What's going on? Why does she sound so unhappy to hear from me?

'Yeah.'

'Can I come over?' I ask warily.

'If you want.'

'I won't if you don't want me to.' I can't help snapping.

'No, it's fine,' she says dully. 'See you in a bit.'

I end the call and stare down at my phone with confusion. Things are going from bad to worse.

I text Stu to let him know my change of plans and he offers to collect me at 5 p.m., which I figure gives me enough time to walk to Natalie's and find out what her deal is.

'What's up with you?' I ask when she opens the door with a sour look on her face.

'What makes you think anything is "up" with me?' she says grumpily, as I step into the hall.

'Have I done something wrong?' I ask, feeling totally on edge.

'You tell me.'

'What?' I pull a face at her. I'm so confused. 'Am I missing something? Did you know that the press have almost found out about me?'

'Not everything is about you, Jessie,' she replies with annoyance, putting me right in my place.

'Then tell me what's wrong.'

'Let's go upstairs,' she says dejectedly.

It turns out that she was properly gutted about Liam at the party on Friday night. So much so that she couldn't even bring herself to call me on Sunday when she saw my news had broken online. She thinks Liam fancies me.

'When you were on the decks, he was watching you,' she explains.

78

'No, he wasn't!' I scoff.

'He was, Jessie,' she says wearily. 'I recognised his look as the same one he gave me at the pub the week before last. And then he saw you, and you blew me out of the water.'

'Don't be ridiculous,' I scoff again.

'He asked me for your number today,' she tells me.

'*What?*' I'm flabbergasted. Poor Natalie. 'I hope you didn't give it to him!'

She shrugs.

'You *did?*'

'What else could I do?' she asks in a small voice.

Now I feel truly awful. 'I'm so sorry,' I say quietly, not really knowing what else *to* say. 'He hasn't called me. I'll tell him I'm not interested if he does.'

'I don't want him any more, anyway.'

'No. No, I wouldn't, either. He's not good enough for you,' I tell her fervently, but she barely cracks a smile.

'Still, I know it's hard to stop fancying someone, even when they're bad for you,' I say. I cringe when I realise I've brought it back to me again, but I really can sympathise.

'You mean Jack, don't you?' She gives me a rueful look.

'Mmm,' I reply. 'But I'm trying to forget about him. I had a date with Tom last night.'

Her eyes instantly light up. 'You did? Did you snog him?!'

I giggle and the rest of our time together passes by in a blur.

Agnes texts me later that night, just as I'm falling asleep. She heard on the grapevine that the British press is pursuing my story and I'm touched that she's thinking of me, even though we don't know each other that well.

79

Again, I wonder what's been going through Jack's mind. He was the one who asked to take *me* out on a date before I left. He *wanted* to stay in touch. So why has he gone cold?

I can't resist grabbing my laptop from my desk and searching for his band, All Hype, on the internet. The most recent picture that loads up is one of him with his arm round Eve, the band's gorgeous lead singer and his on-off girlfriend. I slam my laptop lid shut and put the device back on my desk, feeling sick to my stomach.

I climb back into bed, resolving to put him out of my mind for good.

Laying my head on my pillow, I focus on Tom instead. Did I play it too cool today? I decide to make up for it tomorrow, and remember with a start that it's his birthday on Wednesday. Would it be weird to get him something, seeing as we've only kissed? It's not like he's my boyfriend yet. Is he? What if he thinks that he is? Then he'll definitely expect a present! Oh, man. I don't even know what I'd write in a card. Surely it's too soon to have to think about things like this?!

It takes me a while to fall asleep. But, as dilemmas go, this one I can more or less cope with.

Chapter 8

'Are you playing football again at lunchtime?' I ask Tom when I manage to catch him the next morning.

'I don't think so. You want to hang out?'

'Sure. See you on the field?'

'I'll see you there.'

Smiling, he turns away. I do the same, just in time to see Nina and Michelle smirking at me. I blush furiously, put my head down and hurry to my lesson. But the path to Art, I belatedly realise, is right past them.

'Jessie fancies Tom,' Nina sing-songs at me as I pass.

'Maybe he'll be more interested when he finds out your dad is Johnny Jefferson,' Michelle adds with a snigger.

I can think of nothing better to do than sneer at them. If only they knew how close to the bone they are.

Libby calls to me to wait as I'm walking out of Art. 'I'll catch you up,' she says to Amanda, before joining me. 'Sorry about yesterday.' Her voice is quiet.

'Don't worry about it,' I reply.

'I didn't even get the goss on Tom.' She flashes me a mischievous look.

I give a little shrug, not really knowing what to say.

'Has anything happened with him?' she asks, curiosity getting the better of her.

I was hoping not to have to spill the beans to Libby about him because, while I trust her not to say anything to Amanda about Johnny, it seems a little trite asking her to keep quiet about my love life, too.

'Kind of. Nothing much,' I add, trying to put her off. It doesn't work.

'Like what?' she whispers conspiratorially.

'We went to the movies.' I try to sound casual.

'Did you kiss him?' she asks gleefully.

'Libby,' I reply with a frown. The gesture is contagious because she looks instantly put out.

'What, so now we can't even talk about boys? I won't tell Amanda, if that's what you're worried about.'

Now I feel bad. 'It's not that,' I say, as we walk out of the classroom. 'It's just early days,' I add with an embarrassed look. 'I'm meeting him for lunch.'

She purses her lips. 'Well, good for you.'

I smile awkwardly. 'Er, thanks. See you later?'

'Of course.'

That was uncomfortable, I think, as we turn away from each other.

Lou and I lie on our stomachs with our legs kicked up in the air, occasionally checking over our shoulders for the boys. They must've gone to the cafeteria before coming to the field. I tell her about my awkward conversation with Libby.

We're so engrossed in what we're talking about that we don't see Tom and Chris approach. When a pair of grey Converse trainers appears in my vision, I crane my neck to see Tom smiling down at me.

'Alright?' he says, collapsing on the grass beside me. Chris strikes up a conversation with Lou about the merits of the cafeteria's potato wedges over fries, and Tom and I smile at each other. He holds my gaze for a couple of seconds and I suddenly feel a little shy. I crawl to a sitting position.

'You've got—' he says, reaching over to dust dry grass from the front of my school uniform.

'Oh,' I say, brushing my chest, then meeting his eyes again.

'How was Libby's yesterday?'

'It was OK,' I reply self-consciously. 'We didn't get much time to talk before Amanda came over.'

'Didn't you and Libby used to be best mates?'

'Yeah. Not so much any more,' I admit. 'It's your birthday tomorrow, isn't it?' I ask, diverting him from that particular topic.

His warm brown eyes crinkle as he gives an amused nod. 'It is.'

'Are you doing anything?'

'Just going out for dinner with my mum and sister.'

'Your sister's name is Becky, right? She's a few years older than you?' She used to go to school here.

'Three,' he replies. 'I'm surprised you remember her.'

I know more about Tom than I care to admit. But no need to sound like a psycho this early on in the relationship.

'Is she at uni?' I ask.

83

'Yeah, Edinburgh. But she hasn't gone back yet.'

'Do you miss her?'

'I did last year.' He nods. I bet he missed her loads when his dad left. 'But I've had her around all summer so I'm ready to get rid of her again now,' he adds with a smile.

'So are you not doing anything for your birthday with friends?'

'Nah.' He shakes his head. 'Can't really be bothered. What are you up to this weekend?' he asks.

'Nothing yet.'

'You want to hang out on Saturday?'

'Sure.' We smile at each other.

'What happened to your job at the clothes shop?' he asks.

'I had to quit when I stayed out in America for the summer. Stu called my boss for me, bless him.'

'Are you going to get another one?'

I shrug. 'Maybe. But it's nice having my Saturdays free at the moment.' I don't tell him that I don't really need a job, now that Johnny is giving me an allowance.

'Why don't we go to Windsor for the day?'

'That's sounds great,' I smile.

'What's this?' Chris interrupts. He and Lou have been talking together since Tom sat down. While he fills them in, my attention is distracted by Nina, Michelle and their friends, staring over at us and gossiping. I don't know if they're talking about Tom and me or if they're being bitchy about Johnny again, but my heart rate picks up once more. The secret won't be mine for much longer.

Chapter 9

With every day that passes by without my identity being revealed, I relax a little more. My heart jumps on Thursday when Johnny calls me, and my immediate thought is that he has bad news to break, but he's only calling to say goodbye. They fly home to America the following morning. I'll be in Geography class.

'Look after yourself, chick,' he says. 'Stay out of trouble.'

'I'm making no promises,' I reply, trying to ignore the lump in my throat. It's weird that I feel this strongly about him after such a short amount of time.

'Hey, I've got to tell you something,' he says tentatively.

'What?' I ask warily.

'My dad's coming home with us for a bit.'

'Oh,' I reply quietly.

'I know you wanted to go and visit him, so I'm sorry about that.'

'Yeah.' I don't really know what else to say. I was happy that a part of my new family would be here with me in the UK.

He continues. 'It'll probably be for a few weeks, maybe a month, maybe longer.' There's regret in his tone. He knows this isn't what I want to hear. 'He'd like somewhere warm to recuperate. I think LA will do him good.'

'Yes. For sure,' I say feebly, not wanting to be too selfish.

'I'm sorry, Jess,' he adds in a gentle voice. 'The next few months will fly by.'

'Here's hoping.'

Neither of us speaks for a long moment. I swallow, but the lump remains. I can't believe all of the Jeffersons will be on the other side of the pond. All of them, except for me.

'Hey, how did your date go the other night?' he asks, opting for a different topic of conversation.

'It was good,' I reply lamely.

'Did you kiss him?'

'Johnny!' I exclaim.

He chuckles, then sighs. 'Ah, I wish you'd call me Dad.'

He may as well have lit me up with a torch because, in that moment, everything feels brighter.

'Do you?' I ask, my insides singing. I've never called anyone 'Dad'.

'Yeah,' he replies casually.

'OK, *Dad*.' I force myself to say it, but it makes me immediately giggle.

He laughs, too. 'I'll call you when we land,' he promises.

'OK.' I smile.

'See you—'

'No, wait!' I interrupt him. 'I won't be in.'

'Where will you be?' he asks.

'I'm going out with Tom again,' I admit.

'*Again?*' I can completely picture the frown on his face.

'Yeah, *Dad*. He's a nice guy. You'd like him.'

'Would I now.' It's not a question. 'I'm not sure about your taste,' he says drily.

'You haven't even met him!' I exclaim.

'I met Jack Mitchell. That was enough to go on.'

'Yeah, well, I'm not interested in him any more,' I say, as my heart deflates. 'And Tom is much nicer. Ask Stu, he'll tell you.'

'I might just do that.'

I smirk. 'I'm not bluffing. Ask him.'

He chuckles. 'Alright, I will. Next time we speak.'

We ring off and I sit and stare into space for a while before pulling myself together.

I go out with Natalie on Friday night, resisting the urge to drag her to the pub where Tom is. He's playing pool with a few mates, he told me earlier. He thought he'd celebrate his birthday with some friends after all.

I didn't give him a present on Wednesday, but I did slip a card into his bag, which made him smile. I agonised for ages about what to write, eventually settling on how I was looking forward to Saturday and that lunch was on me. It all sounded pretty lame, but I think he was pleased. I hope so, anyway.

We haven't kissed all week. We've barely touched. But I know he likes me, and he must know that I like him. I can't wait to spend a whole day with him.

On Saturday, when I arrive at the station, Tom is already waiting.

'Hello,' he says, as I wander up to him with a smile on my face.

'Hello,' I reply, my heart fluttering. Even though we're alone, we still don't kiss, but he takes my hand when we're sitting side by side on the train and I'm glad he's starting off the day by being tactile.

'You look nice,' he says. I'm wearing an apricot-coloured, strapless maxi-dress with the black leather jacket Johnny bought for me in LA. 'I like this.' He skims his fingers round the cuff of my jacket.

'Thanks.' I don't tell him that it's designer. 'You too.'

He's wearing light-grey cords and a long-sleeved navy-blue T-shirt. He looks hot, as usual.

Once we're off the train, we walk hand in hand along the old-fashioned platform and wind our way through to the road and the grey stone walls of Windsor Castle.

'Have you ever been inside?' I ask him.

'Yes, when I was little. You want to go in now?' he asks.

'Sure.'

It's more expensive than I remembered, and Tom and I have a little domestic about who's going to pay. Eventually he agrees to let me cover it as part of his birthday present, but he insists on buying lunch. We'll have that argument later.

The truth is, thanks to Johnny, I've now got more money than I can spend. The allowance he's giving me covers anything I want, although I can't fritter away too much without drawing attention to myself. Stu thinks I should go back to work just to keep up appearances, but I'm not keen on that idea, especially now I'm seeing Tom.

We kill a couple of hours until lunch and then head down to the river with a picnic from M&S. The air is cool but not cold, and we sit on a grassy riverbank and watch as families feed the massive horde of squawking ducks and hissing swans. We chat as we eat – about his family, and school – and he asks me about the ribbing Nina and Michelle have been giving me this week.

'Now they're on at me about you,' I tell him, discarding my half-eaten sandwich.

'Are they? In what way?'

'They think I've got the hots for you.'

'Don't you?' he asks with a grin.

'I wouldn't be here if I didn't,' I say boldly, which makes him laugh and wrap his arm round my neck, engulfing me in his warmth. I smile up at him and he presses his lips gently to mine once, twice, three times, before our teeth knock together as we smile. We laugh lightly and pull apart, but that's it: the ice has been broken and we spend the rest of the day kissing and cuddling.

Tom invites me back to his house later that afternoon. It's pretty soon to be meeting each other's families – even though he's already well acquainted with Stu from school, of course – but he's keen for me to say hi to his mum.

He lives in a large, four-bedroomed detached house on a tree-lined street with its own private driveway and a red brick wall out the front. *It's a far cry from my shabby terrace*, I muse, as Tom unlocks the front door.

A tall, slim, blonde woman appears in the hall the moment we step over the threshold.

'You're back!' she exclaims.

'Hi, Mum. This is Jessie,' Tom says casually, motioning for me to come forward.

'Oh!' She looks surprised to see me. 'Hello there,' she says pleasantly, quickly recovering. 'It's lovely to meet you, Jessie. I'm Caroline. Have you two had a good day?'

'Great, thank you,' I reply politely, hovering slightly behind Tom. I'm not normally this shy.

'Is Becky around?' Tom asks.

'No, she's gone into town, but she'll be back for dinner. Is Jessie staying?' she asks.

Tom gives me a questioning look.

'You're very welcome to,' she adds. 'Chicken casserole. There's plenty to go around.'

'If you're sure that's OK?' I say, finding this whole scenario a tiny bit excruciating. I've never had dinner at a boy's house before. Not when it's just me, like this. I met Jack's parents in LA – individually because they've split up – but they were very laid-back. And anyway Jack's older. Eighteen. It seemed to me that they let him get away with murder. *Why am I thinking about Jack?* I try and concentrate.

'Cool,' Tom says, as though he hasn't a care in the world. 'We'll be upstairs.'

'It'll be about half an hour,' his mum tells us as we head towards the staircase.

'Thanks,' I reply, following Tom. As we walk up, it occurs to me that he's done this plenty of times before – with other girls, I mean. I don't think I know of any length of time that he hasn't had a serious girlfriend. Before Isla there was Beatrice, before Beatrice there was Maria, and I can't remember the name of the one before her, but there definitely was one.

With all of these thoughts flying around, I don't feel that comfortable when we go into his room and he pushes the door to, not quite closing it. His room is huge and it smells of him, of his aftershave-slash-deodorant. His walls are covered with posters: his favourite football players, and I immediately see Taylor Swift, Lana Del Ray and Katy Perry, all looking smoking hot and less than efficiently covered with clothing. Humph. I also notice he has a few posters of bands and artists that I like, including cool graphically designed ones for Arcade Fire and Jack White.

I try to ignore Katy's impressively sparkly rack as I go to sit on his bed. It hasn't escaped my notice that it's a double. I wonder if Isla was allowed to stay over. I'm sure they were having sex, and I hate the thought of her being here.

'Are you alright?' he asks, noting my expression. He sits down a little away from me, swivelling to face me so his leg is resting on the bed.

'I'm fine,' I reply, tucking my hair behind my ears. Then I continue before I can stop myself: 'I haven't been in too many boys' rooms before.' His eyes widen. How mortifying. I try to laugh it off, but then a memory of making out with Jack on his bed comes back to me and my face heats up. Double my mortification factor. Things got a little hot and heavy with Jack – and way faster than they should've done. Stop thinking about him, dammit!

'Have you?' I find myself asking.

'What, been in many boys' rooms before?' he asks.

'You're deflecting the question,' I point out with a smirk.

He looks up at the ceiling before returning his eyes to mine. 'I don't know, five?'

'*Five?*' I squeak.

'Hey, I didn't say anything had happened in all of them.' He blushes. 'How many boys' bedrooms have you been in?' He turns the tables on me.

'Two,' I say, my face burning again because one of those boys was Jack.

He frowns. 'Who were they?'

'Dean Smith…'

'*Him?*' he says with distaste.

'It was when we were fourteen!' I laugh. Dean is one of the more badass boys in my year, but I thought he was cute for a while. He plays football, too. 'We only went out for a couple of months,' I tell Tom quickly. 'And we only kissed a few times.'

'Who else?' he asks, to my dismay.

'You don't know him,' I reply, hoping he'll drop it.

'Now I'm curious.' No such luck. 'What's his name?'

'Jack,' I say tightly.

'Does he go to school?'

'No, like I said, you don't know him.' *Drop it, drop it, drop it…*

'When was this? How old is he?'

I answer his second question. 'Eighteen.'

'Does he go to college with Natalie?'

Shit. 'No, he lives in America.'

His face falls. 'Was this over the summer?'

I nod reluctantly.

'Oh.' Great. Now I've really pissed him off.

'Didn't you snog anyone in Ibiza?' I ask.

'No, actually,' he replies, sounding none too pleased. 'I could have, but I didn't want to.'

'Why not?'

He looks pointedly at me.

'Sorry,' I say quietly, realising he resisted because of his feelings for me.

'Who was he?' he asks.

'Just some guy.'

'Nice,' he says sourly.

Wow, I wouldn't have pegged him as the jealous type.

'What do you want to know?' I ask gently, feeling disconcerted by his reaction. I like it that he cares, but I don't like the way it's making me feel: i.e. guilty.

'Have you stayed in touch with him?' he asks.

'No!' *Well, at least, he hasn't replied to my email*, I think to myself. I don't say that I've stayed in touch with Jack's sister. 'We only kissed,' I explain, but I'm not sure that's going to make Tom feel much better.

He flops back on the bed, staring up at the ceiling.

'Do you want me to go?' I ask uneasily after a moment of silence.

'What?' He props himself up on his elbows and stares at me with those very brown eyes of his. 'No!' He shoves his hair off his face and sits back up properly, taking my hands and pulling me towards him. I breathe a small sigh of relief into his mouth as he kisses me. He is *unbelievably* good at this. But then it sounds like he's had a lot of practice...

Jealousy swiftly replaces my butterflies and I tug away, looking down at my hands and then back up at him.

'Why did you and Isla split up?' I ask hesitantly.

'She cheated on me,' he replies darkly.

'What? You're kidding!' I'm amazed. Is she crazy?

'Nope,' he replies flippantly. 'At a party. Snogged some other guy. She regretted it, but it was too late.'

'You couldn't forgive her?'

'No,' he says firmly.

There's a loud knock on the door and it suddenly swings open to reveal a tall, curvy girl with long, dark-brown, wavy hair. Becky.

'Hey!' she says jovially, her eyes landing mischievously on me. 'Sorry, was I interrupting anything?'

'No!' I cry, automatically edging away from Tom.

'Yes!' Tom replies simultaneously. Cringe.

'You really should lock your door, then,' she tells him with a grin.

'I don't have a lock, remember?' he replies wryly.

'That's right. Well, close it, then. Oh, that's right,' she says with a wicked grin, 'Mum's banned you from doing that, too.'

Oh my God, this is humiliating.

'Sorry, *when* are you going back to university?' Tom asks with a hint of amusement, and I realise then that Becky's only teasing.

She laughs and comes into the room, pulling up a chair at his desk.

'You'll miss me when I'm gone.' She fixes her blue eyes on me, narrowing them as she tries to place me.

'You're—'

'Jessie,' I tell her.

'I recognise you. You two go to the same school, right?'

'I'm in Year Eleven,' I say.

'Aah.' She smiles at Tom and he rolls his eyes, but she doesn't make another cheeky comment about me being younger.

Becky stays and chats for a bit until I've relaxed a little in her company. But only a little. She seems like a big personality and she *is* four years older than me. Daunting.

'Anyway,' she says, getting to her feet, 'Mum said dinner will be ready soon, so come down.'

'Will do,' Tom replies with a smile. He's clearly very fond of her.

Dinner is surprisingly relaxed, with Caroline relaying occasional amusing anecdotes about Tom and Becky's childhood. She doesn't ask about my family situation, and I'm guessing Tom filled her in about my mum, so I'm thankful for that.

Eventually it's time for us to call it a night.

'What are you doing tomorrow?' Tom asks me at the doorway while Stu waits in the car. 'I'm playing footie in Grenfell Park if you want to swing by?'

I give him a wry look.

'Not to sit on the sidelines like one of my groupies,' he remembers with a grin. 'We could hang out afterwards.'

'Haven't you had enough of me?' I ask, smiling.

He reaches down and takes my hand, his thumb skimming across my wrist. 'Not nearly enough,' he says with meaning, his face close to mine. He doesn't kiss me, though, not with Stuart in view.

'OK.' I nod. 'What time?'

'Two-ish?'

'I'll see you there.'

He grins and gives me a quick peck on my lips before I break away from him.

'Good day?' Stu asks drily, as I climb into the car.

'Mmm,' I reply, looking dreamily out of the window, the feeling of Tom's lips still buzzing against mine. 'Very good.'

Chapter 10

By the end of the following week, everyone at school knows that Tom and I are a couple. Seeing him every day, I feel like we've been together for a lot longer than we actually have. We even talk to each other at night before we fall asleep.

Now it's Saturday and I'm going over to his house for dinner. I think I'm going to come clean about my dad tonight. Johnny said that I could tell people that I trust. And I trust Tom. Definitely.

Johnny stuck to his word and asked Stu about Tom, which made me feel oddly giddy. It's surreal to know that my father's a superstar who's concerned for my welfare. I don't think he – or Stu – would be too thrilled to hear that Tom's mum is out tonight, though, so I've kept this information to myself. The thought of being alone with Tom in his room without having to worry about the door being open makes me feel jumpy. In fact, we'll have the whole house to ourselves because Becky's not there, either.

*

'Hey,' Tom says with a warm smile when he opens the front door. He looks past me to wave at Stu and I do the same, before watching him drive off down the road. Luckily Stu didn't insist on saying hi to Caroline.

'Has your mum left already?' I ask, as I step into the hall.

'Just,' he replies, closing the door behind me. 'She was late leaving.'

'Did she know I was coming over?'

'She helped me cook you dinner,' he admits with a shy grin, leaning against the wall and crossing his arms.

'You've cooked me dinner?' I grin, as I slip off my jacket and hang it over the banister. 'I thought we were getting takeaway?'

'Changed my mind.' He holds his arms out to me and I step into them, tilting my face up to his. He kisses me gently.

I'm relieved to hear that his mum knows I'm going to be here. I didn't really relish the thought of going behind her back. But if her date goes badly and she comes home early… Damn, I hope she doesn't.

'What have you cooked?' I ask, pulling away and sniffing the air. There's something distinctly delicious-smelling coming from the direction of the kitchen.

'You'll see.' He leads me through to the living room where *The X Factor* is on the telly.

We sit together on the sofa and Tom puts his arms round me, practically pulling me onto his lap. I giggle and snuggle closer to him, turning my face towards the telly.

'Oi,' he gently chastises, tilting my chin back in his direction. We kiss, gently at first, while Simon Cowell drones on at someone. Tom fumbles around and the sound cuts off, making me giggle. There goes this week's viewing.

'Let me put some music on,' he says, tapping my thigh so I edge off him.

He lopes over to the speakers and delves into his pocket for his iPhone. I love his body: the boyish but defined biceps that protrude from the short-sleeved T-shirt he's wearing. He's so tall that he makes me feel smaller than my five foot six inches. His hair is falling down across his forehead and I want to brush it back from his face. As he sorts out the music and returns to the sofa, I remember that I can.

My fingers slide through his soft hair as The Temper Trap's 'Sweet Disposition' kicks off in the background.

'I love this song,' I say.

'Me too.'

We have pretty similar tastes in music, which I'm pleased about, but I think I respected Jack's taste even more. There I go again. I wish I could stop comparing Tom to Jack, but, much as I try, the latter is never far from my mind. It's so confusing. Maybe, when I see Jack at Christmas, I'll realise that whatever we had is well and truly over.

Hopefully.

It's not long before Tom's lips find mine again, and my head is swimming with the reminder that we're completely alone. His hands move to my waist and I shiver involuntarily as he slides them along my curves. My breathing quickens, but I don't stop kissing him. Once more he manoeuvres me onto his lap and I wriggle to get comfortable. My legs end up straddling his and shivers rocket down my spine as he pulls me closer. He sighs, shakily, into my mouth, then draws away slightly, moving his hands up to run his fingers through my hair. He smiles crookedly at me and I gaze down at him.

'You're so beautiful,' he murmurs with a seriousness that makes my insides melt. This has gone past 'like' and Jack feels a million miles away.

I bend down to kiss him again, pressing my chest against his. He draws a sharp breath and then his hands are on my waist, edging me away from him. He flashes me a self-conscious smile and I realise as he glances down that, oh, God... I quickly slide off him.

'Sorry,' he mutters with embarrassment, adjusting his jeans.

I bite my lip and blush profusely, looking at him from underneath my lashes.

'That look you're giving me is not helping,' he comments, not without humour. It breaks the ice and I laugh lightly and fiddle with my hair.

His head falls back onto the sofa cushion and he gazes sideways at me, his dark eyes burning into mine.

'I'm going to ruin dinner,' he whispers.

I look past him to the open-plan kitchen. A thin trail of smoke is coming out of the oven. 'I think you already have.'

'Bollocks!' he exclaims, leaping up from the sofa and rushing over to pull the oven door open. I follow him in time to see more smoke spill out. 'Argh!' He looks around hopelessly so I hand him an oven mitt and he draws the dish out. Its contents are charred black on top.

'We'll just scrape the burnt bits off,' I say, feeling sorry for him as he swears and places the dish down hurriedly on the hob. 'Look, it's not that bad.'

He peers dubiously at the blackened pieces of chicken as I hunt around for some cutlery to see if I can repair the damage.

We're in good spirits again soon afterwards because, despite the overcooking, it tastes delicious. We sit at the kitchen table lit by candlelight and he pours me a glass of wine. I feel very grown-up, even though I don't really like wine that much.

He catches me gazing at him and pauses for a moment.

'Is it OK?' he asks, nodding at my food.

'It's lovely,' I reply. 'Did you really cook this?'

'Well, I had quite a lot of help from Mum, but I did peel the carrots.'

'Is that all?' I laugh.

'And the potatoes. I peeled the potatoes.'

'Wow, that's really something,' I joke.

'I also crumbled up a stock cube.'

'Gordon Ramsay in the making.'

He laughs.

'It was nice of your mum to do this,' I say.

'She likes you,' he replies.

I wonder if she liked Isla more… Luckily, before I can even think about asking, he speaks again.

'I hope I can meet your dad one day. Is he coming back to the UK any time soon?'

'I don't know. Not for a while,' I say, chewing on my lip.

Now's my chance.

'What?' he asks, seeing my expression.

'There's something I need to tell you,' I say, as his face freezes. 'About my dad,' I add.

'Jeez,' he exclaims, slumping back in his chair. 'I thought it was going to be something bad, then.'

'Hey?' I'm confused.

'I thought you were going to tell me you've kissed someone else or something.'

'No!' I cry, horrified and then amused.

He visibly relaxes. 'So what about your dad?' he asks, and then it's my turn to feel tense again.

I've been here before and it didn't go down well on either occasion. Neither Libby nor Natalie believed me when I told them about Johnny.

'Actually,' I say, a brainwave coming to me, 'it might be easier if I show you.'

'Show me what?'

'Who he is,' I reply, getting up to retrieve my phone from my bag in the hall.

'Who he is?' he calls after me like a parrot.

I type some very familiar words into the search engine of my phone. The story about me being a local girl comes up, complete with pictures of me in my sunglasses at the riverside restaurant in Henley.

Nervously, I show Tom the pictures. 'That's me,' I say quietly. He takes the phone from me and scrutinises it, then his eyes widen. He's completely and utterly lost for words.

'I'm sorry I didn't tell you before,' I say, but he's still speechless. 'I haven't been able to tell anyone,' I almost whisper. 'Libby and Natalie know, but they've been sworn to secrecy. I haven't even told Lou yet,' I add, to deafening silence. 'Are you going to say anything?' I ask finally.

'I— He— What?' he splutters. 'What? How? *How?*' he repeats.

'My mum went out with Johnny before I was born.' My face warms. 'She fell pregnant, he went off to become a world-famous rock star,' I say a touch sarkily, 'and she didn't tell me because she didn't want me to run off and go to live with him.'

'You're Johnny Jefferson's daughter?' Tom says in not much more than a whisper himself.

'Yes.'

101

'You're not kidding about this, are you?' he checks.

'I swear on my mother's grave,' I say solemnly.

'Bloody hell,' he exclaims, but my surge of relief is soon replaced with uncertainty.

The way he's looking at me… It's different. It's almost like he doesn't know me any more.

'I'm sorry I didn't tell you sooner,' I say in a small voice. 'But it's all been so confusing. Such a strange summer.'

'Come and sit down,' he says suddenly, nodding at the sofa.

'What about dinner?' I ask.

'I'll heat it up later.' He takes my hand as we fall onto the sofa beside each other.

I tell him everything. How I found out, how I met Johnny's solicitor, how I went to LA to stay with the Jeffersons for a while. I tell him the truth about my half-brothers and their real names. I tell him about Brian. He listens to every single word, asking questions where appropriate, and I feel a heavy weight that I didn't even know I'd been carrying lift from my shoulders. I'm so glad he knows everything.

'Johnny wants to meet you,' I say finally, and his face freezes comically.

'He knows about me?' he asks, flabbergasted.

'Of course he knows about you,' I reply.

'Johnny Jefferson knows who I am?' he says again, more slowly, as though still not quite believing it. 'I can't believe you're Johnny Jefferson's daughter,' he says, unable to take his eyes from mine.

'Believe it,' I reply.

He shakes his head with astonishment. 'You really do look like him, you know.'

I shrug slightly.

'God!' he erupts. 'Weren't Nina and her friends teasing you about this?'

'Yes!'

He laughs suddenly, a slightly crazed laugh that I can't help but join in with. 'Jesus Christ, what did Mr Taylor say?'

We carry on talking until, to our surprise, we hear the sound of a key in the lock. I realise with dismay that Caroline is home already.

'Hello!' she says brightly, appearing at the doorway, her eyes darting between us. She probably thinks we've been sitting here, making out.

'How was it?' Tom asks her.

'Great!' she exclaims, coming into the room.

'You're home early.' He sounds almost accusatory, as though he doesn't believe her when she says she had a good time.

'It's eleven thirty,' she replies.

'Is it?' Tom and I both say at once.

'You didn't eat your dinner!' she exclaims, spying the leftovers of our food still laid out on the table.

'I burnt it,' Tom replies apologetically, quickly getting to his feet. 'Sorry, Mum,' he adds.

'Oh, dear,' she says with regret. 'Are you still hungry? Do you want me to make you something else?' She looks at me.

'No, no, I'm fine, thank you,' I reply, getting up also and feeling bad that we haven't even cleared the table. 'I didn't realise how late it was.'

'Time flies when you're having fun,' she says with a smile, picking up our plates. I quickly grab what I can and take it through to the kitchen.

'I'll do this,' Tom says hastily, taking the items from me. 'Mum, leave it,' he adds, as I stand there awkwardly while they fuss between themselves about who's going to clear up. 'Can I give Jessie a lift home?' he asks eventually.

'What, in the car?' His mum sounds alarmed.

'Yeah, with you in the passenger seat,' he replies. He only had half a glass of wine, and that was hours ago now.

'Oh, I see! Yes, I don't see why not. Are you ready now?'

I nod, thrilled at the thought of seeing Tom drive. If he gets his licence soon, we'll be able to go anywhere together.

I sit in the middle at the back, watching his toned arm in the darkness as he changes gear. I can see the goosebumps on his forearm. It's cold out, but he shrugged off his mother's suggestion of a jacket. The journey is smooth and easy, and Caroline doesn't have to say anything about his driving. My heart is bursting with pride by the time we pull up outside my close, and then I feel a sudden spike of humiliation as I realise his mum is peering out of the window at my shabby house.

It's my mum's house, I think defensively. If Caroline doesn't like it, tough.

Tom hops out of the car and opens my door, taking my hand as I step out. We walk hand in hand to the front door.

'Sorry my mum came home like that. I feel like there's still so much to talk about,' he murmurs, his face close to mine in the darkness. 'Shall I – shall I call you when I get back home?' he asks tentatively.

My face breaks out into a smile and I nod. He kisses me quickly with his mum watching and walks away with a spring in his step. I go inside to wait for his call.

Chapter 11

By the end of the weekend, I feel so close to Tom. He cancels football on Sunday and we spend the day together, and that night we talk on the phone for an hour.

Stu thinks it's a bit ridiculous, but I know he's not really annoyed. He likes Tom, and I can tell he knows that Tom doesn't mess girls around. He'd still be with Isla if she hadn't cheated on him. I feel uneasy as that thought occurs to me.

We're even more tactile than usual that week at school and I'm not oblivious to the occasional snigger.

I only realise just how far the gossip about us has gone when Libby corners me in the corridor outside the library.

'What is it?' I stutter, as she pulls me into the thankfully deserted space.

'I just—' She looks uncomfortable.

'Spit it out,' I say, not unkindly.

'It's just that I heard… Have you and Tom…?'

'What?'

'You know,' she says, as the blood drains from my face. 'Have you…'

'No!' I exclaim. I can't believe she's even asking me. We've only been together a few weeks!

'I just heard—'

'What?' I demand to know. 'What have you heard?'

'That you two have done it.'

'Jesus!' I erupt. 'No! We're just closer than we were! I've told him… I've told him everything,' I say significantly, and her hazel eyes open wide with surprise.

'About your dad?' she asks.

'Yes!'

'Do you trust him?'

'Yes!' I say even more firmly.

'Well, I just… I thought you'd want to know,' she says quietly.

'Thanks for telling me,' I force myself to say, trying not to shoot the messenger.

She nods abruptly and we walk out of the library together.

Tom, Lou, Chris and I go to a party at Natalie's house that night. She called earlier in the week to tell me about it. Her parents are away this weekend and, when that happens, she and her older brother Mike tend to make the most of it. Her parents are massively laid-back, so I don't think they mind. Perhaps they don't even care, although Natalie doesn't say a lot about her mum and dad, neither negative nor positive. We don't really talk about personal stuff, which is partly why I like her. She's all about having fun.

Initially, Tom and I were supposed to be going to the movies tonight, but Natalie was having none of it.

'I haven't seen you for ages,' she interrupted. 'You have to come!'

'Can Tom—'

'Yes, he can come, too,' she said wearily. 'Do you two live in each other's pockets now?'

She claimed that she was joking when I didn't answer, ending our call with, 'Of course he can. The more the merrier.'

She meant that last part. Her place is more packed than I've ever seen it, and it doesn't take long for me to see that Isla is here, too. My grip on Tom's hand unwittingly tightens when I see her walk into the kitchen. Tom looks past me, clocking who I've seen. I let go of his hand.

'Hey,' he complains, reaching over to take it again and flashing me an enquiring look. I shrug and shake my head, reaching for my cider and taking a large swig. Natalie, Em and Lou are outside smoking, but I haven't had a cigarette since LA. It helps that Tom doesn't smoke. I know he doesn't like it.

Later, we find ourselves in the crowded TV room where Natalie has got PlayStation SingStar up and running. Usually she'd persuade me to join in, but I'm refusing all of her attempts tonight because I'm not drunk enough. I only ever sing in front of other people when I'm wasted.

No, that's not true. I sang with Johnny when I was stone-cold sober. I still can't believe I did that. He was in his private studio playing one of his new songs to his friend Christian. I went in to have a listen and, the next thing I knew, Johnny was asking me to accompany him.

'Get in here,' he said from inside his glass-windowed box.

'Go on!' Christian urged me.

'Forget it.' I shook my head determinedly. 'I don't sing in public, remember?'

107

And then Christian told me I'd regret it if I didn't and I realised that he was right.

God, I loved being in that studio with Johnny. We sang an acoustic version of one of his big hits. I just did a few harmonies to start with and then joined in and sang with Johnny until the end. Christian's reaction shocked me. He was blown away and I was on such a high.

I'd give anything to feel like that again. SingStar can't compete.

Still, it's damn funny watching Natalie and Lou give it a go.

After a while, Tom heads off to get us some more drinks and I discover to my deeply unpleasant surprise that I have his ex's attention. She's with two of her friends and they're all looking over at me, then turning back to each other.

I stare back at them defiantly.

'Jessie! Come on, please!' Natalie implores when the Guns N' Roses song she and Lou were murdering finishes. I shake my head with a grin.

'Go on,' Chris urges, as a hot-and-sweaty-but-still-utterly-gorgeous Lou joins us. He wraps his arm round her neck.

'No,' I reiterate, noticing one of Isla's friends looking over and saying something that makes Isla laugh nastily.

I excuse myself to go to the loo, hoping I'll find Tom on the way back, but Isla and her friends are at the bottom of the stairs and I have to walk past them.

'*Slag…*'

White noise fills my head at Isla's jibe and suddenly I see red.

'You might've shagged him and then screwed someone else, but I've got more restraint!' I bite back.

Her face flushes and the looks on her friends' faces could kill me right there on the spot. As I walk past them, one of them shoves me. I stumble, but don't fall.

'Stupid bitch,' Isla hisses after me.

Blood rushes into my face. Tom only told me she kissed another guy – not slept with him – but I wanted to hurt her. I think I've just gone too far. I glance into the TV room only to catch Tom's eye before I hurry out through the kitchen to the garden. A moment later he's caught up with me.

'Jessie?' he asks with alarm. 'What is it?'

I gulp back a sob. There's a bench at the end of the garden which, thankfully, is empty. I sit down and angrily brush away my tears and try to take a deep, shaky breath as Tom sits beside me, his dark eyes regarding me with worry.

'Is this about your mum?'

'No.' I stare at him and then look around, bemused. 'We've been here before, haven't we?' I say, sidetracked for a moment.

He nods slightly, a sympathetic smile on his face. Before anything had happened between us – when we'd only spoken a couple of times – he comforted me on this very bench. I had heard a song that we'd played at Mum's funeral and it had set me off. That was when he told me about his dad leaving.

'What's wrong?' he asks.

'Isla called me a slag.'

He looks horrified, but his expression swiftly transforms into disgust. I can tell he's furious with her.

'But what I said was worse.'

Feeling ashamed, I repeat my words.

'Well,' he says, 'maybe she did shag him, I don't know. And I don't care any more. I can't believe she said that to you when we haven't even done anything!'

I don't know how or why, but the look on his face makes me laugh. I think I might be feeling a tiny bit hysterical.

'Come here,' he says, wrapping his arm round me and pulling me close. Some of the ice in my stomach is instantly thawed, but there's something that's bothering me so I may as well just get it over with. I pull away and look at him. 'Were you her first?'

He looks uncomfortable, but he answers me with a nod.

'Urgh,' I can't help but mutter, edging further away. 'How many girls have you slept with?'

The expression on his face tightens. 'Just Isla.'

Why oh why did I ask? I'm a virgin, too. Will he be comparing me to Isla, if we ever make it that far?

'Stop it,' he berates me, seeing the look on my face. 'I'm with you. You,' he says firmly. 'Don't ruin it. She broke my heart.'

'I don't want to hear that,' I moan.

'I'm not telling you to hurt you. I'm telling you because the way I feel about you… It's stronger. I don't want to spoil this, so I'm not going to push you to do anything you don't want to.'

I manage a small smile and he cups my face and kisses me.

'Please don't care about what people say,' he begs. 'They'll find something else to gossip about soon.'

He's not wrong. The very next day, in fact. And it blows my liaison with Tom right out of the water.

Chapter 12

When Stu wakes me up, I know instantly that something's wrong. Mum's face flashes into my mind. But no one's died this time. This is about me.

The whole of the front page of our local paper, in fact.

Me.

Me.

Me.

I'm completely and utterly screwed.

I read the story online because Stu hasn't left the house to buy the paper yet. Wendel was the one who called to tell us about it.

> Two short months ago, Maidenhead resident Jessie Pickerill was a very ordinary fifteen-year-old girl. But then her stepfather revealed a secret

that would turn her whole life upside
down. Her biological father is
superstar Johnny Jefferson...

I skim over the words as my blood pumps with adrenalin.

Her mother, who sadly passed away
earlier in the year, never told Jessie
the truth. 'It was such a shock,' our
source tells us...

Source? What source? I meet Stu's eyes. 'Who told them?'

He shakes his head. 'I don't know.'

'Does Johnny know? Does Wendel? Why hasn't Johnny called?'

'It's the middle of the night in LA,' Stu replies. 'Wendel hasn't told him yet.'

I feel a spike of loneliness. I wish he would. I wish he'd call his flipping client and wake him up so he can reassure his goddamn daughter.

'What's the time here?' I think to ask.

'Six a.m.,' Stu replies.

No wonder my head and eyes hurt so much. Add that to the anxious pain in my stomach and I'm really not doing so well.

The phone rings and we both jump. 'Here it goes,' he says resignedly.

'It might be Johnny,' I say, but he puts his hand on my arm to keep me seated at the table while he answers the phone. I wait with baited breath, and then he says: 'No comment.' My heart sinks as he ends the call. I notice that the curtains in the kitchen are still drawn.

'Are they… Is anyone outside?' I ask with stunned horror.

'I'm afraid so,' he admits.

'Oh, God,' I say with a gulp. This is it. This is really happening. I won't be able to stay here…

'Oh, God!' I say again, pushing my chair from the table and running up the stairs into the spare room. 'Mum,' I say out loud, as my voice shakes, and then my whole body. I sit on the bed among her things, enveloped by the smell of her, and Stu leaves me alone as I begin to cry. This is it. I'm going to have to leave this house. Leave Mum.

Johnny is on the other end of the phone half an hour later. Stu decided 'to hell with Wendel' and called him himself, rousing him from his sleep.

'You need your dad,' he mutters, wincing slightly. He hands over the phone and I sit up from my foetal position in the spare room. Johnny is *angry*.

'Meg and Annie are already in the office,' he tells me.

'Do you think they'll find out who the source is?'

'Honestly? No,' he says, a hardness to his tone. 'Do you have any idea?' he asks me.

'No. I mean, hardly anyone knows,' I say, feeling a wave of sickness engulf me once more. 'I've only told Natalie, Libby and Tom.'

'Natalie and Libby hadn't said anything so far,' he says, and I hate where he's going with this.

'It's *not* Tom,' I cut him off, my voice rising. He can't make me doubt Tom. 'It could be anyone.' I will him to believe it, clutching at straws. 'There are girls in my school who teased me that I looked like the picture in the papers. Maybe they've realised it really is me?'

'I doubt that,' Johnny states. 'Is it possible that one of your friends told one of their friends? You need to know who you can trust.' He's speaking from experience.

'No!' But, deep down, I'm not so sure. I've always been worried that Libby would tell Amanda, and Natalie and I haven't been as close recently. Our other friend, Em, is a huge Johnny Jefferson fan. If she knew, I'm not sure she'd be able to keep quiet. Word would spread like wildfire until someone blabbed to the press.

'Are you absolutely certain about Tom?' Johnny asks again, and at that moment I really don't like him very much.

'It's not him!' I say angrily. 'He wouldn't have told anyone! He cares about me too much!' A lump springs up in my throat. It can't be him. He's made me happier in these last few weeks than I've been in months. I'll be heartbroken if he has anything – anything at all – to do with this. Could he have told Chris? No, he wouldn't. What about his mum? Becky?

Oh, God, no, please no.

'I've gotta go,' I say to Johnny.

'You know you can't leave the house,' he says sharply. 'I'll send security for you. You and Stu can relocate to my place for now.'

I start to cry.

'Jessie,' he says gently, and his voice is torn. 'You've *got* to.'

Stu comes back into the room and takes the phone from me. I barely hear his half of the conversation because my head is spinning so much. I'm going to have to leave my home, and I have no idea how long it will be before I'll be allowed to come back.

As soon as Stu ends the call, he stares down at me kindly.

'Go pack a suitcase,' he says. 'Two if you like. Just your most important things.'

My most important things, I already know, are my memories, but I'll also take my photo albums and Mum's dressing gown that still smells of her. My other stuff can be packed up at another time.

Stu leaves to pull the plug out of the wall before the phone calls start up again, and I return to my room to ring Tom from my mobile.

'Don't use your mobile,' Stu's voice calls from the landing outside my door.

'What? Why?' I exclaim.

'It could be tapped,' he says, poking his head round the door. 'You don't want to give the press anything else to gossip about, do you?'

'But I have to call Tom!'

'It's not a good idea, Jess.'

'It wasn't him,' I say angrily, just in case Johnny has got to him.

'I'm not saying it was,' he replies firmly. 'But Johnny has someone coming within the hour and you can call Tom once we're at his place where we know the line is secure.'

'I can't not call him! He'll be worried if he wakes up and finds out about all of this!'

'Send him a text. But that's it. I'm warning you, Jess,' he adds when he sees me wavering. 'Don't make this worse for yourself – or him.'

I nod tightly and he leaves the room, giving me privacy to type out a text for Tom:

The press know about me. It's in the papers. I've gotta go to Johnny's house, but I'll call you when I get there.

I keep it neutral – just in case the press have ways of tapping into text messages, too.

The car arrives an hour later. By then I have my bags ready in the hall and my sunglasses on the top of my head, ready to put on. Not that it matters. The picture of me on the front of the paper is enormous. It's a close-up so I can't see what I'm wearing, but I don't recognise it. I don't know when it was taken. I'm smiling and looking almost straight into the lens. Wendel says it's likely to be a pap shot and I wouldn't have even known they were there. It could have been taken anywhere, on the street, at the park, and I was completely oblivious to them waiting and watching. It makes me feel sick. Sicker than I already feel.

'OK?' Stu asks me, clearly not expecting an answer. I don't give him one. A burly man dressed in a black suit with an earpiece strides in and takes my bags. Another man is right behind him.

'Miss Jefferson?' he asks me.

'Pickerill,' I correct him, putting my sunglasses in place and feeling Stu's eyes on me.

'This way, please,' he says firmly, and then I'm being shoved out of the door and herded towards the car while the sound of cameras clicking and people jostling reaches my ears. Seconds later I'm in the car with Stu beside me.

'Bloody hell!' he exclaims, and I'm surreally aware that I hardly ever hear him swear.

Stu won't have seen anything like that before, but I got a taste of it when I was in LA with Johnny. The frenzied attention he receives from the press, not to mention his fans, is mind-blowing.

The two men in black are suddenly in the front seats and the car moves forward. The windows, they assure me, are completely blacked-out from the sides, but they can barely get the car past the pushy paps taking shots from the front.

'Haven't they ever seen a celebrity's daughter before?' I ask out loud.

'Not one with your story,' the second bodyguard replies.

I glance out of my window, back at our tired old house, its front garden overgrown with weeds and one of the curtains in the living room hanging slightly off the rail.

No, I don't suppose they have, I think, a touch bitterly, before turning my eyes to the front and the life that lies ahead.

Chapter 13

It's very strange to be back in Johnny's house without the warmth and chaos that his family's presence brings. My family's, I guess.

When Bruce – the second bodyguard – finally closes the door behind us to give us some privacy, Stu and I just stand there in the hall, not really knowing what to do.

We've been told the housekeeper is on her way to get the house ready for us, but it all looks pristine to me.

'Cup of tea?' Stu asks.

I nod and follow him into the kitchen. Bruce took our bags upstairs, but I'm too shell-shocked to go and explore. I wonder which room Stu will be staying in.

Stu opens the fridge and peers inside, but of course there's no milk.

'Don't worry about it,' I tell him. 'I'm sure Helen will be here soon.'

Johnny's Henley housekeeper is only part-time when he's

abroad. I hope she doesn't mind coming into work for my sake. This is so weird.

'Can I go and call Tom?' I ask Stu. Bruce confirmed that the phones in the study have secure lines.

'Sure,' he says. 'I might put the telly on for a bit.'

I feel nervous as I dial Tom's number. It only rings once before he picks up.

'Are you OK?' he asks with such concern that my eyes prick with tears.

'I'm a bit freaked out,' I reply weakly.

'What happened? I thought you were safe. I didn't think…' His voice trails off.

'Someone must've told them.'

'But who else knows?'

'Only Libby and Natalie. You didn't—'

'No!' he exclaims, sounding alarmed. But I have to ask. Despite my unwavering belief in him when I was speaking to Johnny, I can't help the toxic doubt that is creeping in.

'Not even your sister?'

'Jessie, it *wasn't* me,' he says firmly. 'Christ, did you think that it was?' He sounds hurt.

'No, I didn't! But I had to ask.'

'I didn't even tell my mum!' he exclaims. 'Her face nearly fell off a cliff earlier.'

Relief surges through me. I believe him.

'You don't have any idea, then?'

'No,' I admit. 'You were the third and last person I told.'

'Johnny doesn't think it was me, does he?'

'Um…'

'Oh, shit, he does.'

119

'He doesn't know what to think.'

'Bloody hell,' he mutters. 'Great way to impress your dad,' he adds in a sullen voice.

I can't help but smile. 'I think we have worse things to worry about right now,' I say gently.

'Sorry,' he says quickly.

I laugh a little, but the smile quickly falls from my face. 'I can't quite believe this is happening. I don't know when I'm even going to see you next.'

'What? Why not? Won't you be at school?'

'Not this week, apparently. I don't know when I'll be allowed to come back. When this all dies down, I guess.'

I feel like a caged animal that week. I stay inside because, despite what Johnny said about it being illegal to print photos of people taken on their own private property, I hate the thought of the press spying on me. Stu has to return to work and the bodyguards stay out of my way, so I feel very alone.

I speak to Tom every day before and after school, and I'm pleasantly surprised when Libby calls me every evening. Apparently I'm all anyone is talking about. I feel bad that Lou found out about me along with everyone else, but she says that she understands.

The story hits the nationals, and the local paper runs pieces every day, quoting various sources. I recognise some names, including Nina's and Michelle's, but then the headmaster sends home a letter forbidding anyone else from talking to the press.

Towards the end of the week, there's a story about Tom which makes me freak out even more. There are no direct quotes from him, of course, but I hate that he's being dragged into it all. I hope his mum isn't too angry.

'She's not,' he tries to reassure me when we speak on Friday night. 'Honestly, Jessie, it doesn't matter. They'll get bored soon and will leave us alone.'

'What do you mean? They're not harassing you, are they?'

'There's at least one man waiting outside the driveway, but it's fine,' he says.

'What?!' I had no idea anyone was 'doorstepping' him. That's the technical term, apparently.

'It's fine.' He laughs. 'He's just a fat nacker with nothing better to do. And I think Mum might find it all quite exciting, if I'm being honest.'

I sigh and he chuckles quietly.

'What are you up to tomorrow?' he asks.

'Nothing,' I reply miserably.

'Want some company?'

'Are you kidding?' I respond excitedly. 'Will your mum let you come over?'

'She reckons it can't hurt, now that the press know about me.'

She had wanted him to keep his distance, earlier on in the week.

'Oh my God, that would make me so happy!' I exclaim. 'I feel like I'm going insane here.'

The next day can't come soon enough, and my heart jumps when I see Caroline's car pull up at the gate. I almost fall flat on my face in my eagerness to get downstairs, throwing the door open before Tom can even press the doorbell.

'Hey!' he says with a laugh, as I practically knock him over.

121

'Hello!' Stu chirps, coming out into the hall to join us.

I break away from Tom to say hello to Caroline, and Stu offers her a cup of tea that she doesn't refuse. Her eyes dart around the hall as she follows us in, and it strikes me that being in Johnny's house must feel very surreal to her. Tom, too, no doubt.

'I'm just going to show Tom around,' I call after Stu and Caroline, as they go into the kitchen. I'm desperate to get him alone.

We hurry into the first door off the corridor, which happens to be the living room, and shut it behind us. He doesn't waste time kissing me.

I sigh against his lips, then press my face into his neck. He wraps his arms round me and we stand there for a long time. He makes me feel so safe.

Voices in the hall break us apart and the door opens, Stu leading Caroline in, both of them cradling mugs of tea.

'Whoops,' Stu says, seeing us.

'So this is the living room,' I blurt, flashing Stu and Caroline a cheeky grin, before taking Tom's hand and pulling him out of the room. Caroline smiles after us as we go.

'I can't believe we're standing in Johnny Jefferson's house,' Tom says eventually, after we've been – and kissed – in every room. It became a bit of a joke after a while: darting inside, kissing quickly, then darting out again. I've left my room until last. I'm in the Orange Room again. I love it, but I know it will never feel like my own, even with two suitcases' worth of belongings in the wardrobes.

'It's weird, isn't it?' I agree. 'It still feels surreal to me, too.'

'I bet.' He flashes me a sympathetic smile. 'Have you found out any more about who spilt the beans?'

'No,' I admit. 'I don't know if I ever will.'

'Tom!' Caroline's voice comes up the stairs.

I follow him back out onto the landing.

'I'm off,' she calls up to us with a warm smile. 'I'll come back for you tonight, OK?'

'OK.' He nods.

'Bye!' I call down to her.

'Be good,' she says, giving him a meaningful look, and then Stu appears behind her and I see the back of Tom's neck flush.

'Mum!' he mutters with annoyance and embarrassment, but she just smiles and turns to Stu. Tom flashes me an awkward look and then we both go back downstairs. Clearly my bedroom is off limits.

We have a lovely day together, and I almost forget what's been happening outside the walls of the Jeffersons' mansion. I even hunt out the photos of Johnny's mum and that prompts me to show Tom the pictures of Mum I brought with me. Stu, for the most part, leaves us alone. But I'm all too aware of the clock ticking down to the time that Tom's mum will come to collect him. I think Stu senses my unease because he doesn't even so much as raise an eyebrow when we both turn down dessert after dinner and go upstairs to my room. I guess he's indulging my need for privacy. I'm not going to get much of that any more.

Inside my room, Tom takes my hands, but I'm the one to pull him onto the bed. We kiss slowly, languidly, exploring each other's mouths with our tongues. He shifts to lie on top of me and I feel light-headed at the sensation of being under the weight of his solid, fit body. He props himself up on his forearms and breaks away, but I don't want him to stop kissing me. I slide my hands up inside his T-shirt and he breathes in sharply as my fingers trace the definition of his abs. When he kisses me again, it's with a passion that I haven't felt before. I kiss him back, just as heatedly, and then he lets his weight settle back over me so his body is completely flush with mine. A dart of desire shoots through me, but, before I can react, he rolls onto his back and pulls me on top of him, holding me at arm's length. He stares up at me, his eyes seeming even darker than usual.

'Mum's going to be here in a minute,' he whispers.

'I wish you could stay over,' I comment, then blush when I realise how he might take that sentence. We're not *there* yet.

I realise he's watching me, studying my face. Self-consciously, I move off him so we're lying side by side. He sighs and reaches out to stroke my hair away from my face. We stare at each other in silence for several moments, and then the doorbell rings.

'Hmm,' he says sadly.

'Hmm,' I disconsolately agree.

'When do you think you'll be allowed to come back to school?' he asks.

'Maybe Monday.'

'Really?' His eyes light up.

'Apparently Johnny's going to call me tonight with a plan.'

An hour later that's exactly what Johnny does.

'I'm sending Sam over,' Johnny says. 'He'll be with you first thing in the morning.'

'Sam?' I ask with surprise. 'As in Samuel?' His American bodyguard?

'I don't trust anyone else as much as I trust him,' Johnny states.

'But Bruce seems nice.' I don't want to put poor Samuel out and make him fly over from the States.

'Nice isn't safe,' Johnny snaps. 'At least, not safe enough. I don't know Bruce. If you're going back to school, I want Sam to take you.'

'Please don't tell me he's going to be following me around to my lessons,' I say in a pleading voice.

'He will at first—'

'*Johnny!*' I cry with dismay.

'But you'll get used to it.'

'Oh, God, this is going to be mortifying!'

'It's just a short-term solution, Jess.'

'What's that supposed to mean?' I ask sharply.

He doesn't answer at first. 'We'll talk about it when all of this dies down.'

'I'm not moving schools!'

'Jess…'

'I'm not!'

'In that case, Sam is going to have to sit GCSEs in Maidenhead.'

'Jesus, Johnny!' I erupt.

'What happened to Dad?' he asks, his tone softening and his words tugging at my heartstrings.

'There's a lot I'm still getting used to,' I say finally.

Chapter 14

True to his word, Samuel turns up on Sunday, and on Monday I return to school. Tom comes in early to meet me, earlier even than usual. It's only seven in the morning, but Samuel wanted to beat rush hour.

Stu lets us hang out with him in the staffroom, which is a novelty, but, as the time passes, my nerves increase. I can see students wandering past outside the windows, completely oblivious to my presence. A small part of me still hopes that people will leave me alone.

No such luck, of course.

Even the teachers stare at me. It's completely disconcerting, especially when Mr Hillman, the headmaster, makes a point of coming over to me to pass on his best wishes. Stu told me he feels somewhat responsible for the students that blabbed to the press.

Eventually Tom takes me by the hand to walk me to my tutor room, but we have to traipse through the busy courtyard to get there.

It's the weirdest thing. I suddenly feel like the school has gone all *The Matrix* on me, with everything moving in slow motion. People turn to gape, mouths drop open, conversations are cut short – and then the whispering starts, the commenting, the pointing. Tom squeezes my hand and tugs me forward.

'Haven't you got anything better to do?' he snaps suddenly at a group of especially rowdy Year Tens, making me jump. I didn't have him down as the confrontational type. 'She's just a girl, get over it!'

A few metres later he bends down and murmurs in my ear: 'You're not just a girl, by the way. You're *my* girl.'

The butterflies in my stomach carry me the rest of the way to my classroom. I'm relieved when I see Libby and Lou already seated.

'Jessie!' Lou cries, getting up.

Libby does the same, but Mrs Rakeman is already at the front of the class.

'Settle down!' she snaps, putting an end to the whispers and commotion.

I go to take a seat next to Lou, noticing a flicker of resentment cross Libby's face as she glances at Lou and then at Amanda. Amanda also looks at me with an odd smile.

As soon as we're released to go to our first lesson, my classmates are all over me.

'I can't believe it's true!' Nina cries. 'It WAS you!'

'We said you looked just like her!' Michelle exclaims. 'We bloody well knew it!'

'Would you all leave Miss Pickerill alone!' Mrs Rakeman has to shout over them to make her voice heard.

Lou and Libby usher me out of the room and I'm vaguely

aware of Amanda hanging back. She's probably jealous that Libby is paying me so much attention.

At break, we go to the library and Lou nips off to tell Chris and Tom where we are. It doesn't take long for news to spread and the library is soon busier than it's ever been. We huddle in the corner behind some bookshelves. Again, Amanda is noticeably absent. I'm pleased that Libby is here, though, and I'm thankful that Lou is, too. But, above all, I'm grateful for Tom.

I'm sitting closer to him than I ever have before at school – nestled between his legs, with his arms round my waist. I just want to be protected by him. I look around at all of my friends – Chris, Lou and Libby – and feel relatively at peace, despite everything.

And then I think of Natalie and begin to ponder how strange it is that I've barely heard from her since the news broke. Would she have…?

No. I don't believe she was the one who ratted me out to the press. I know Stu doesn't like or trust her, and Libby never has, either, but she wouldn't do that to me. So why has she been so quiet? I know we've grown apart a little, but surely not that much?

I call her that night and her phone goes straight through to voicemail. My unease increases.

The next morning, I'm in the sixth-form common room with Tom, with the consent of the headteacher. Libby finds me there, and I'm touched that she made the effort to come in early to check on me, so I kiss Tom goodbye, and Libby and I head to the library to hang out.

The courtyard is pretty empty – it's still only eight thirty – but the few students who are there watch me as I pass.

I don't think I'll ever get used to being stared at, and this is just at my school. What's it going to be like when I go out in public? Especially with Johnny and Meg…

Thankfully, Samuel isn't following me around the school grounds, but I know he's outside the gates, and every so often I spy him doing a circuit of the perimeter. I haven't forgotten that Johnny said I could be a kidnap risk once the news got out, but honestly I think he's being over the top.

My story hasn't been in the national papers for days and, once everyone gets used to the sight of me at school, I can't believe that Samuel will be necessary. It seems crazy that I can't go home.

I figure that if enough time passes – maybe a week or so – Johnny will realise he's overreacting and will let me go about my business without a bodyguard watching over my every move. I just have to keep my head down.

It takes me a while to notice because I'm too consumed with everything else, but, by that afternoon, I realise that Amanda and Libby are barely talking to each other. Between Maths and English, I pull Libby aside and ask her about it.

'What's up with you and Amanda? Have you fallen out?'

'No,' she replies. 'I just haven't seen that much of her lately.'

'Why not? I thought you were BFFs.'

She snorts slightly. 'No.'

'Really?' I frown at her.

'She's grating on me a bit,' she eventually admits, and I stifle a giggle.

She laughs and hooks her arm through mine and we walk the rest of the way to English together.

Chapter 15

I try calling Natalie again that night, but, once more, her phone goes straight through to voicemail. I sit in Johnny's study and chew my bottom lip thoughtfully. Her lack of contact is definitely worrying.

My nerves eat away at me and, by Thursday, I can stand it no longer. On the way home from school, I direct Samuel to take me to Henley College.

'I can't let you go in there without me, miss.'

'Call me Jessie, Samuel! How many times do I have to tell you?' I can't help snapping.

'OK, Jessie, but I still can't let you go in alone.'

'Let's just wait here for a bit. We'll see if she comes out.'

'Cool,' he rumbles, in his trademark deep voice.

Stu is working late tonight. Apparently *he's* not a kidnap risk. It's alright for some.

'Heard any good jokes recently?' I ask Samuel after ten minutes of bored silence.

'Not lately,' he replies.

He seems to have left his sense of humour in LA.

I sigh heavily and stare at the double doors of Henley College.

'I cleaned the attic with my wife the other day,' Samuel says suddenly. I look at him with interest. I didn't think he was married. 'Now I can't get the cobwebs out of her hair,' he continues.

I stare at him with confusion for a moment before bursting into laughter.

'I'm glad I made you smile, girl.'

'Jessie,' I correct him.

'Then you should call me Sam,' he replies.

'I thought only Johnny called you Sam?'

'True, true.' He pauses. 'You remind me of him, you know.' I smile as I look out of the window again, and then I see her. Natalie.

'There she is!' I exclaim, pulling on the door handle. I tug and tug, but it won't open. 'Sam!'

'Hang on, I'm comin',' he grumbles, climbing out of the car.

What, now I can't even open my own door?

He opens it and I stumble onto the pavement. 'Natalie!' I shout.

Her head whips round and she stares at me and then at Sam, her face freezing in shock.

Em, our other friend from college who's much closer to Natalie than to me, comes out of the door behind her and clocks me almost immediately. 'Oh my God!' I can't hear her from this distance, but I can read her lips. She comes hurrying towards me in her high-heel boots and I'm aware that several other students have stopped to stare. I guess I must look pretty conspicuous, even if people don't know I'm Johnny's daughter. Here I am, standing in front of a black Mercedes with a bodyguard in tow who's about ten times the size of me. I watch warily as Natalie follows her.

My heart is pounding as I wonder whether Nat sold me out to the press. The look on her face when she saw me… I don't know what to do. Do I confront her? Here and now?

'Oh my God!' I hear Em cry again, as she approaches. 'I heard the news!'

Em throws her arms round me and glances with slight trepidation over my right shoulder to where Samuel is standing. 'Who's that?' she whispers. She looks more orange than usual. She's clearly been overdosing on fake tan.

'This is Sam, my, er, bodyguard,' I mumble.

Em's grin looks like it's going to split her face in two. 'Flipping hell!' she cries. 'I can't believe it!'

'Shall we go somewhere more private?' Natalie mutters, looking around.

'I think that would be a good idea,' Sam interjects, standing back and ushering us into the car. 'Is there anywhere you ladies would like to go?' he asks when we're safely ensconced in the back seat.

'Maybe back to ours?' I suggest. Sam's living at Johnny's, too.

'We're supposed to be meeting Aaron and Dougie at the pub,' Natalie reminds Em.

'Screw them,' Em snaps good-naturedly. 'They can wait.'

'I'll text them,' Natalie says moodily.

'Oh my God!' Em screeches suddenly. It's not an uncommon phrase for her, but it still takes me by surprise. 'When you say "ours", do you mean Johnny Jefferson's mansion?'

'Um, yeah,' I reply awkwardly.

She screams. Literally.

'Bloody hell, Em!' Natalie erupts and Sam's brown eyes look amused in the rear-view mirror.

Em is one of Johnny Jefferson's biggest fans, and when we arrive at the house she gleefully asks for a tour. I comply, and Natalie berates her for being nosy while we're walking around.

'We don't have a lot of time,' Nat points out grumpily. 'Will your, you know, *bodyguard* give us a lift to the pub? Otherwise we're going to be really late.'

'I'm sure he will,' I reply, disappointed at how unpleasant she's being. We've barely said more than two words to each other. Em, on the other hand, has talked non-stop with excitement.

I realise that Natalie doesn't appear at all fazed that this is Johnny's house. *Libby would love to be here*, I muse with affection. Maybe I'll invite her over this weekend. And Tom, Lou and Chris. We could watch a movie in the private cinema… Maybe Tom could drive everyone! *If* he passes – he's got his test tomorrow…

The smile drops from my face seconds later when it occurs to me that perhaps Natalie is trying to act like she doesn't care about my famous dad so I don't suspect her of ratting me out.

I once read in *Heat* magazine about a celebrity who planted certain inaccurate stories about themselves with friends that they weren't sure they could trust. When one of the stories showed up in the papers, the celebrity knew exactly who it was who'd been blabbing. I narrow my eyes as I look at Natalie now. Even if I ask her outright, I'm sure she'll lie and say she didn't tell anyone, but I have to find out who's been stabbing me in the back.

I rack my brain for a story to tell her, but, coming up with nothing, I decide to let it lie for now.

The next day, to my delight, Tom passes his driving test, and on Saturday he drives Lou, Chris and Libby over. We have the best day, hanging out and watching movies in the private cinema, but they have to leave all too early because Libby has family plans.

Later, I try calling Tom and discover that, on the way home, he, Chris and Lou dropped in to someone called Will's place for a game of pool. From the level of the background noise, it sounds like there's a house party going on. I begrudgingly tell him to have fun, but, when I hang up, I'm overcome with irritation at being stuck in Henley on my own.

I know that I could wake up Sam and demand that he take me to Will's house, too, but the thought of him hanging around outside or, God forbid, *inside* fills me with mortification. And anyway Stu wouldn't want me to go out this late at night.

My phone buzzes to let me know a message has come in and I snatch it up, hoping it's Tom, but it's from Lou. My heart stops.

Urgh, Isla is here. Don't worry, I've got your back.

Great. Now I can add paranoia to my unpleasant mix of emotions.

Despite my better judgement, I call Tom again. When he doesn't answer, I ring Lou's number instead.

'I tried to call Tom,' I say, then have to repeat myself twice because she can't hear a word over the loud music playing.

'I think he's outside!' she shouts back.

134

'Can you go and find him for me?'

'Sure!' she replies.

In a muffled voice, I hear her tell someone that she's going to find Tom, and Chris responds with what definitely sounds like, 'He's outside with Isla.'

The most sickening, uneasy feeling instantly overcomes me.

It feels like the longest twenty seconds of my life and, when Lou comes back on the line, I can barely speak for the debilitating fear of what she'll say next.

'I can't see him outside. Maybe he's inside somewhere,' she says.

'Did I just hear Chris tell you he's outside with Isla?' I ask her straight.

'Yeah, but he's not. Anyway, I'm sure they're only talking,' she adds quickly.

'Can you see her?'

'Er, no, she's not out here, either.'

A memory hits me of Tom and Isla sitting at the bottom of the stairs at another party before the summer holidays. They were talking intimately, their heads pressed together. I didn't like the sight then, and I damn well hate the thought of it now.

'Will you tell him to call me back as soon as you see him?' I ask her, hating how needy my voice sounds.

'Of course I will,' she replies, and the sympathy in her voice makes me feel even worse.

I end the call and throw my phone down, covering my face with my hands. Tom has never done anything to make me doubt him, but it's hard to compete with his first love. And my life is so insane at the moment. Perhaps it's too much drama for him.

My phone buzzes again and I snatch it up, but this time when my heart stops it's for an entirely different reason. Because the text is from Jack:

> **J! Hear you've been making waves in the press again.**
> **Thought of you recently at Wombats gig. When you**
> **back in LA? Jack x**

Despite how much I care for Tom, a jittery feeling that is strictly Jack-induced starts up in my stomach.

Jack *has* been thinking about me.

In a split second, my mind is full of him: his grey-blue eyes and tousled black hair. The memory cuts to him kissing me, hot and passionately. I involuntarily shiver and try to push the image away. I shouldn't be thinking about him like that.

But I'm confused. Why is he texting me now? Why didn't he reply to my email? Should I ignore him?

Like me, Jack's life isn't normal, either. His dad was a rock star, too. Still is. It's not something you just grow out of, apparently, even if you're not making music any more.

On impulse, I text him back:

> **So jealous re Wombats. Back around xmas. Things a**
> **bit crazy here. Missing LA...**

Not 'missing you' exactly. I don't sign off with a kiss.

To my surprise, he replies immediately:

> **Man, that's ages away. Call me sometime? Lottie still**
> **trying to get us on show but Eve threatening to quit.**

I experience a little rush of adrenalin. He wants me to call him? I scan the rest of his message. Lottie is trying to get All Hype a slot on her TV show, but the band's lead singer – the beautiful, stunning girl who made it very clear to me that Jack was hers – is talking about quitting. I wonder what that means. Are she and Jack done for good?

Whoa, keep me posted.

I don't answer his question about calling him, and I'm annoyed at how disheartened I feel when he doesn't reply. I turn off my phone and try to stop thinking about him.

Chapter 16

I switch my phone back on late the next morning and it soon starts to buzz with two text messages and two voicemails. They're all from Lou asking me to call her urgently.

With my heart in my throat, I ring her number, squeezing my eyes shut for whatever awful news she's about to disclose. Please don't let it be about Tom and Isla… Please, please, please…

'I tried calling you last night!' she exclaims.

'What is it?' I prompt.

'I think I know who told the press about you,' she says.

Not Tom, please not Tom. I squeeze my eyes shut.

'It was Amanda,' she says.

My eyes fly open. 'Amanda?'

'Her ex-boyfriend was there last night and he got really drunk and started spouting off to one of his friends. I was standing right behind him – he didn't know I was eavesdropping. He was boasting about it! Chris managed to find out who he was. He goes to sixth-form college, apparently.'

My head is spinning. 'Amanda? But how did she… Libby,' I say, as my heart contracts.

'It must've been,' Lou confirms flatly.

'That's why they've fallen out.' But wait… 'That means Libby has known all along that it was Amanda!'

'That's what I've been thinking,' Lou says sympathetically.

'But I thought it was Natalie!' I exclaim.

'No. It was definitely Amanda who went to the local press. Apparently they paid her quite a bit of money for her story.'

I feel sick. 'I've got to call Libby.'

'Are you alright?' she asks worriedly.

'Not really,' I reply, trying to be strong. 'But it is what it is.'

'I'm so sorry,' Libby whispers when I come right out and ask her. She doesn't deny it.

'When did you tell her?' I demand to know.

'A few weeks ago. Oh, Jessie, I'm so sorry.' She sounds close to tears. 'I swore her to secrecy. I really thought I could trust her.'

'And I really thought I could trust *you*,' I say, anger rushing through me.

'Please forgive me,' she begs. 'Amanda really let me down—'

'Amanda let *you* down?' I interrupt bitterly. 'Libby, I *begged* you not to tell anyone. You *promised*! I can't believe you've done this!'

'I'm so sorry.' She starts to cry, but I don't have the strength, or the will, to comfort her.

'I've gotta go,' I say, ending the call.

My whole life – this cage that I'm now living in – is all because my oldest friend couldn't keep her mouth shut. And there I was blaming Natalie, my new friend, the one Stu doesn't like or trust because she's a bad influence. Maybe she *is* a bad influence, but she's never let me down like Libby just has.

Poor Natalie. There I was, planning on planting a story to catch her out. She didn't even do anything wrong. I don't know what's been up with her lately, but I owe it to her to find out. I text her to ask if she's at home before calling Tom to fill him in. He offers to cancel football and drive me over to her house, but Sam puts a stop to that.

'For God's sake!' I explode when he tells me that he doesn't want Tom driving me. 'This is ridiculous! The press have stopped hounding me, there's no one outside the gates—'

'Not true,' he interrupts. 'There was a pap sneaking around out there this morning.'

I sigh heavily. 'Aren't you bored, Sam?' I ask with exasperation. 'I mean, don't you have better things to do than babysit me?'

'It's my job, miss.'

'Jessie! My name is Jessie, and I'm a person, not a job!'

His brown eyes regard me steadily. I storm off in a huff and call Tom again. It's only after we hang up that I realise I didn't even ask him about his conversation with Isla last night.

'Jeez, what's up with you?' Natalie asks when she opens the door to my scowling face.

'It was Libby. Libby told Amanda and she was the one who blabbed to the press.'

'Shit!' she gasps, leading me into the TV room.

'I thought it was you,' I admit.

'What?' She looks horrified.

'I'm so sorry. It's just that you've been acting so distant lately.'

'*I've* been acting distant?' She sounds irate. 'You're the one who's got a new boyfriend!'

'Tom hasn't stopped me from seeing you,' I say hastily. 'We came to your party, didn't we?'

'Whoopie doo,' she says sarcastically.

'Wait, you're not annoyed about the extra time I've been spending with him, are you?'

'I just want the old Jessie back, alright? I miss you!' she erupts.

My mouth gapes open like a goldfish before snapping shut again.

'But I'm right here. I've been here all along,' I say hopelessly.

'You're not Jessie Pickerill. Not any more. You're Jessie Jefferson.'

'Don't say that.' I shake my head. 'I haven't changed. I'm still the same person.'

'That's not true, Jessie. You've been Jessie Jefferson for a while, ever since you came back from LA. Even before the truth came out about you.'

'I don't know what you mean.'

'That night at Liam's house…'

'Oh, no, not this again. I didn't fancy Liam!' I erupt. 'I didn't lead him on!'

'I'm not saying that you were,' she tries to explain. 'But it was the way he was looking at you—'

'That's not my fault!' I chip in defensively.

'The way *everyone* was looking at you! The way you were behind the decks. You seemed so confident… So cool. You looked like Johnny Jefferson's daughter. Suddenly you just seemed way out of my league.'

'What—? Way out of *your* league?' I'm stunned that she would think that. She's always been the confident, cool one.

'You haven't really needed me since you came back,' she adds.

'Of course I still need you!' I reply, feeling a little emotional.

She leans in and gives me a hug. 'Good. Because I'll always be here for you, you know.'

'Me too,' I murmur.

We sit and chat and catch up on everything we've been missing out on and it's so refreshing to be sitting in her TV room and not in the vast mansion that's felt more like a jail than a home in the last couple of weeks.

Suddenly I'm desperate to be in my own house, surrounded by its familiar smell. I say goodbye to Natalie and go outside to ask Sam to take me home. He complies without a fuss, but I still feel pissed off that I have to ask permission. I look out of the window moodily, watching houses and streets flash past. Soon we're pulling into my close and I'm tugging at the car door, crying out in exasperation because I can't even let myself out.

Hot tears sting my eyes as I wait for Sam to come and release me. I try to shove past him, but he's a brick wall and I end up stumbling. His big hands steady me, but I shrug him off and go to unlock the door.

'Jessie,' he says.

I ignore him. Why isn't the door opening?

'Jessie,' he says again, more firmly.

Finally I look at him to see that he's holding a set of keys.

'We had to change the locks.'

Of course they bloody did. Mum gave out spare keys to friends and neighbours. Johnny wouldn't have trusted anyone with them.

Sam opens the door and then moves aside to let me pass. I shut the door in his face, not caring that I'm acting like a petulant child.

The familiar smell engulfs me, filling me up from the inside out. I walk slowly down the corridor to the kitchen and look around, picturing my mum standing at the toaster, buttering my toast. My eyes prick with tears and I back out of the room and head up the stairs, my body feeling heavier with every step. In my bedroom, my little bed looks so inviting, so comforting. I know that I'm tired, I know that a decent sleep would probably do me the world of good, but I can't leave Sam on the bloody doorstep.

I wish Tom were here.

I glance at the window as a thought occurs to me. A thought that is distinctly Jessie Pickerill.

Sturdy new locks have been fixed to the window from the inside, but, as I'd hoped, I can open them. I lift up the window and breathe in the autumn air. Then, without so much as a second thought, I climb out.

Chapter 17

'Stop looking so worried.'

'It's just… I don't know, Jessie, you've got a bodyguard for a reason.'

I scowl out of the window at the scenery flashing past. 'Yeah, and it's ridiculous,' I mutter under my breath.

I had to persuade Tom even to drive me home. He was in the middle of a football game at the park just down the road and his face lit up when he saw me, abandoning his teammates to run over and sweep me up in his arms. He was all hot and sweaty, but I couldn't get enough of him. It was a few minutes before I remembered to ask him about his conversation with Isla last night and, when I did, I couldn't help but sound accusatory.

'I only talked to her for a bit,' he replied defensively.

'Was she calling me a slag again?' I demanded to know.

'No,' he said firmly. 'In fact, she apologised for that.'

'Did she?' I was astounded. 'How did that come about?'

'She asked after you. Obviously she's heard about your dad.'

'Obviously,' I chipped in sarcastically.

'She was being *nice*, Jessie. She seemed genuinely happy that things were going well for us.'

I didn't believe a word of it, but I let it lie.

Tom doesn't reply to my '*It's ridiculous!*' comment and, when I look back at him, his jaw is rigid with tension. My eyes travel along the length of his long, lean arms until they rest on his tanned hands gripping the steering wheel. He looks so sexy behind the wheel. It's the first time he's driven me anywhere without his mum in the passenger seat.

I'm suddenly tempted to unclick my seatbelt and climb closer so I can press my lips to his warm neck, but I know that would be pushing my luck. And anyway I'd better not distract him. He glances in the rear-view mirror and his frown deepens.

'What is it?' I ask, my thoughts still on kissing him.

'I don't know,' he murmurs. 'That white van has been behind us for a while.'

I swivel in my seat and look through the back window, but I can't make out anyone in the driver's seat. 'You're being paranoid,' I say, brushing him off, and then he's swerving off the main road into a smaller one.

'Whoa!' I gasp, trying to stay upright. The van flies straight past us on the main road. 'See?' I exclaim. 'Nothing to worry about. Jeez! Pull over.'

He doesn't bother indicating as he crunches to a stop at the entrance to a private driveway. I flash him a dark look and wrench open the door, hopping out onto the gravel.

'Oi,' he calls. 'Where do you think you're going?'

'I need some air,' I state, slamming the door shut.

A moment later he joins me. I glare up at him.

'Come on, maybe we should go to your dad's place,' he says gently, his brown eyes crinkling with concern.

I stare at him, incredulous. I can't believe he's saying that to me. 'No!' I raise my voice. 'I'm sick of feeling like a prisoner! I just want some alone time with my boyfriend – is that too much to ask?'

'Hey,' he says softly, sliding his arms round my waist and pulling me against his firm chest. To my surprise, I discover I'm fighting back tears...

'Kiss me,' I demand, tilting my face up to him.

He touches his lips to mine, but withdraws all too quickly. 'We're parked in somebody's driveway,' he says uncertainly.

I start to laugh, but the sound is verging on manic, the laugh of a crazy person who's been locked up for too long.

I take a few steps backwards, away from him. He snatches my hand and pulls me towards him and this time he kisses me like he means it. The sun, surprisingly warm for October, beats down on our heads as his hands circle my waist and then he pushes me back against the car door and traps me with his body. We kiss like it's our last, and it is so, so sweet. I draw a sharp breath as he wrenches his lips away from mine and stares past me, over the car roof. His whole body tenses.

'The van,' he says in a low, urgent voice.

Before I can roll my eyes, I hear it, like thunder, hurtling towards us. And then it screeches to a stop and my heart stops with it because I *know* we're in danger.

'RUN!' I scream at the sight of the two men in the front seat. I shove Tom away from me. 'RUN!'

146

But he grabs my hand to pull me with him and then, suddenly, Sam's car squeals into the road. He crashes his car straight into the back of the van and it lurches forward, then Sam is out of his vehicle and running around to the front and, oh my God, he has a gun!

'Get out of the car!' he shouts in a commanding voice.

But the driver revs the engine and screeches forward. Sam holds his ground, but doesn't fire, and then the driver swerves towards him and I scream Sam's name, distracting him for a split second before he leaps out of the way.

'SAM!' I scream again, as I see him fall to the ground. The van roars off up the hill, away from us. Somewhere in the distance, police sirens are wailing.

'Get into Tom's car!' Sam shouts at me, before speaking into a CB radio attached to his belt. He's clutching his left leg and I can see that he's hurt.

I run towards him, yanking my hand away from Tom.

'Stay back, goddammit!' Sam shouts at me, but I ignore him.

'What happened?' I gasp, as I reach his side.

'Got hit by their van,' he replies gruffly. 'Now get back into Tom's car *right away*, or so help me God…'

Everyone is angry with me. Stu, Sam and Johnny. Especially Johnny.

'What the hell were you thinking?' he shouts down the phone later that evening, after I've been discharged from hospital. Tom and I were both treated for shock, but Sam had to stay in – he has a small fracture in his leg, which will put him out of action for a while.

'Sam could've been killed! YOU could've been killed!'

'I know,' I mumble.

I'll never forget the look on Caroline's face when she arrived at the hospital. She was terrified and I felt so bad. It was all my fault.

The sound of me crying softens Johnny's tone somewhat. 'We're going to have to talk, Jess,' he says. 'You can't go on like this.'

Things are changing so fast and there's nothing I can do about it. I think for the first time that maybe I don't *want* to be Johnny Jefferson's daughter. Then I bury the thought guiltily.

Needless to say, I'm not allowed to go back to school. The story about 'the Jessie Jefferson kidnapping plot' was on the front page of three of the nationals today. Poor Tom has had to go and stay with his uncle because his house is under siege.

Sam had been in contact with the police from the moment he'd realised I was missing, and they apprehended the would-be kidnappers at the top of the hill. The men are now in custody. They'd been following Tom only since that morning, hoping an opportunity would present itself, and I gave them one on a platter.

Bruce returns to cover security temporarily, but Sam comes to the house as soon as he's out of hospital. I find him in the hallway, leaning on crutches as he talks to Stu. It's strange to see him out of a suit, in his simple grey T-shirt and denim jeans.

'Sam!' I cry, running down the stairs.

'Careful,' he warns. 'Don't trip.'

I throw my arms round him.

'Oof,' he grumbles.

'I'm so sorry,' I say, the tears in my eyes threatening to spill over.

'S'all good, Jessie. Could've been a lot worse.'

'I'll never forgive myself,' I whisper.

'Don't beat yourself up. I should've known what you were up to sooner.'

'No, I'm entirely to blame,' I say fervently. 'Johnny is furious with me. But how *did* you find us?' I ask him. I know now that the kidnappers were watching Tom, but the question of how Sam tracked us down has been plaguing me since it happened.

'I put a tracker on Tom's car.'

'What?' I gasp.

He raises one eyebrow at me. 'Your boyfriend gets his driving licence and you're not gonna make a run for it? I wasn't born yesterday.'

I throw my arms back round him and hug him tightly, feeling more grateful to him than I could ever express in words.

I hope he knows it.

Johnny is the one to break the news to me. He wants me to go to LA.

'Not forever, just until things settle down over there. I know you don't want to leave Tom, but you owe it to him and your friends to let the attention die down.'

I'm so desperate to escape this mess that it doesn't take much for me to agree, but it breaks my heart to be leaving Tom and Stu, and all my friends.

Tom, Lou, Natalie and Chris come over the day before I leave. I don't ask Libby. She's called me several times, but I can't

149

forgive her. Not yet. Not when she's contributed to everything that's happening right now. Still, I can't help but miss her and, in the end, I regret not inviting her.

Sam will return to LA with me, but Bruce is staying on to look after Stu, just to be on the safe side. He'll be able to go home soon, though.

Sometime towards the end of my leaving do, I take Tom off to my bedroom. We don't have long, so I don't want to waste time talking. I don't know when I'll get to kiss him again.

'I'm going to miss you,' I say against his lips, as we lie side by side on the bed. He makes a sound that tells me the feeling is mutual. I run my hands through his hair and kiss him passionately as he clutches my body tightly against his.

I don't want to leave him. I don't want to lose him, so I cling to him like I'm trying to cling to my old life.

With a low groan coming from somewhere deep inside his throat, he pulls away from me. His face is flushed, his pupils are dilated and we're both breathing heavily. My eyes follow him as he climbs off the bed and paces the floor for a moment. Then he reluctantly turns round and holds his hand out to me, offering me a regretful smile. I take his hand with a sigh and stand up.

As goodbyes go, that was pretty sweet. But now it's time for me to return to the City of Angels, to the land of the rich and famous, to the house of my superstar dad.

I don't feel anywhere near ready, but it's time to be Jessie Jefferson.

Chapter 18

Sam and I sit side by side in First Class, barely speaking during the whole flight to LA. Davey, Johnny's friendly-faced limo driver, is waiting when we arrive. Davey has a big smile and a personality to match, and he clasps Sam's hand warmly before turning to me.

'Miss Pickerill.'

'Jessie,' Sam and I correct him at the same time.

Davey's eyes are bright with amusement as they dart between us. 'Well, I see you two have become better acquainted during your time in the UK.'

'Mmm-hmm,' Sam rumbles wryly and I flash a rueful glance at his crutches.

Sam sits in the front with Davey, so I have the rest of the limousine to myself. It's ridiculously roomy, the bench seat running all the way down one side and along the back of the car. I reach across to open the fridge and smile when I spy little cartons of milk. A burst of excitement explodes in my gut at the thought of seeing my half-brothers again.

I feel slightly wary of seeing Johnny and Meg. Johnny must certainly still be angry with me and surely that means Meg is, too. She adores Sam and I could have got him killed.

Eventually we're driving through the gates of Bel Air and, despite the tension in my stomach, I put the window down and stick my head out. It's a warm and sunny afternoon, not a cloud in the sky, and I inhale deeply, the smell of freshly-cut grass filling my nostrils.

We start to climb into the hills and I smile at the sight of Charlotte Tremway's house behind a high brick wall. It's practically a palace.

I'm a little nervous as we pull up at the gates to Johnny's mansion. Lewis, another one of Johnny's security staff, waves at his colleagues from the guardhouse and smiles broadly at the sight of Sam.

The car travels along the winding driveway and the trees that obscure the house come into view. Their leaves have turned yellowy-orange and have started to drop. I see my bedroom window through the branches. My bedroom. The front door opens and Meg comes out, closely followed by Johnny – and then Gramps! It cheered me up to hear that our paths would cross – he's heading back to the UK in a few days.

Davey opens the car door, and then Barney is upon me.

'JESSIE!' he shouts, and I giggle as he jumps up and down with excitement. I didn't even see him come outside.

'Come and see my helicopter!'

'Hello!' Meg calls with a smile, engulfing me in a hug as soon as I'm close. 'Thank God you're OK!' she says on an exhalation of breath.

Isn't she mad at me?

I pull away and look at her in confusion, but she steps back to make way for Gramps.

'Glad you're OK, kiddo,' he says, giving me a quick squeeze before releasing me, and then Johnny's arms are around me and he's holding me tightly and stroking my hair. It's easily the longest hug he's ever given me, and I'm so taken aback that I extract myself first. His green eyes are full of concern as he stares at me and shakes his head.

'Aren't you angry with me?' I ask.

'Yes.' He nods decisively.

Oh.

'Furious,' he adds.

Whoops.

'But I'm glad you're safe,' he continues, to my relief. 'If anything had happened to you…' He shakes his head.

Yes, I imagine he *would* feel guilty. But maybe there's more to it than that…

Just as I think that thought, he pulls me back into his arms. My stomach goes all fluttery. This is my dad. My real dad. And he cares about me. Quite a lot from the length of the hug going on here. OK, now it's getting hard to breathe.

He pulls away. 'Don't ever do anything like that again!' he warns angrily, the smile gone from his face.

'I won't.' I shake my head vigorously.

'I mean it. Security is there for your protection. If I say you need a bodyguard, you need a bodyguard!'

'I get it.'

'Good.' He grins and gives me another squeeze, making me think he's got some sort of personality disorder which sends him bouncing from happy to mad in seconds.

'I really am sorry,' I say sincerely.

He shakes his head, wrapping his arm round my neck and walking me towards the house. 'No. This is my fault.'

'Come on, Jessie!' Barney distracts us.

'What?' I say to Johnny, baffled by what he's just said. 'No, it's not, it's—'

'We'll talk about it later,' he cuts me off, nodding with a smile at his young son jumping up and down at our feet. 'More important things to attend to.'

I smile at him and follow Barney into the living room.

The first time I saw Johnny and Meg's house, I was lost for words. Set high up in the hills, floor-to-ceiling panes of glass look out onto the sun-drenched terrace with its infinity pool and view of LA far down below in the valley. At night, the stars above have to compete with the city lights, and inside it's just as stunning.

In complete contrast to their opulent English mansion, this pad is slick and modern, with large, spacious areas and cool designer furniture. The living room runs almost the entire length of the back of the house and is mostly a double-height space, with the kitchen off to one side. Polished concrete stairs in the middle of the living space lead up to a landing safeguarded by a low wall, with the bedrooms and Johnny's studio leading off it. Underneath the bedrooms, behind the living room, are the office, a gym and a private cinema.

After being momentarily blinded by the afternoon sunshine spilling in through the enormous windows, I spy Phoenix watching CBeebies on the huge flatscreen telly.

'Phee!' I cry, scooping him up into my arms and kissing one of his chubby cheeks.

'Phee?' Meg asks me with a smile. 'I think that's going to stick,' she says.

Phee and Bee, my little brothers.

Apparently Meg has lined up a tutor for me. I'll be taking lessons at home so I won't fall behind on my GCSEs. But this week I'll just be settling in and getting over my jet lag. I didn't sleep at all on the plane – too much adrenalin – so now I'm hitting the ground running, trying to go for as long as possible before I call it a night. I don't want to be waking up at 3 a.m. to a silent house and be raring to go.

I do, however, slip out after a while to call Stu – and Tom.

'I can't believe you're gone…' Tom's deep voice travels down the line. 'It's only just starting to sink in.'

'I know what you mean,' I reply. 'It all happened so fast.'

'I'm going back to school tomorrow,' he says. 'It won't be the same without you.'

'So soon?' I ask with surprise.

'I need a distraction,' he replies glumly.

'Will you call me after school?'

'Sure. Should I use your mobile?' he asks.

'No, let me give you the home number.' He waits while I fidget through my phone and relay it to him. 'Did you get that?' I ask.

'Yeah.' He laughs and I can almost see him shaking his head. 'I still can't believe you're staying with Johnny Jefferson.'

'Mmm,' I reply with a smile. I don't tell him that I'm already loving it.

It doesn't take long for Agnes to call to arrange a catch-up. Within a few days, Davey is driving me to see her with Lewis in tow. Sam still hasn't returned to work full-time – he's certainly not up to being a personal bodyguard – and Johnny is taking no chances.

Agnes and I are meeting at one of our old haunts, the Skybar in the Mondrian Hotel in Hollywood. She's already there when I arrive, sitting in the warm autumnal sunshine, tapping away on her iPad. She's taller than me by a couple of inches and her black hair is cut into an edgy, blunt bob. Her eyeliner, as usual, is drawn on thick, but today her lips are neutral. She wants to be a fashion designer and always looks very cool. Today she's wearing a yellow minidress, her legs still tanned from summer.

She's so engrossed in what she's doing that she doesn't see me until I'm standing right over her table.

'Good morning,' I say in a plummy English accent, making her head whip up in surprise.

'Jessie!' she gasps, getting to her feet.

'Hello.' I giggle as she hugs me.

'I can't believe you're back!'

'Neither can I,' I admit, a bit unhappily.

'I heard what happened!' she whispers, her face paling slightly as she pulls me to sit next to her on a bench seat running the length of the city-view window. 'Are you OK?'

'I'm alright.' I shrug, bizarrely aware of Lewis standing on the other side of the bar, near the door. I notice I'm getting a couple of curious glances from the clientele at the bar, but people are used to seeing full-blown A-listers here in Hollywood, so hopefully I'll be mostly ignored. '*None* of this feels real, to be honest. It hasn't for months.'

Her eyes narrow. 'Why didn't you tell me you had a boyfriend?'

'Sorry.' I don't know why I didn't. Or maybe I do.

'Obviously I read about what happened,' she adds significantly.

'It felt pretty hairy there for a minute,' I admit with a small shrug.

She calls out to a passing waitress. 'Excuse me!' The waitress comes over and Agnes turns to me: 'What would you like?'

I order a latte and then fall into a thoughtful silence. I should have told Agnes about Tom. It's not like we haven't texted back and forth a few times. The truth is that I didn't want Jack to know. Being with Tom means I'm strictly off limits, but I guess I wanted to see if Jack would contact me of his own accord.

And he did.

Enough of that. Now Agnes needs the gossip. So I plaster a smile on my face that soon becomes genuine as I tell her all about Tom Ryder, the hottest boy in school.

'Do you love him?' she asks, a slight crease between her dark eyebrows.

'I don't know,' I reply carefully. I glance at Lewis, but he's pretending not to pay us any attention. 'I think so, but we haven't said it yet.'

She takes a sip of her coffee. 'Jack told me he texted you.'

My heart unwittingly spikes at the mention of his name. 'Yeah.' I try to nod casually. 'That was sweet.'

'So you don't have the hots for him any more?'

I'm not surprised by her directness – Agnes is nothing if not direct – but I still tense up.

'You said it yourself, he's trouble.'

'That didn't exactly answer my question,' she points out.

'I'm with Tom now.'

'Still not answering my question,' she notes with amusement.

'What does it matter?' I exclaim, my blush deepening under her scrutiny.

'It matters,' she replies with a smirk, and then, thankfully, the waitress returns with my latte.

'It's so strange to be back,' I say, looking around.

'Oh, no, you're not changing the subject that easily,' Agnes says. 'Jack almost came with me today.'

I nearly choke on my drink. 'Did he?' I manage to ask between coughs.

'He missed you when you left.'

'That's what you said last time. Wasn't it: "He was bummed when you left" or something like that?'

'More or less.'

'Well, he didn't bother to reply to my email. Anyway!' I cry. 'What does it matter? He's not boyfriend material, and he's on the other side of the Atlantic.'

'Not any more,' Agnes says with satisfaction. I get the distinct feeling that she's enjoying herself.

'Well, I have a boyfriend now, so it doesn't matter, anyway.'

'Even though *he's* now the one on the other side of the Atlantic?' she enquires sweetly.

'He won't be for long. I'll be going home soon.'

'How do you see that panning out?' she asks. 'What's the point of going back? Life won't be as you left it. You'll have to go to private school; you won't be able to stay in your house. Everything's going to change.'

'Don't I know it,' I mumble.

'Why don't you just stay in LA?' she asks. 'You know, move here. Permanently. You could come to school with me!' she exclaims, her look of glee faltering when she sees my face. 'Or not,' she adds, reaching for her coffee and freezing in mid-air. 'Oh, God, I meant to tell you! Lottie's having a Halloween party next weekend. You've got to come! We'll go shopping for an outfit together. Can we?' she asks when I don't answer.

'Sure,' I reply with a smile. 'Why not?'

'Great! What are you doing tomorrow?'

Chapter 19

It's the following weekend and, as Johnny won't let me go anywhere without Davey or Lewis or both, we've swung by to pick up Agnes.

Meg took me aside earlier and gently encouraged me to indulge Johnny until he gets over the kidnapping scare. But I hope he chills out soon. There's only so much babysitting that I'm going to be able to take.

'Oh my God, you look amazing!' Agnes cries, climbing into the limo beside me.

'So do you!' I give her a kiss, being careful not to get my blood-red lipstick all over her.

We've seen each other's outfits already – we went shopping for them together, after all – but now our hair and make-up are done and we look properly scary. And hopefully a little sexy, too. At least, that was the plan. She's dressed as a witch, in a black sequinned bustier and flared miniskirt, with dark make-up, messy blue-black hair extensions and a sparkly hat. I'm the Bride of

Dracula, in a shredded white lace wedding dress, my blonde hair backcombed all over the place, my eye make-up muted, but my lipstick making up for it.

'Is... Is Jack coming? Does he need a lift?' I dare to ask, stuttering slightly, despite my attempts to sound cool and unbothered. Dammit.

'No, he's meeting us there.'

My heart falls at her no, but skips at the second part of her sentence. I shouldn't care if he's going or not.

We all live up in the hills, so it doesn't take long to get to Lottie's house. Davey drives us in through the back entrance and I'm surprised to see that all of the mansion lights are off. It looks deserted, but Lottie lives in a log cabin guesthouse in the garden and I can hear the music pounding through the limo doors as we approach. The mansion probably has twenty bedrooms, but Lottie still finds it cramped, thanks to her dislike of her dad's most recent wife.

Johnny has deemed the security at the Tremway mansion sufficient, so Lewis doesn't have to babysit me tonight. Davey promises to come back for me as soon as I call him and reminds me of my midnight curfew. I've only just got over my jet lag so I think I can just about cope with that.

Agnes hooks her arm through mine and, as Davey's headlights turn away from us, our eyes adjust to the darkness.

Agnes said Lottie's Halloween parties were not to be missed. She wasn't lying.

The log cabin is lit only by the light of hundreds of candles and a multitude of red lanterns hanging from the branches of the surrounding trees. There are dozens of pumpkin lanterns lining our path and resting on every visible surface, all carved with gruesome faces. I can't even imagine how much time it took to do them – the house staff have probably been working on them all week. I bet there was a professional party planner involved. Fake cobwebs drift down from the trees and I can see the shadowy shapes of spiders set within them. The whole effect is spooky and very, very cool.

There must be about thirty or forty people here already, but I don't recognise anyone, not helped by the fact that they're all in fancy dress. Suddenly a girl comes over, her face hidden in the darkness behind a red hood glittering with sequins.

'Hey!' Agnes addresses Little Red Riding Hood with delight. A moment later I realise that underneath the hood is teen star and host, Charlotte Tremway.

They hug and gush a few compliments before Agnes indicates me.

'Jessie!' Lottie exclaims. 'Agnes told me you were back.'

'Yeah,' I say with a small shrug, although I'm pleased with her happy reaction to seeing me.

'Come get a drink!'

A bar has been set up on the deck outside the cabin and there's a hot, goth-like barman mixing cocktails and pouring drinks. Cut-glass bowls full of red punch sparkle on the surface, lit from within with glowing, plastic ice cubes in the shape of eyeballs.

Lottie pokes her head between ours. 'The punch is amazing,' she drawls.

'*How* amazing?' Agnes asks meaningfully.

'Pretty amazing, but it will get more amazing as the night wears on,' she says with a sly smile. 'Although I've got to be careful. Colleen will have me arrested, given half a chance.'

Colleen is her stepmother.

There are DJ decks set up on the other side of the cabin and loud music is blaring out of the speakers. I take a sip of my drink – *yum* – and look around. Some of the costumes defy belief. One girl is dressed up like a comic-book character with bright orange hair and black spots dotted all over her face to make it look as though she's been pixelated. There are the usual mummies, ghouls and superheroes, but everyone has gone to such an effort. *Then again, I suppose they have the money to pay for it*, I think to myself.

I recognise a few people from the last time I was here, but, unfortunately, the one person I don't want to see is Lissa, a girl who has always been a total bitch to me. But there she is, looking more like a stripogram than Britney Spears, in high black patent boots and a low-cut top, her boobs pushed to the limits. Lissa's eyes land on me and I hold her gaze, fighting the urge to run away. A moment later she comes over.

'So the rumours are true,' she says with what is more of a sneer than a smile. 'You're back.'

'Be nice,' Lottie warns.

'I'll be nice,' she replies, straight-faced. 'I heard what happened.'

'You were so lucky,' Lottie chips in breathily.

I flinch as the memory of it comes back to me. The two men in the front of the van… Their angry, determined faces… Sam falling to the ground…

'You don't have to talk about it,' Agnes chips in.

I'd certainly rather not. Agnes and I got papped when we were out shopping for costumes. I thought maybe the photographer had mistaken me for someone else, until he started speaking.

'Hey, Jessie! How are you feeling after the kidnapping attempt? What's it like staying with your famous dad?'

Luckily Lewis fended him off. I'm still hoping all the kidnap stuff will blow over and they'll leave me alone…

'Jessie Jefferson?' I hear a male voice call and turn to see Fred from *Scooby-Doo* coming towards me, all tall, blond and buff.

'Peter?' I ask with surprised delight, welcoming a chance to move away from Lissa. I met him in the summer – he's an actor and plays Lottie's character's long-lost brother on *Little Miss Mulholland*.

'Hey!' he says, sweeping me up in a hug. 'I heard you were coming back!' Then his grin fades. 'Man, I also heard what happened.'

I stifle a sigh. I think I'm going to get a lot of this tonight.

When Jack arrives half an hour later, I recognise him instantly, despite his disguise, and my heart skips a beat. He and his bandmates, Brandon and Miles, have come as vampires and they look like something out of *The Lost Boys*: messy hair, pale faces, guyliner and fake blood trailing down from their lips. They're wearing all black: skinny jeans and tight-fitting shirts. Brandon, who's as tall and slim as Jack, and who normally wears his blond hair in a slick quiff, is wearing a leather jacket. Miles, who's shorter and slightly stockier, still has the tips of his black hair dyed orange and is wearing a long-sleeved shirt, open at the neck.

And then there's Jack. He's had a haircut and it's now very short behind, but longer on top. It's wavy and messy, a few dark tendrils falling down across his forehead.

Brandon is carrying a DJ bag and goes straight over to the guy behind the decks. Jack scrapes his hair out of his face and my eyes fall on his slim wrist encircled with several leather straps, and the comic-book-style POW! tattoo on his forearm. I see him notice the girl dressed as a comic-book character and his eyes skim over her with appreciation. I knew he'd like her costume. I hope he doesn't like her, too. But why should I care? I shouldn't.

And then his eyes are on mine and everything freezes. A moment later I gather my wits and nod a hello as crowds of people pass between us. He makes his way towards me and I'm aware of my heart quickening and my body tensing. My knuckles are white as I grip my punch glass and I'm vaguely conscious of Agnes relaying a story to Lottie that I really should be paying attention to.

'Hi,' he says, looking down at me, his blue-grey eyes seeming darker than usual.

Before I can reply, Lottie has her arms round him and is hugging him hello. Miles and Brandon join us and she breaks away from Jack as Brandon slides her hood off her head and kisses her cheek. She grins and touches the trail of fake blood running down from one side of his lips.

'Don't get me all bloody,' she warns.

'People are Strange' – one of the songs from the *The Lost Boys* soundtrack – starts to play out of the speakers. Miles looks over his shoulder and salutes the DJ with amusement before heading to the bar with Agnes.

'Is that Morgan?' I ask Jack, nodding towards the guy behind the decks.

'Yeah,' he says, glancing back at me.

'Are you playing a set later?' Such an ordinary conversation for such extraordinary circumstances. The last time I saw him he was teasingly singing about kissing me.

Tom, Tom, Tom, I chant inside my head.

He nods, casting his gaze over my outfit. 'You look cool.'

'Thanks. So do you.' I try to ignore the thrill I feel when he compliments me.

Lottie and Brandon are standing off to one side, flirting and talking, their heads close together.

I wonder if Agnes has told Jack that I have a boyfriend.

'Oh, wow,' Lissa interrupts with a nasty smile, materialising beside us. 'Bride of Dracula and *Dracula*?' She lets out a horrid little hoot of laughter.

'Nice to see you, too, Lissa,' Jack replies coolly.

'Did you guys go shopping for your costumes together?' she asks. 'Or did fate intervene?'

Fate or Agnes, I think to myself. Did she know her brother was coming as a vampire when she encouraged me to buy this dress? I glance over my shoulder, wondering where on earth she is with our drinks.

'I don't suppose a guy like you would care that she has a boyfriend,' Lissa continues.

Oh, here we go…

'Here you go,' Agnes interrupts. 'Sorry, Lissa, I didn't get you one,' she says, before leaning past her to hand out glasses and, in doing so, forcing Lissa to step back. Agnes closes the gap in our circle, excluding her from the group.

'Cheers!' Agnes says, prompting us to all chink glasses. A moment later I'm aware of Lissa stalking off.

'Was she being a bitch again?' Lottie asks, finally dragging her attention away from Brandon to notice what's going on.

'No more than usual,' Agnes replies flippantly. 'I don't know why you keep inviting her to these things,' she adds.

'Yeah, you do,' Lottie replies with a pointed look before turning back to Brandon.

I raise my eyebrows at Agnes. 'They've known each other all their lives,' she explains with a shrug. 'They're practically related. Not that that's any excuse to behave like a total bitch.'

'She wasn't being that bad,' I feel compelled to say.

'Have you forgotten that she sold you out to the press?' Agnes asks.

I could never forget that. It was when I was last here and the news had just broken about Johnny having a fifteen-year-old daughter. The press didn't know who I was yet, but Lissa called them and told them that I was at Lottie's house, so they tailed me home to try to snatch a picture. I was with Agnes and Jack, and I still remember the feeling of Jack's arms around me in the back seat, hiding me, protecting me, while his sister drove us home… I remember it a little too well unfortunately.

'Selling me out to the press seems to be all the rage these days,' I reply to Agnes, and I can't keep the trace of bitterness from my voice.

'I meant to ask you about that,' Agnes says with concern. 'Who blew your cover?'

I fill her in about Libby and Amanda. Her lips turn down in sympathy and then Miles asks her something and I turn away, downing half my drink.

'How's the punch?' Jack asks.

'Nice,' I reply. 'But not very spiky.'

'All the better for drinking more of it, my dear,' he says in a low voice.

'Was that supposed to be the Big Bad Wolf?' I ask, laughing. 'You're talking to the wrong person.' I nod at Lottie in her Red Riding Hood outfit.

'She looks pretty happy with who she's talking to,' he replies, as Lottie cracks up at something Brandon has said.

Jack hooks one of his thumbs in his jeans pocket. He's wearing a studded black belt, but his jeans would sit perfectly on his hips regardless. I spot black ink underneath the leather straps on his wrist and grab his arm to scrutinise it.

'You got another tattoo,' I say.

'Yeah.' He moves the straps aside to show me. The black ink looks like a bracelet circling his wrist.

'It's cool, I like it,' I semi-shout above the music.

He stares down at me, raising one eyebrow. 'So, boyfriend, huh?' I drop his hand like a hot potato.

'You kept that quiet in your texts,' he says offhandedly. 'Agnes mentioned it.'

I shrug. 'His name's Tom.'

'Serious?'

I shrug again, aware that I'm being unacceptably evasive. 'Yes,' I say, finally injecting some authority into my voice. 'We've been going out for a few weeks.'

He shakes his head. 'That's not serious.' He sounds dismissive.

'That depends on how you define the word,' I say crossly. 'I doubt you've *ever* had a serious girlfriend.'

To my surprise, he doesn't argue. Instead he grins and rakes his hand through his hair, fixing his attention on the other partygoers.

I take another sip of my drink and watch him furtively. The red lanterns are reflected in his eyes.

'How are things going with the band?' I change the subject. 'Is Eve still talking about quitting?'

'She quit,' he replies, glancing back at me.

'No! When?'

'Yesterday.'

'Shit! What are you going to do?'

He smiles a little, clearly amused by my reaction.

'Get someone else,' he says.

'How?'

'Audition.'

'Wow. And what about *Little Miss Mulholland*?'

'Yeah, what about *Little Miss Mulholland*?' Jack asks loudly for Lottie's benefit. Her head whips round. 'Jessie's asking when we're going on your show.' He's teasing her.

'Well, it was looking pretty good,' she responds. 'But now that Eve's quit...'

'Eve Shmeve, we'll find someone else,' Brandon chips in, placing his hand on Lottie's shoulder. 'Can you sing?' he asks her.

'No.' She laughs. 'But nice try.'

'Dude, your set's up,' Miles says suddenly, nudging Jack. They both look over at Morgan on the decks.

'OK, sure,' Jack says. He glances at me as if to say something, but seems to think better of it. 'Catch you later,' he says, half over his shoulder.

I watch him walk away. Was he going to ask me to join him at the decks? The last time I did that was the first night we kissed.

My heart hurts slightly at the thought that it's over between us – whatever it was that we had.

I turn back to see Agnes studying me.

169

'*Definitely* still like him,' she says with satisfaction.

'No, I don't,' I reply with nowhere near enough conviction.

'He was annoyed you didn't tell him about Tom.'

'Was he? He didn't seem annoyed just now.'

'He was,' she says.

'Would you stop stirring things?' I snap, half amused and half irritated. 'Look at him, he doesn't care in the slightest.'

He's stopped to talk to Comic Book Girl, but my nonchalant comment masks the contracting of my stomach. His lips are close to her ear and his hand is resting on her arm.

'That's just Jack,' Agnes replies, nonplussed. 'He's always been tactile.'

'Is that what you call it?' I say wryly, then realise I'd better make a concerted effort from here on in not to give Agnes any ideas that I'm still interested in her brother.

Chapter 20

On Monday morning, I have to drag myself down to breakfast. I would've stayed in bed, but my new tutor starts this morning, and I want to make a good impression.

'Over your jet lag, then?' Meg asks with a smile as I walk into the kitchen and almost stumble into the chair at the end of the table.

'Yes.' I nod, trying to stifle a yawn and then giving up, letting it damn near break my face in half. Meg laughs.

Last week my jet lag had me waking at the crack of dawn, but, since Saturday night, I haven't been able to sleep. I didn't doze off until the early hours of this morning, so it's not surprising I've overslept.

To my intense annoyance, I haven't been able to get Jack off my mind.

We barely spoke for the rest of the party. After his DJ set, he resumed his conversation with Comic Book Girl. In the end, I left early, freaked out that if I stayed I'd catch him kissing her.

'You're all dressed and ready, then?' Meg says.

I nod. I just threw some clothes on, but didn't bother with make-up. I might go for a swim after my lessons. Apparently I'm only being tutored for four hours a day. I guess I'll have extra lessons if I need them, but one-on-one is allegedly quite intense.

'What do you want for breakfast?' Meg asks, picking up Phoenix's spoon from the floor. He bashes it against the table and then lets it fly again.

'Phee!' she snaps, swooping down to pick it up.

I smile at her use of the nickname I came up with. She notices.

'I told you it would stick,' she says with a grin.

I root around in the cupboards for some cereal, amused as always at the sight of the super-sweet kiddie stuff. The boys don't eat any of it – it's all for Meg.

I pour some muesli into a bowl and sit at the table. I miss Gramps already. He was only here for a few days after I arrived, but his presence was cheery. I hope he comes back soon. If I don't go home first.

'How are you feeling today?' Meg asks me.

'Tired,' I reply with a yawn.

'You seemed quiet yesterday,' she comments carefully. 'Are you OK?'

'I'm fine,' I say. 'Just settling back in.'

'You know that Stu can come and stay any time he likes.' She's mistaking my quietness for homesickness. 'We'll cover his ticket.'

'Thanks, that's really kind,' I say and sigh.

Meg cottons on. 'You miss Tom and your friends.'

'Mmm.' I nod, aware that my thoughts last night were centred predominantly on Jack. I need to refocus.

172

'What's he like?' she asks.

'Gorgeous.' I glance up at her and smile. 'You want to see a picture?'

'Yes, please!' she says eagerly.

I get my phone out and scroll through my photos. My heart clenches at the sight of my sexy, brown-eyed boy. I hand over my phone wistfully.

'He's lovely!' Meg exclaims.

'Who's lovely?' Johnny asks crossly, wandering into the kitchen, looking almost as knackered as I feel.

'Jessie's boyfriend.'

'Aah.' Johnny smiles sleepily and ruffles my hair. 'School today, hey?'

'Yep,' I reply, feeling a familiar warmth at the attention from him.

'What time's she coming?' His eyes dart between Meg and me.

'Nine o'clock,' she replies. 'And it's a he.'

'A he?' He looks taken aback. 'I thought you said her name was Jan.'

'I said *his* name was Jan,' Meg replies deliberately. 'He's Polish. And it's actually pronounced *Yann*. That's the problem with emails,' she says to me.

'Hang on, are you telling me that Jessie has a male tutor? How old is he?' Johnny wants to know.

'What's your problem?' Meg replies, slightly outraged. 'Don't be sexist!'

'*You* had a crush on your French teacher,' Johnny accuses her. I suspect a run-in with the green-eyed monster. 'Don't think I've forgotten,' he adds.

'Oh, no, you never forget anything,' Meg says sarcastically. 'It's

173

just as well my memory isn't so good, or God knows where we'd be.'

That shuts him up, and then the doorbell goes. 'I'll get it!' I cry, shoving my chair back.

I'm keen to see this tutor of mine now. I hope he *is* hot. That would make lessons more interesting.

I wrench the front door open and my jaw nearly hits the floor. Standing in front of me is a buff, olive-skinned hottie with short black hair and dark eyes. He's wearing long shorts and a tight vest that does little to cover up his taut six-pack, or his well-defined biceps.

'Jan?' I ask weakly. *I am never going to be able to concentrate in lessons!*

'Hello,' he replies with a pearly-white smile. 'I, er, I'm here to do the pool?' he says uncertainly.

'Oh! I thought you were my new teacher!' I stupidly tell him.

'Er, no,' he confirms, shaking his head, while I blush profusely. 'I'm Gino.'

Behind him, a car pulls up in the driveway, revealing a middle-aged, dour-looking man in the driver's seat.

Johnny appears at my shoulder.

'Aah, Jessie, I see you've met Santiago's cousin,' he says with deep amusement. 'He's covering for Santiago while he's on holiday. You know what you're doing?' Johnny asks Gino while I wish the ground would open up and swallow me.

'Yes, sir,' Gino replies.

'Give me a call if you need anything.'

Gino nods and sets off without so much as a backward glance at me.

'Bad luck,' Johnny murmurs to me with a cheeky smile as the person who I can only assume is Jan climbs out of the car, old-fashioned briefcase in hand.

'You must be Jan!' Johnny calls merrily.

'Hello!' he calls back in a thick Polish accent.

I inwardly groan. There goes my eye-candy moment.

'Oh, God, it was awful.' I laugh down the phone to Lou the following Saturday.

'I'm still jealous of you,' she snaps jokily. 'I can't believe you finish school at lunchtime.'

'The hours drag, believe me,' I tell her with a groan. 'I even miss Maths class with Stu.'

'Aw, Mr Taylor,' she says fondly. 'I can tell he misses you, you know.' She sadly adds: 'We all do.'

'I miss you, too. How are things going with Chris?'

'Good,' she replies and I can tell she's smiling. 'We hang out every lunchtime.'

'With Tom, too?' I hate the thought of him feeling left out.

'Sometimes. He's been playing a lot of football, though,' Lou reveals. 'Chris hurt his foot so he's not playing so much.'

'Oh, no!' I say. 'Is he alright?'

'I think so. It's only his big toe.'

'At least he has you. How are you?' I ask, worrying about her being on her own in classes.

'I'm OK, actually.' She pauses. 'Libby and I have been hanging out a bit,' she says hesitantly and I immediately stiffen.

'Really?' I try not to show how much this bothers me.

'She's not friends with Amanda any more, so I felt kind of sorry for her. You don't mind, do you? She really is very sorry for letting you down,' Lou says quietly. Her voice trails off and we both fall silent.

'It's fine,' I force myself to say, wishing I'd called Tom first. 'Listen, I'd better go. I want to catch Tom before he goes out.'

'OK,' she says uncertainly.

'Good to talk to you.'

'Jessie, are you sure you're alright?' She sounds worried.

'I'm fine,' I lie.

After we end the call, I sigh deeply and give myself a minute to chill out before dialling Tom's number. It rings and rings and my heart sinks. But then he picks up. I feel weirdly nervous suddenly.

'Hey!' he practically shouts down the line.

'Hi! Where are you?'

'Home.' He sounds breathless. 'I just got out of the shower. I'm dripping water all over the carpet.'

'Oh!' An image of his fit body streaked with water comes to mind and I flush. 'Do you want to get dressed?' I ask.

'No,' he replies, 'but can you hang on a sec?'

'Sure.'

I hear rustling in the background. Finally he comes back on the line.

'That's better,' he says.

'What did you do?'

'Got into bed. It's freezing here. What's the weather like in LA?'

'It's, like, twenty degrees or something. It's all Fahrenheit here. It's hard to work it out. Warm, though.'

'It's alright for some,' he mutters good-naturedly.

His familiar voice makes my stomach squeeze suddenly. 'I miss you,' I blurt out.

'Aw,' he says gently.

'I hear Lou's been hanging out with Libby.'

'Mmm, yeah,' he replies.

I don't bother to moan to him. He'll just think I'm being bitchy. The thought makes me feel lonely.

I change the subject. 'Have you still got paps hanging out on your doorstep?'

'Nah, they're long gone,' he replies.

'Everything's back to normal, then.' I feel oddly empty.

'Not with you on the other side of the pond it isn't,' he says firmly.

I hear someone calling to him.

'Coming!' he calls back.

'Is that Becky?' I ask, recognising her voice.

'Yeah, she's back for the weekend. We're just going to grab a quick bite to eat.'

'Why quick?' I ask.

'A few of the lads are going out in Marlow for Dave's birthday. I said I'd drive,' he adds. 'Teach me to get my licence before anyone else,' he mutters.

'Well, have a nice time,' I say quietly. 'I might give Nat a call.'

But the person I call instead is Agnes.

'Oh my God, you have to come over!' she shouts down the phone. She has to shout because the noise of music pounding in the background is deafening.

'Why? What are you doing?'

'All Hype are auditioning for a new singer!' she yells. 'It's damn entertaining!'

'I'll be there in half an hour,' I tell her.

I need a distraction. I don't have to be asked twice.

Chapter 21

Jack and Agnes live on a hill overlooking the city in a huge Spanish-style villa with sandy-coloured walls and a red tiled roof. The house is hidden behind a tall white wall, a section of which forms a camouflaged gate that slides open to allow access into a tiled courtyard-cum-driveway.

I text Agnes when I'm almost there and she comes out of the large, intricately-carved wooden front door to let me in. Johnny agreed to let me come without Lewis. Davey will pick me up later.

Agnes and I walk along the right-hand side of the villa, under fat, shady palm trees towards the back of the house and the games room – or 'game' room as Agnes and Jack call it, with their American accents.

The back garden has a view similar to Johnny's, but the grounds are even larger, set on a hill with three flat expanses of green lawn, each separated by a steep slope. A swimming pool is situated on the first flat expanse, within a terrace of peachy-coloured floor tiles.

One set of the four double doors of the games room are wide open and music is spilling out. I recognise this song, but it's not one of All Hype's. I think it's by Metallica.

My confidence wavers as we approach. Will Jack mind me coming here to watch? He doesn't so much as look my way as we walk in; he's too busy pounding on his guitar and watching the guy singing, his brow forming a slight frown.

At the head of the raised platform that makes up the small stage is a skinny blond dude wearing a lot of leather. His shirt is open halfway down his chest and he has long, seemingly blow-dried hair. He looks like he's making out with the microphone.

'It's going from bad to worse,' Agnes says with a giggle, leading me to the far wall and pulling me down to sit on an oversized beanbag. Back here we can gawp openly.

'He's got a good voice, though,' I say, trying not to fix my attention entirely on Jack – he's even more attractive when he's playing his electric guitar.

'Yeah, but look at him.'

The guy starts to headbang and swish his long hair around.

Agnes wants to go to art school to be a fashion designer, so she *would* be more concerned with how a band member looks, whereas for me it's more about their voice.

'I thought they'd replace Eve with another girl,' I muse.

'They're open to a guy this time. Thought they'd change it up a bit.'

'Really?' That shouldn't make me happy, but it does.

'At least, Miles and Brandon want a guy,' she continues.

'Oh?'

She smirks at me and shrugs her shoulders, looking back at the band.

179

'Oh.' This time the word sounds flat as realisation dawns on me. 'They don't want to have to worry about Jack getting off with their lead singer?' I say this slowly.

She shrugs and glances at me as if to say something, but the song comes to an end.

'Next!' she says instead in a loud whisper.

'Thanks,' Jack drawls, taking off his guitar strap and propping his guitar up against the wall. 'We'll be in touch.'

When the eighties rock god wannabe has gone, Jack turns his blue-grey gaze on us. His eyes widen slightly at the sight of me, but he recovers quickly.

'Going well?' Agnes asks, trying to keep a straight face as he comes over.

'Hmm,' he replies, looking down at me. 'Hey.'

'Hi,' I reply.

'*You* can't sing, can you?' he asks drily.

'Uh-uh. No girls,' Brandon interrupts before I can react, hooking his arm round Jack's neck and dragging him away.

Actually, I can, a little voice inside my head whispers... But I don't sing in public. Do I?

Jack rolls his eyes, but lets Brandon shove him stageward. Miles returns with the next auditionee and they all gather in a circle to discuss whatever it is they need to discuss, before hooking back up with their instruments.

I watch Jack furtively, then snap myself out of it and think about Tom instead.

I wonder what he's doing right now. He'll be out with his mates and girls are probably eyeing him up. Will people still know that we're together or will they think 'out of sight, out of mind'? I don't like the direction my thoughts are taking me so I force myself to focus on our earlier conversation when he was lying in bed, naked and damp from the shower.

'What are you thinking about?' Agnes asks knowingly.

'Tom,' I reply without missing a beat.

From her expression, she wasn't expecting that answer.

'What's up with you and Miles?' I ask.

Nor was she expecting that question.

'Nothing,' she replies a little defensively.

'You're always talking to him when we're out. Lottie's always flirting with Brandon and you're always talking to Miles.'

'Oh, Lottie and Brandon. I wish they'd just get it on already.'

'What, you mean they haven't?' I'm surprised.

'No. He's got a girlfriend.'

'Does he?' He doesn't act like he has a girlfriend.

'They've been together for years. He never lets her anywhere near us.'

'That's a bit weird.'

'You're telling me.'

'Anyway, how did we get on to talking about Lottie and Brandon? I asked you about Miles.'

'Shh, I'm trying to hear this song,' she says, nodding at the stage. I barely give the boys a second glance as I reply.

'Are you a master of distraction or something?'

She purses her lips, but doesn't meet my eyes. 'I dig that description.'

'Yeah, well, you're not getting away with it. Do you like him or not?'

'Of course I like him,' she says, giving me a sideways glance. 'I've known him since seventh grade.'

'You know what I mean,' I say.

'He's always acted like more of a brother towards me than a potential boyfriend.'

'And?'

She hesitates and I think that *finally* I'm getting somewhere.

'And, yeah. That hurts,' she admits, chewing her thumbnail and watching the stage. 'I've only felt like this for a few months,' she clarifies. 'He doesn't feel the same.' I lean closer so I can hear her over the music. I've barely looked at the current auditionee, but his voice is too raspy for my liking. 'Don't say anything,' she adds quickly.

'Of course I won't!' I snap. 'Anyway, who would I tell?'

The band finishes up and Miles sees Mr Raspy out. I don't catch Jack's eye again, but I see his shoulders heave with a sigh. Miles returns with the next singer.

Agnes instantly sits up straighter in the beanbag and hits me on my stomach.

Whoa. He's tall and slim with messy brown hair and piercing green eyes.

'Jeez,' Agnes breathes. 'Please let him be good, please let him be good.'

I don't know whether he's got supersonic hearing or can just sense the excitement radiating from the back of the room, but Jack glares at us. Agnes and I are rigid with anticipation as the band begins to play, the hottie nodding his head to the music and hanging off the microphone like a proper rock star. And then he starts to sing.

'Damn,' Agnes mutters, as my heart sinks. *Sooooo* very flat.

The afternoon doesn't see much improvement. The next couple of guys either look good or sing OK, but no one has the 'whole package' as Agnes puts it.

When the last auditionee leaves, Agnes and I get up to join the boys.

'No luck?' Agnes asks Jack, as we wander over to them.

'Nope,' he says glumly.

'We'll have to cancel San Fran,' Miles says.

'No,' Brandon states firmly.

'What's happening in San Francisco?' I ask.

'Upcoming gig for unsigned bands,' Jack explains with a sigh.

'I booked it before Eve quit,' Brandon explains, flashing Jack a dirty look that he chooses to ignore.

'It's a pretty big deal,' Miles tells me. 'But I don't see what else we can do. Whoever we take on has to learn all the songs.'

'How many did you audition today?' I ask.

'Seven,' Jack replies.

'I thought the first guy I saw sounded pretty good.'

Jack raises one eyebrow at me as if to say, '*Really?*'

'He did!' I exclaim. 'I know he looked like Jon Bon Jovi reincarnated, but he sounded good.'

'I don't think you can reincarnate someone who's not actually dead,' he points out reasonably.

'Should Jon Bon Jovi be concerned for his life?' I ask.

'He should be concerned for his career,' Jack retorts, delving into his jeans pocket.

'Ouch,' Agnes interrupts. 'Don't let Dad hear you talking like that.'

'I'm kidding!' Jack replies, putting up his hands in acquiescence. I notice he's now holding a packet of cigarettes. 'You know how I feel about Jon.'

The way Jack says it makes me think he knows Bon Jovi

183

personally. I wouldn't be surprised. His dad, Billy Mitchell, was pretty successful in the eighties.

'I need a drink,' Brandon says.

'I need a smoke,' Jack replies, popping a cigarette between his lips.

Agnes groans.

'Next week,' he promises her, then to Brandon: 'There are some beers in the fridge. Help yourself. I'll be right back.'

As I watch him go, I have a sudden craving for a cigarette, too, and I'm annoyed with myself. I had no desire to smoke when I was with Tom. What is it about Jack that brings out the bad girl in me?

'What does "next week" mean?' I ask Agnes when he's gone.

'Next week is when he plans to quit smoking,' she replies with a roll of her eyes.

'He'll never quit,' Miles says with gruff amusement. 'You do realise that, don't you?'

'I can but try,' she says, looking straight at Miles, and I see the beginnings of a blush creeping up her neck.

'Can I grab a drink?' I ask to distract her. It's easier to hide a crush when you're the only one aware of it. I bet she wishes she hadn't told me.

'Of course.' She heads to the fridge. 'What do you feel like?'

'I don't know, a lemonade or something?'

I hear her small sigh as she bends down to retrieve a couple of cans, but I don't comment on it.

We've barely cracked our drinks open when Jack returns, a certain buzz emanating from him.

'I have someone in mind,' he says.

'Let me guess,' Brandon interjects drily.

'Hear me out,' Jack continues with a grin. 'I met her at Lottie's.' A dark feeling settles over me. 'She was cool. She was dressed like a—'

'—comic-book character,' I interrupt.

He glances at me with surprise. In fact, everyone does. 'I saw her, too,' I say. 'She looked amazing,' I add begrudgingly.

Jack gives me an odd look before continuing. 'Yeah, well, she said she's a singer-songwriter. She might not be interested in trying out, but we could ask her.' He glances at me and quickly looks away again. He seems slightly disconcerted.

'And I take it you've got her number?' Miles asks wryly.

'Yeah.' Jack shrugs.

'Fine,' Brandon concedes, and my heart sinks. 'But if she works out, and you screw this up, we'll be auditioning for a new guitarist, too,' he warns.

'I won't touch her, I swear.' Jack grins and holds up three fingers of his right hand. 'Scout's honour.' Then he pats his back pocket and pulls out his phone. 'I'll call her.'

He doesn't look at me as he finds her number and puts the phone to his ear, wandering casually towards the games-room door. I hear him say hi in a deep, warm voice as he steps over the threshold.

I suddenly don't want to be here any more.

'Well, that was fun,' I force myself to say to Agnes in a cheerful voice, as I get out my phone to call Davey.

'Are you going?' she asks with surprise.

'Yeah.' I try to look sad. 'Got to get back for dinner.'

Before she can say anything else, Davey answers. He says he'll be with me in five.

'That's a shame. I was hoping we could hang out.'

185

I feel a stab of regret. 'That would have been nice, but… Next time?'

'Sure.' She smiles and I take another gulp of my lemonade before placing it on a counter in the small kitchenette. Agnes is seeing me out when Jack comes back.

'Are you going?' he asks.

'Dinner with Johnny and co,' I reply. 'See you soon.'

I try to resist glancing over my shoulder at him, but the magnetism that drew me to him in the first place refuses to comply with my intentions. As Agnes and I turn the corner, I look back and catch his eye.

Sometimes it feels like there's a cord that connects me to him. It's almost painful to pull away, but I force myself to turn to the front and keep walking. I have to believe that one day that cord will snap for good. But only if I want it to, I guess.

Chapter 22

That night, I have a nightmare about Mum, and it's one that I've had before.

I'm in my house, but it's not really my house. I'm trying to find Mum. The corridors are long and winding and I keep screaming out for her, but she doesn't reply. Eventually I stumble into a large, echoing living room and almost cry with relief when I see her sitting in her favourite place on the sofa. But she doesn't look at me, and her face is pale and lifeless. I run to hug her and my arms close round nothing. Then I remember.

I wake up, sobbing for real. I miss her so much. If she were here, she'd hold me tightly and stroke my hair and tell me that everything is going to be OK. But she's not here. So I can't imagine that everything will be OK ever again.

And everything is so crazy. Until now, it hasn't truly sunk in that I'm living in limbo while everyone else I know is carrying on as normal. Stu is back at work, back at home, no longer a prisoner at Johnny's house. Tom is playing football, going out with his mates. Even Libby and Lou have become friends, and Natalie left school months ago.

It's almost as if I were never there.

I can't shake off my slump that week. My lessons with Jan drag by at a slow and painful pace, and afterwards I feel so overwhelmed with exhaustion from my sleepless nights that I spend the afternoons dozing in my room. I'm happy to be in LA, I am, but everything suddenly feels really overwhelming.

My nightmares about Mum keep recurring. I wake up every day in a mess, and I miss her more than ever now that I'm further away from our home in the UK. I miss Stu, too, and Tom, of course. I often want to call him, but it's rarely the right time – he's either at school or getting ready for it.

Coming back from LA after the summer, I felt the happiest I'd been since Mum died. But now I feel like I'm back to square one.

Tom had so much to do with my feeling safe and content. Tom and Johnny. But life for the Jeffersons is also continuing as normal, and I'm just an add-on.

Johnny is often in his studio. Other times he's gone for meetings with his record label without bothering to tell me.

Things are always better when Barney gets home from school. Playing with my little brothers is the one thing that seems to cheer me up, but they both get tired – Barney especially – so I tend to retreat after a while, rather than risk tantrums.

Towards the end of another week, Meg stops me from going upstairs to my room after my lessons.

'Do you fancy coming for a swim with Phee and me?' she asks.

'Not really,' I reply. 'I'm a bit tired, so…'

'It's a beautiful day…'

'It's always a beautiful day here,' I reply.

'Not true!' she insists. 'Go on,' she encourages. 'Come and chat to me.'

I hesitate, only because I don't want to offend her. But company is the last thing I feel like.

'I'll go and get changed,' I say eventually, and she smiles, looking pleased.

Upstairs in my room, I throw myself down on the bed, barely having the energy to strip off my clothes. As the minutes tick by and I lie on my side, staring into space, I can't even bring myself to care that Meg will be outside with Phoenix by now, wondering where I am. I don't know how much time passes before I drag myself to a sitting position and slowly unbutton my dress, but then the urge to cry overcomes me and suddenly I'm fighting back tears again. I give up, flopping back down on the bed and sobbing into my pillow.

After God knows how long, Meg comes to find me.

'Jessie!' she exclaims in dismay, rushing to my side and wrapping one arm round me. 'What's wrong?'

I'm incapable of formulating a response, so I continue to cry instead while she rubs my back and makes soothing noises. Finally my tears subside and my blurry vision clears enough for me to see that her face is etched with concern.

'I'm so sorry,' she says to my surprise. 'I thought you seemed quiet this week. Is it anything in particular or it is, well, is it *everything*?'

I sniff. 'It's just all starting to sink in, you know?' My voice sounds croaky and I swallow, fighting back a fresh onslaught of tears.

She nods solemnly and strokes my hair. 'I do know.'

'I feel like I'm in limbo.'

She nods again encouragingly.

'I don't live there, I don't live here. Everyone else is carrying on as normal and I feel like… Is Phee OK?!' Panic shoots through me as this thought strikes me.

'He's fine,' she reassures me. 'Eddie's got him in the kitchen.'

I nod. 'Oh, I don't know. It's all just a bit messed up.'

'Do you like your tutor?' she asks.

'He's alright.'

She frowns at my lack of a glowing reference.

'He's a good teacher. He's just not very pretty to look at.'

That makes her laugh.

'I'll be OK,' I say with a sigh. 'Things will settle down.'

'They will,' she agrees with a nod.

I don't know when Meg speaks to Johnny, but I assume that she does because on Friday afternoon he comes to find me.

'You and I are going out for dinner,' he tells me.

'What, just the two of us?' I ask with surprise.

'Yep. To The Ivy, for a pizza, on my bike.'

'Your motorbike?' My heart skips a beat. Is that safe?

'Yep. You up for it?'

'Um…' What would Stu say?

Stu's not here.

'OK!' I agree.

Meg helps me to get ready. I wear jeans and my leather jacket and she suggests I tie my hair back in a ponytail. Johnny gets stopped by Annie, his PA, asking a question, so Meg walks me out to the garage to try on a couple of helmets.

'Does he drive fast?' I ask her nervously.

'Oh, yes,' she replies firmly with a grin. 'But I'm sure he'll take it slow with you on the back. He's a very good driver.'

'Has he asked Stu?' *Why oh why did I say that?* The question slipped out without me even thinking, but I don't want Johnny to change his mind.

'I don't think so,' she replies, frowning. 'Do you think he should?'

'No!' I exclaim. 'No, it's probably better that he doesn't.'

'You've got me worried now,' she says. 'Will Stu flip out?'

'No, I'm sure he trusts Johnny. And anyway Johnny's my dad. He's allowed to take me on his motorbike if he wants, right?' I sound on edge. Can she tell?

'Well, yes, OK, I'm sure you're right,' she says with a smile. 'I was just thinking that it's about time your dad showed you LA. I can't believe he didn't do this in the summer.'

'Someone must've told him I needed cheering up,' I say pointedly and she looks down, before meeting my eyes.

'Don't blame him for being a bit hopeless sometimes,' she says, her hand on my arm. 'He's still not that used to having to look out for anyone but himself,' she adds with a smile.

I grin back at her.

'Are we ready?' Johnny's voice calls and we start away from each other to see him walking towards the garage, his helmet dangling from one leather-clad arm.

'Yep!'

He nods at my head. 'Helmet fit OK?'

'Perfectly.'

He puts his hands on it anyway to check, moving it around a little. I can't help but look up at him, at his tanned face, the stubble on his jaw, his green eyes furrowed with concentration

191

as he tightens the strap under my chin. He meets my gaze and smiles. 'Good. Come on, then.'

My heart starts to pound a little faster with adrenalin as he leads me to an enormous black, shiny Ducati. He pulls his helmet on, followed by gloves, and then throws one leg over and flips the kickstand up, balancing the bike between his legs. He nods at the seat behind him.

Meg helps me to climb on, placing my feet on the footrests behind Johnny.

'Keep your toes here,' she says, 'not your whole foot, so you're out of his way.'

I nod because at that moment he starts up the engine and it fires into life. Whoa. Noisy.

'Have fun!' Meg shouts. Johnny squeezes her arm and she smiles back at him.

'Hold on tight!' he shouts at me, so I wrap my arms round his waist and a moment later he drives out of the garage.

Eek! He's going pretty fast!

He slows down as we reach the gate, saluting Sam in the guardhouse. Then he pats his gloved hands on mine and sets off down the hill.

ARGH! OH MY GOD!

The breath is sucked right out of me and I hang on for dear life as he takes a corner. I thought the driveway ride was fast, but that was a snail's pace compared to this. I've never been so scared in my life! I can't even scream, I'm so terrified.

He pats my hands again. 'LET UP A BIT!' he shouts.

What? No! I'm not loosening my grip – I'll fall off!

'AM I GOING TOO FAST?' he shouts.

I scream my response.

192

His ribs shake as he laughs. 'Sorry, I'll slow down.'

He does. Marginally. But after a while I get used to the speed and actually start to enjoy myself. We're at the bottom of the hill in no time, and it isn't long before we hit traffic. At first, I don't like it when he rides so close to the cars, but soon I see the benefits of being able to go straight to the front of queues waiting at traffic lights, and I also realise after a while that he's avoiding the busy roads when he can, cutting through backstreets where it's safer. By the time we pull up outside the white picket-fence entrance of The Ivy, I don't want the ride to stop.

He climbs off the bike and hands the keys to a waiting valet before helping me off. Then he removes his helmet and rakes his hands through his dark-blond hair to mess it up a bit.

'That was awesome!' I say, as he takes off my helmet and grins down at me.

A moment later I hear the clicking.

Oh, no… Paparazzi. Lots of them.

'It's cool,' he says quietly, touching my shoulder to steady me. 'Alright, lads,' he says to the people with cameras who are darting around in front of us. To my surprise, Johnny wraps one arm round my shoulder and pauses for a moment, facing them. 'Want to get a couple of me with my daughter and then leave us in peace?'

They shout their affirmation and then Johnny leans down and whispers in my ear: 'Smile.'

It's over very quickly. A moment later his arm is guiding me up the front steps of the restaurant and the maître d' is welcoming us with menus. The outside of the restaurant looks lovely, dotted with fairy lights and greenery, but we're led to a table inside and I'm thankful for the privacy.

'OK?' he asks once we're alone and seated opposite each other, bread and water already on the table.

'That was mental,' I say under my breath.

'Which part?' He looks amused.

'All of it.'

'Sorry about the paps,' he says. 'I should've warned you they'd be here. They always hang around outside this place.'

I'm confused. 'You seemed happy to pose for them.'

He shrugs and reaches for a bottle of water on the table, pouring us both a glass. 'I figure the sooner they get used to seeing you around, the sooner they'll lay off you. We've gotta face them sometime, right?'

'Oh. Yes, I suppose.'

He glances down at his menu. 'What do you feel like? I come here for the pizzas, but everything's good.'

I try to focus on the words swimming in front of me. I'm having one of those surreal, Oh-my-God-I-am-Johnny-Jefferson's-daughter moments.

'I'll go for a pizza, too,' I decide, putting the menu back down.

'This is one of my favourite restaurants in LA,' he tells me. 'I still remember the first time I brought Meg here.'

He smiles, and swirls the water around in his glass before taking a gulp.

'Was it your first date?' I ask, encouraging him to open up to me.

'No!' He shakes his head, grinning cheekily as he places the glass back on the table. 'No, that was when she was working for me as my PA. I had a girlfriend at the time.'

'*Really?*' I'm a little bit outraged.

'It was totally innocent!' he exclaims, leaning back in

his chair. 'I dragged her here to keep me company, that was all.'

He stares past me, lost in his thoughts for a moment.

'I bet you fancied her, though.'

'It was hard not to,' he admits flippantly. Suddenly he's leaning forward again, his elbows resting on the table. 'So what about you? How are things with Jack Mitchell?'

'Can we order?' I ask, but the blush is already warming my face and he laughs. I roll my eyes. 'I have a boyfriend,' I point out.

'I thought we'd just established that you can still have the hots for someone when you're with someone else.' I know he's only teasing me, but I want to throw some bread at him in any case.

'I'm not talking to you about Jack. Anyway, the only reason I've seen him since I arrived has been because of his sister. I like Agnes a lot.'

He nods, seeming to approve. 'I'll have to meet her. When are you catching up next?'

'I don't know. Tomorrow, maybe.'

'Why don't you ask her over for lunch?'

'OK, I'll text her when we get home.' I wonder when Comic Book Girl is auditioning. Maybe she already has. 'Jack's auditioning for a new lead singer of All Hype,' I tell Johnny, trying to sound upbeat.

'Did the other girl quit?'

'Yeah.' I don't want to tell him why. Thankfully, he doesn't ask.

'That's a big loss,' he says. 'She was good.'

'I know.' As a singer, Eve was amazing. As a person, I was less keen. But that might have had something to do with the fact that she rubbed her on-off relationship with Jack in my face. I didn't even know they had a thing going… I suppose I can't blame her.

Johnny jolts me out of my thoughts. 'Not tempted, are you?'

'What?'

'To audition,' he says casually. 'I mean, I can't say that I want you hanging out with Jack Mitchell, but I dig his band. Might be good for you to have something to take your mind off stuff.'

'Are you joking?'

'Why would I be? Your voice is incredible.'

His unexpected compliment makes my heart swell, but I return to earth with a bump.

'I don't know how long I'll be here. And anyway I don't sing in public, remember? Not unless I'm very, very drunk.'

'Oi,' he berates me. 'Not on my watch. Besides, that attitude is never going to get you anywhere.'

The waitress comes over then, full of smiles and tucking her hair behind her ears. Johnny is polite, but doesn't encourage her blatant flirtation.

'I'll have the same,' I say after he's ordered, my head still spinning at his words. 'And a Coke, please.'

'Make that two Cokes,' he adds.

'Double trouble,' she comments with a grin.

I smirk at him once she's gone. 'How does Meg cope with all the attention you get?'

'What? *Her*?' he asks with a frown.

'Yes!'

'She was more interested in you than she was me.'

'Me?'

'"Double trouble." You're going to get that a lot, you realise. You and I look crazily alike.'

My insides feel warm at the reminder – especially as it's come from him.

'You've been in your studio a lot lately,' I say, trying to make conversation. 'What are you working on at the moment?'

'I'll show you tomorrow, if you like.'

'That'd be great.'

'Actually, I could do with your help on some of the harmonies.'

I narrow my eyes at him.

'I mean it,' he stresses. 'If you don't mind,' he adds.

'Of course not,' I hurriedly reply. I'd help with anything he asked.

Does he really think I have an incredible voice? I'm not going to be able think about much else tonight.

It occurs to me later, when I'm tucked up in bed, that maybe Johnny only asked for my help to "take my mind off things", as he put it. But I realise that I don't even care. It's the thought that counts. And the fact that my dad cares about me.

I fall asleep that night with a smile on my face, dreaming of the sparkling lights of LA that I saw from the back of his bike on Mulholland Drive on the way home. For the first time that week, I don't have any nightmares.

Chapter 23

I'm sitting on a stool in Johnny's recording studio. He's beside me, a guitar in his hands, hooked up to an amp.

I'm a little nervous – the studio door is wide open – but Meg is downstairs with the kids and I'm hoping they won't pay us any attention. I think Johnny has left the door open on purpose. He wants to get me over my phobia of singing in front of other people.

He starts strumming his guitar and nods at the notepad I'm holding. I've been reading his lyrics and now I'm about to hear them to music.

When he sings, the voice I've heard on countless radio stations over the years fills the room, reverberating through my entire body. He sounds so familiar, yet it could not feel stranger to be sitting right next to him.

'That's where you'd come in,' he says, still strumming. He continues to sing, nodding as if to say, 'Now.'

I'm pretty sure he doesn't expect me to sing this time – I need to listen to the whole track first – but in my head I'm already working out the harmony. He strums the last note.

'What do you think?' he asks, lowering his guitar.

'I love it,' I say. Surely he knows how good it is.

'I wrote it last week. You're the first person to hear it.'

Oh, wow!

'Let's go again,' he says, shifting his guitar back into place. 'You going to come in this time?'

'Um. Yeah, sure,' I say uncertainly. 'Can I shut the door?'

'No,' he replies with a grin. 'You have a great voice. You need to start believing it.'

I start off quietly, feeling slightly mortified at the sound of 'me' coming through the amps. But he nods encouragingly.

'Louder!' he yells.

I ramp up the volume and he smiles.

'Better.'

It takes me a while, but I begin to get into it. I don't know how much time passes, but, when Meg appears at the doorway with Phee balanced on her hip and Barney running in behind her, I falter.

'Don't stop!' Johnny warns.

Meg's eyes are wide open, her mouth gaping slightly as she nods with encouragement. I glance at Johnny to see him grinning. He cocks his head towards me as if to say, 'See?'

I kind of wish I could climb out of the window and disappear, but I force myself to keep singing, as much as it's killing me.

'That was incredible!' Meg gasps, as soon as we've finished the song. 'I had no idea you could sing like that!'

'I've sung in front of you before,' I say, trying to shrug it off. But my insides are burning with pride.

'*Thomas the Tank Engine* doesn't count,' she replies firmly.

I once joined in when Johnny sang it to the boys.

'I told you,' Johnny says with a grin. I glance at him, but he's talking to Meg. He told her about me?

'You did,' she says. 'But whoa. That was nuts.'

'Shall we do another one?' Johnny asks me.

Without an audience?

He must see the look on my face because he says to Meg, 'Give us a bit of time to practise.'

'Yes! Of course. Come on, Bee.'

Barney, at this point, has his face squashed up against the studio window. 'No!' he exclaims.

'Let's go,' Meg says, holding her hand out to him and waggling it about.

'I want to hear Daddy and Jessie!' he cries.

'Later,' Meg says, but now I feel bad.

'He can stay,' I blurt.

'Are you sure?' she asks.

'Absolutely.'

'Hop onto the seat, buddy,' Johnny calls to him as Meg leaves the room. Phoenix starts to wail at being taken away.

'He'll be fine,' Johnny brushes me off. 'Let's try something else.'

He reaches across and plucks his notepad from my grasp, flicking back a few pages until he settles on something. He passes it back over and starts to play.

I look down at his lyrics. I'm just about getting used to his messy handwriting, but that in itself is astonishing. These lyrics are so raw – just scribbles really – but he trusts me with them. It's one of the best compliments he could pay me.

With my stomach bubbling away with happiness, I look at my dad and smile.

Barney lasts for a whole twenty minutes before he happily runs out of the room to find Meg. By then, we're well into our third song.

'That sounds awesome!' Johnny exclaims, pounding at the strings of his guitar. It's a much more upbeat number. 'I might have to get you to lay these down.'

Lay them down?

'Nick has to hear them.'

'Who's Nick?' I ask.

'From my label.'

What?

'Let's try the chorus again,' he says.

I feel a bit dizzy.

'Louder!' he shouts over the music.

I nod and do as he asks. He grins and God, I love this feeling. I'm impressing my dad!

I look around the studio – not needing to focus on the words on the pad any more. I could feel at home here, I realise. I *do* feel at home here. Could I really do this? Could I be a singer like my dad?

Barney returns to the room, but the smile freezes on my face and my voice falters because he's not alone. Jack is with him. And he's staring at me with disbelief.

Chapter 24

'Oh my God!' Agnes exclaims, shoving past her brother.

'What are you doing here?' I demand, getting to my feet. Johnny strums a final note and places his guitar at his feet. I notice the look of amusement on his face.

'You invited me over for lunch,' Agnes replies, barely refraining from adding, 'duh'. 'Your little bro told us to come inside. He said you were singing, but I had no idea.'

'Sorry!' Meg calls from the doorway, looking apologetically at me. She obviously didn't mean for them to interrupt, but I'm guessing Barney was a force to be reckoned with.

'No worries,' Johnny says, pushing the glass studio door open. I follow him out, a blush staining my cheeks. 'Agnes, right?' Johnny shakes her hand.

'Hello again!'

'Have we met?' he asks, perplexed.

'When I was much younger,' she explains. 'My dad took me to one of your concerts. We came backstage.'

'Oh, right,' he says with a grin. 'Haven't seen Billy since…
Well, not since your gig,' he says to Jack, his smile diminishing
slightly as he reaches out to shake his hand. I glance at Jack to
see him looking awkward. The last time he saw Johnny, Johnny
was staring him down because he'd just pissed me off. What's he
doing here?

'Shall we take this downstairs?' Meg suggests. 'Eddie's doing a
barbeque on the terrace.'

'Sweet!' Agnes says.

'Are you staying for lunch, Jack?' Meg asks him.

'No—'

'He was just giving me a lift,' Agnes interrupts.

'You're very welcome to,' Meg offers, glancing at me for
approval.

'Thanks, but I've got plans,' he replies. He nods at Agnes.
'Call me when you need a ride.'

'I'll see you out,' I say.

'It's cool, I can find the front door,' he replies, barely looking
at me as we walk back downstairs. 'Nice to see you,' he calls to
Johnny and Meg at the bottom of the stairs.

A moment later he's gone and I feel strangely unsettled.

We head outside to the terrace. It's another beautiful sunny
day in the Los Angeles hills – nineteen degrees – and I'm only
wearing a light cardie and a summer dress. I can't believe we're
having a barbeque in November.

'Good night last night?' Agnes asks after I've introduced her
to Eddie. We're sitting at the outdoor stone table with the city
of LA below us. Johnny is chatting to Eddie, and Meg is getting
some drinks together at the outdoor bar. Phee and Bee have
gone back inside to play with their toys.

'Great. We went to The Ivy.'

'I know.' She smiles.

'Oh, yeah,' I say with a touch of embarrassment. Photos of Johnny and me were all over the tabloids and online gossip sites this morning. For the first time, it didn't freak me out. Is it weird that I found it strangely exciting?

'Has Jack got more auditions today?' I ask, trying not to seem bothered that he left so quickly.

'Yeah, he's got some singer called Susan coming over to meet Brandon and Miles.'

'Comic Book Girl?' I ask.

'I don't know.' Agnes looks confused. 'He met her at Lottie's. She came over on Thursday to audition *personally* for him.' She gives me a knowing look that makes my stomach twist.

'What a surprise,' I say sarcastically. 'I thought he wasn't going to do that.'

She smirks. 'He said he kept it professional. But you know Jack…'

Yes. Unfortunately I do.

'Hey, have you got plans for tonight?' Agnes asks.

'No, why?'

'Drew's DJ'ing at a new venue that's just opened up downtown. You wanna come?'

Drew is her older brother and in the summer she was barely on speaking terms with him. She couldn't forgive him for being so cosy with their dad after he constantly cheated on their mum.

'You patched things up with him?' I ask.

'Partly thanks to you,' she replies. 'It was something you said to me,' she explains, 'about not taking your family for granted.' She glances at me and I remember. I was thinking about Mum

204

and how much I'd lost. 'Anyway, after you went back to England, Jack arranged for us all to meet up. Things have been better.'

'I'm so pleased to hear that,' I say warmly. 'Jack must've been happy.' He told me how much he hated being caught in the middle.

'He was.' She nods. 'So what do you think? Wanna come out tonight?'

'I'll check with Johnny and Meg, but yeah, I'd love to.'

'Great! Jack can collect us both from here and we can get ready together at mine.'

Hmm, I'll have to persuade Johnny. 'Is your car in the garage?' I ask, wondering why she didn't drive herself over.

'No.' She shrugs, her face turned up to the sun. 'Jack just said he felt like the drive.'

I fall silent. Maybe he wanted to see me? No. I shake myself. Not likely. 'Is he going tonight?' I try to keep my voice steady.

'Yep,' she says. She purses her lips, but doesn't look over to see me squirm.

'You let me go on the back of a motorbike, but you won't let me go in a boy's car!' I say crossly. My attempts to convince Johnny to let Jack drive me back to his and Agnes's place – let alone a club – are failing massively. Agnes is up in my bedroom, rifling through my wardrobe, trying to decide what I'm going to wear tonight. Yes, she really did make it sound like it was her decision.

'I let you go on the back of *my* motorbike,' he corrects me. 'I wouldn't let you go anywhere near anyone else's.'

'So you trust yourself, but not Jack or Agnes,' I say. Agnes was planning on driving us to the venue later so Jack can drink.

205

'Exactly,' he says.

'Well, *I* trust them. Doesn't that count for something?'

He cocks his head to one side, thinking. I interrupt before he can speak again.

'Come on, they've driven me around before.'

'That was before anyone knew who you were.'

'But who cares if the paps get pictures of me now?' I ask.

'You've changed your tune,' he says drily.

'Everyone knows I'm your daughter,' I continue quickly. 'The more shots they get now, the sooner they'll get bored of me and move onto the next D-lister.'

'D-lister,' he mutters with disgust, before falling silent. Is he wavering?

'Come on, *Dad*.' I force the last word out of my mouth. It still feels weird. His eyes dart towards mine and I grin cheekily.

'Is that how it's going to be? You'll only call me Dad if you want something?'

'I'm still getting used to it,' I reply sweetly, pursing my lips.

'Oh, go on, then,' he says gruffly, ruffling my hair.

It worked! 'Thanks!' I chirp with glee. I'm allowed out! On my own! Could this day get any better?

'But I'm going to need the full address,' he calls after me before I run upstairs to tell Agnes.

'Why?' My brow furrows.

'Lewis will follow you there.'

My shoulders slump. 'You have got to be kidding me.'

'Not kidding, chick.'

He's not. He's really not.

'He'll stay out of your way,' he adds, trying to placate me. 'You won't even know he's there.'

I stare at him with dismay. 'None of the others have got a bodyguard.'

'Don't test me, Jess. I almost lost you. I'm not risking it again. I'm OK with you going to Jack and Agnes's house without him, but Lewis will be following you later to the club and Davey will bring you home. I'm going to need that address,' he says firmly.

'OK,' I agree moodily, walking out of the room.

'Hey, I'm still letting you go out!' he calls after me.

'Thanks,' I call back with a distinct lack of enthusiasm.

Chapter 25

Jack barely speaks in the car on the way back to his and Agnes's house, but his sister rabbits on as though we haven't just spent all afternoon in each other's company. I'm still annoyed that Lewis is going to be there tonight, that I can't just have an evening out with my new friends without worrying about someone watching me. But then I think about Sam and how he still can't walk without crutches and I mentally shut up.

I'm sitting behind Agnes and I can see Jack's hands on the steering wheel, his long-sleeved T-shirt pushed up his forearms, revealing the POW! tattoo on his right arm.

If we were in England, the steering wheel would be on the other side of the car and I wouldn't be able to see his tattoo, I think to myself distractedly.

'Thanks, bro,' Agnes says when we arrive, leaning across to cheekily peck him on his cheek. He bats her away.

'Yeah, thanks,' I say, as I unclick my seatbelt.

'Sure,' he says, not looking at me.

I climb out of the car and shut the door, meeting his eyes momentarily over the car roof. He looks away immediately, making me feel slightly rattled.

'What time shall we leave?' Agnes asks her brother.

'You're driving,' he reminds her.

'I know,' she says.

'Eight?'

'Cool. We'll go get ready.'

He wanders off to the games room. I wonder if Comic Book Girl is still here.

Agnes and I get ready in her room. I'm wearing black jeans and heels with a black, long-sleeved lace top. Agnes has backcombed my light-blonde hair and styled it up into a ponytail, high on top, and my eye make-up is a lot darker than I would normally wear, outlined in shimmery gunmetal-grey eyeshadow. When she's finished, I look about ten years older.

'You know I don't have any fake ID,' I point out. 'I'm not going to get served no matter what you do.'

'You can try,' she says with a grin. 'There's no age limit on the door tonight, by the way.'

'Phew.' I wouldn't want to go to all this effort and still not get in...

We come out of her bedroom and I inadvertently glance down the corridor towards Jack's room. I know where it is because I've been inside. On his bed. Kissing him. The memory makes me flush.

Agnes goes and knocks on the door.

'All Along the Watchtower' by Jimi Hendrix is blaring out of his speakers.

'Jack?' she shouts.

A moment later the door whooshes open.

'Coming,' he says, glancing past her to me. His eyes quickly skim over my outfit, but he doesn't say anything. He goes back inside to switch off his music, joining us on the landing. He's wearing skinny black jeans and a grey T-shirt with a hot-pink line drawing of a house on the front.

We all traipse back downstairs together, but this time every nerve-ending in my body feels electrified.

'Bye, Mom!' Agnes calls out.

'Have fun!' she calls back, popping her head out from the upstairs sitting room. She has long, dark, wavy hair and is tall, slim and attractive. I said hello to her earlier, but, from what I gather, she lets her children do pretty much whatever they want. I think, as parents go, Agnes and Jack's are very laid-back. A bit like Natalie's, only with a lot more money.

'You can sit in front,' Agnes directs me.

'Are you sure?' I glance at Jack, but he's already climbing into the back seat. I wonder why he's being so *off* with me. I'm going to have to force him to speak to me. I swivel round in my seat.

'I heard Comic Book Girl came over earlier.'

'Yeah,' he says, meeting my eyes reluctantly before looking out of the window. 'She was good.'

Beside me, Agnes pulls a face, smirking into the rear-view mirror.

'What are you looking like that for?' he snaps. 'She sang, period.'

'Sure she did,' she replies in a breezy voice, clearly trying to wind him up.

He rolls his eyes. Agnes drives us out through the gates, unable to keep the smile from her lips.

'Who's that?' Jack asks, sitting up in his seat.

I look out of the window to see a black car.

'Lewis,' I reply. 'One of Johnny's bodyguards. My dad won't let me go far without security at the moment.'

'Jeez,' Jack says under his breath.

'Don't worry, you won't even know he's there. Johnny promised.' I can't keep the trace of bitterness from my voice.

'Hey, we don't care,' Agnes tries to reassure me. 'It's no big deal. It's not worth risking it after what happened.'

Out of the blue, Jack leans forward in his seat and hooks his left arm round my waist, giving me a quick squeeze. Before I can react, he's sitting back in his seat.

'What was that for?' I ask him with surprise.

'Aw, are you feeling protective?' Agnes says fondly.

He shrugs and looks out of the window. He's one of only a few people who haven't demanded details about the kidnapping attempt. I thought he didn't care. Now I'm so surprised at his sudden display of affection that I don't know what to say. After a moment, I lean forward and switch on the radio, searching for a song I like. When I find one, I turn it right up. We ride most of the rest of the way in silence.

There's a queue snaking out of the front door of the venue, but Jack exchanges a look with Lewis and leads us round the side to the back entrance. He pounds on the door and a man opens it.

'We're with Drew,' Jack says.

The man frowns and looks past him to Lewis. His face breaks into a grin. 'Lew!' he says, swinging the door open wide.

'Hey, Mike,' Lewis says, coming forward to clasp his hand. The doorman waves the rest of us inside. 'I'm not really here,' I hear Lewis say.

'Gotcha,' Mike replies, glancing at me.

The venue is already busy. The walls are painted midnight blue and the lighting is low with yellow booth seats all around the edges. The dance floor in the middle is already busy with people, although no one is dancing yet. There are DJ decks set up on the stage. It looks like they might do gigs at this venue, too.

'Have you guys played here?' I ask Jack, having to shout over the music.

'No.' He shakes his head and nods towards the bar. 'You wanna drink?'

He's back to barely looking at me, I realise with disappointment.

'Sure. A Coke or something, I guess.'

'I'll get you a beer,' he says, placing his hand on my forearm and leaning past me. 'Agnes?' he asks.

I don't hear what she replies because I'm too aware of the heat radiating from his palm. A second later he lets go, but I can still feel the pressure from his fingers.

I really need to have a word with myself.

I haven't spoken to Tom today. When was the last time he called? I have to rack my brain, and eventually it comes up with Wednesday. Days ago. I haven't even checked my phone today, I realise with alarm.

'You OK?' Agnes asks me.

'Sorry, I'll just be a sec,' I reply, getting my phone out of my bag. Oh. 'Whoops,' I say out loud.

'What is it?' she asks.

Two missed calls and one text. I show the screen to Agnes. 'It's from Tom,' I say.

Hey, you OK?

'I'd better reply to him,' I say, quickly typing out a message:

Sorry, been busy today and out now, but I'll call you tomorrow!

I stuff my phone back into my bag, just as Jack returns with our drinks.

'Thanks. Oh, you really did get me a beer!'

'That OK?' he asks with a frown.

'Yeah, great, but how did you get served?'

'I have a buddy behind the bar.'

'And he has a fake ID,' Agnes chips in. 'You really should hook Jessie up with your guy,' she says with a grin.

'What, and have her dad set his dogs on me? Actually, crap,' he says with alarm, looking around. 'You'd better give me that beer back. I forgot Lewis was here.'

'No way,' I say, tightening my grip on the bottle. 'Anyway, Johnny won't mind if I have a couple.'

'WOOHOO!' I hear Brandon a split second before I see him, and then his arm is hooked round my neck and his other arm is hooked round Jack's.

'Dude! Watch where you're sloshing your drink!' Jack complains, detaching him. Brandon laughs, not removing himself from me. I kind of like the familiarity of the gesture, so I don't mind.

Miles appears and says hi, and I keep my gaze away from Agnes so she doesn't feel uncomfortable.

'No Lottie tonight?' Brandon asks Agnes.

She rolls her eyes. 'No. She's filming. Where's Maisie?'

I take it that's his girlfriend. He shrugs. 'Out with her friends.'

Agnes frowns at him and he shakes his head innocently. 'What?'

Out of the corner of my eye, I see a flash of orange. Brandon laughs at the look on Agnes's face and releases me, but I barely notice.

Comic Book Girl is here.

Jack breaks away from us to greet her. I watch as he bends down to speak in her ear and I feel a stab of jealousy as she smiles and nods at whatever he's saying.

I thought her bright orange hair was part of her Comic Book Girl get-up, but obviously not. She's wearing it forties-style in a sleek bob with wavy curls. She's not that much shorter than him, which means she's much taller than me. She looks über-cool.

Jack puts his hand on her lower back and guides her towards us.

'Hey, guys!' she says with a grin at Brandon, Miles and Agnes. Her gaze eventually rests on me. 'Hi,' she says, holding her hand out. Is it my imagination or does her smile not reach her eyes?

'Jessie,' I say, as I shake her hand. Her grip is bony and pincer-like.

'Susan,' she replies, and I swear she doesn't look at me again for the next five minutes.

'There's Drew!' Agnes says after a while. 'Come meet him.'

I'm only too pleased to be dragged away after standing there like a lemon.

Drew is even taller and broader than Jack. He's wearing a T-shirt, but his arms are decorated with tattoos and he has short dark-blond hair like his dad.

'Aggie!' he shouts, scooping her up in his arms. She squeals as he squeezes her a little too tightly.

'Put me down!' She screws her nose up and flaps her hand at his face. 'Urgh, you stink of cigarettes!'

He grins, unfazed, looking past her to me. 'Who's this?'

'Jessie,' she replies with a smile.

'Ah,' he says with amusement, clasping my hand in his. 'So *you're* Jessie. We meet at last.'

He has Jack's eyes, I realise with a start.

Suddenly Jack himself is between us, slapping Drew on the back.

'Bro!' I hear Drew shout in his ear, as he engulfs him in a bear hug. I have a feeling he's a bit drunk. 'Thanks for coming down.'

I don't hear what else is said between them because the music is too loud and their heads are huddled together. 'I Bet You Look Good on the Dance Floor' by Arctic Monkeys comes on so I pat Agnes's arm and indicate the dance floor. She nods. Drew notices us leaving and he smiles as I wave bye. I catch Jack's eye a split second before we walk away.

We dance for a while and then Drew plays his set so, by the time we exit the floor, I'm hot and sweaty and a little bit tipsy. Agnes manages to grab a couple of seats in a booth and I'm grateful because my feet are aching in my high heels. Looking round, I spy Lewis leaning against a wall.

Johnny was right: he's stayed out of my way. I wouldn't know he was there at all, except when I look for him. He's rarely in the same place twice, and he certainly hasn't given anyone the impression that he's here for me. So far tonight, I've been able to go incognito. No one has given me a second glance.

215

'I'll go to the bar,' Agnes tells me. A moment later Jack slides into her recently vacated space. He turns to face me, his knee up on the seat and his left elbow resting on the table. For the first time in what feels like ages, he stares at me directly.

'Why didn't you tell me you could sing?' he demands.

'You're talking to me now?' I reply. He's been drinking whiskey. I can smell it from here.

'Don't change the subject. Why didn't you tell me?'

I shift in my seat and look away from him, my heart pounding against my ribcage. 'You didn't ask.'

'I did, actually.'

'You were joking!' I exclaim.

He still hasn't taken his eyes from mine. 'Brandon and Miles want you to try out for the band,' he says.

'*What*? How do they know I can sing?'

'I kinda told them,' he admits.

'Well, I don't sing in public.' I shake my head determinedly. Is he being serious?

'Jessie,' he says firmly and I jump as his hand rests on my hip.

'Jack,' I reply warningly, glancing down at his hand and then back at his face.

He takes his hand away. 'Yeah, yeah, I know you've got a boyfriend.' He rolls his eyes. 'I won't touch you, I swear. But come over tomorrow. Sing for the guys.'

'What happened with Susan?'

'She's good, but you're better.'

My stomach flutters.

'Have you got something else to do?'

His question stumps me because no, actually, I've been bored out of my brains and I could do with a distraction.

At that moment, Agnes returns with our drinks. 'Beat it,' she snaps at Jack, who's sitting in her place.

He leans in towards me, so close that I can feel his breath on my skin. 'Think about it,' he says with a significant look.

'What was that about?' Agnes asks the moment he's gone, leaving me in a bit of a tizz.

'He wants me to try out for All Hype.'

'Does he now?' She sounds sardonic. 'I thought he'd hold out at least a coupla days before asking.'

I narrow my eyes at her.

'You're awesome, Jess,' she says matter-of-factly. 'I wish I could sing like you. I'd kill to be in their band.'

'You would?'

'Yeah, but I can style you instead,' she decides with a grin.

I can't believe I'm actually considering this.

Chapter 26

The next morning, I wake up early and full of nerves. Did that seriously happen last night? Am I really trying out for All Hype today?

Brandon and Miles turned on their charm when Agnes and I rejoined them. They were so amiable and encouraging that I somehow found myself agreeing that no, it couldn't hurt to go to Jack's today.

My nerves intensify, but when I think of Susan, and how cold and catty she seemed, it bizarrely stiffens my resolve. I'd hate her to be their lead singer, but it looks like she's next in line if I don't step up.

For a moment, I picture myself onstage with the band and it gives me a thrill. But the jitters soon take over again.

Eventually Johnny emerges from his room after what feels to me like the longest lie-in in history.

'I need to talk to you,' I say, dragging him into the studio before he can go downstairs.

'What's wrong?' he asks, still looking only half awake.

'Nothing's wrong.' I come straight out with it. 'Jack wants me to audition for All Hype.'

'Now why doesn't that surprise me?' he asks drily, slumping into a swivel chair.

'I think I want to as well,' I tell him, still feeling a little uncertain as I sit down opposite him.

'Yeah?' he asks with interest, before his expression transforms into a frown. 'Of course you do.'

'What's that supposed to mean?' I ask.

'I know how you feel about Jack Mitchell.'

'No, you don't,' I bite back. 'I'm with Tom.' Oh, and I must remember to call him later.

'That won't stop Jack from trying it on,' he says and my face heats up.

'Yeah, well, even if he does, which he *won't*,' I add pertinently, 'he won't get anywhere.' I'm resolute about this. 'Anyway, Miles and Brandon will kill him if he comes onto another band member.'

Johnny reels backwards slightly, but Meg interrupts us before he can comment.

'Oh, you're awake,' she says, coming into the studio.

'Hey.' He tugs her onto his lap.

'Have you told her yet?' she asks him over her shoulder.

'Not yet,' he replies with an amused smile.

'Told me what?' I ask, confused.

Meg smiles at me mischievously. 'How do you feel about adding singing lessons to your daily tutoring sessions?'

It turns out Annie knows someone who's recently graduated from music school and is looking for new students to fill his

219

books. Johnny and Meg thought it would do me good to balance my compulsory subjects with something that really interests me. I'm touched that they care enough to look into it.

I turn to Johnny, seeking his approval. 'Did you ever have lessons?'

'No,' he admits. 'But I never had confidence issues with singing in front of people,' he adds pointedly.

Another flurry of nerves swirls through me. If only I could've started my lessons a week ago…

Davey has the day off with his family so Johnny offers to drive me to Jack's. I ask if we can go on his bike.

Agnes looks delighted when she comes outside to buzz us into the courtyard. Johnny helps me down from the back of the bike and flips his visor up. I take off my helmet and shake out my hair, then glance at him to see his green eyes are crinkled at the corners.

'Have fun.'

'Thanks.' I smile at him and he looks past me, raising one hand in a half-wave.

I glance over my shoulder to see that Jack, Brandon and Miles have come out of the games room. They're looking a little overawed.

Johnny flips his visor back down and revs his engine loudly, roaring out of the drive. God, I love my dad.

And I do, I realise, as my heart expands. It might have been a casual thought, but I discover that I meant it.

'Sweet ride,' Miles says, his goggle-eyed expression distracting me from my warm thoughts.

'For sure,' Brandon agrees. 'You ready?'

I nod because my sudden anxiety has rendered me speechless.

'You sure know how to make an entrance,' Jack murmurs as we walk down the side of his house.

We reach the games room and I put my jacket and helmet off to the side, taking a few deep breaths to calm down. I turn round to see that Miles is already behind the drum kit and Brandon is standing talking to him, gripping his bass guitar by its neck and swinging it slightly. Jack is front and centre, lowering the mic stand for my height. I remember that Susan was here yesterday and she's much taller than me. I don't even know what I have to live up to. What if they still choose her?

Jack jerks his head at me, indicating that I should join them. I slowly walk forward.

'How's this?' he asks of the microphone height, moving back to make room for me.

'Good,' I reply, far too aware of his body heat beside me.

Agnes is sitting at the back, grinning at me. I take another deep breath and offer her a shaky smile.

Jack reaches for his guitar, slipping the strap over his head. 'Any requests?' he asks.

I cast my eyes over his bandmates, looking at me expectantly.

' "Hit Me With It", ' I reply. It's the name of my favourite All Hype song.

Jack looks impressed. 'One of ours,' he says, glancing at Brandon and Miles. Miles grins and twirls his drumstick around in his right hand and then immediately starts to bash on his kit.

I jolt. This is all happening very quickly.

Brandon brings in the bass, then Jack starts to pound on his guitar strings and I realise with horror that the lyrics have completely flown from my mind.

Oh, God, oh, God… Focus, Jessie!

I feel like a rabbit caught in the headlights as I look at Agnes, and then the first line comes to me like a bolt of lightning and I don't have time to think any more, only sing.

I step up to the mic and let rip.

'Jeez!' Brandon is the first to speak afterwards.

'Told you so,' Jack says flippantly as I try – unsuccessfully – to look cool, calm and collected.

'I messed up on a couple of lines,' I apologise.

'No, man, that was good,' Miles says, impressed. 'Shall we go again?'

'OK.' I nod. 'What next?'

'What else do you know?' Brandon asks.

'How about 'Disco Creep'?'

He nods and grins – it's another one of theirs. I glance at Agnes and she gives me the thumbs up. I bite my lip. I feel like I'm buzzing.

Two songs later we take a break. Agnes gets me a can of lemonade from the fridge.

'Done deal,' she says with a significant look, glancing at the boys. They're deep in discussion. I see Jack nod and then Brandon comes over.

'We usually have basic band practice on Monday, Wednesday and Thursday afternoons, but we'll have to ramp up rehearsals in the lead-up to San Fran.'

'Maybe we should still cancel,' Jack chips in.

'Not yet,' Brandon states firmly.

I'm staring at them, flummoxed. 'What, that's it? I'm in the band?'

I glance at Jack to see him dig his hand into his pocket. He stares back at me, his eyebrow slightly raised.

'If you wanna be,' Brandon says.

'Um, yeah. I mean, *yes*. Definitely.' I thought I'd have to jump through a few more hoops.

Agnes whoops melodramatically, prompting laughs from Brandon and Miles.

Er, shouldn't I tell them I'm going back to England at some point? I push the thought aside, just wanting to enjoy the moment. I'll cross that bridge when I come to it. One question is plaguing me, though.

'What about Susan?' I glance at Jack.

'Who?' Brandon asks cheekily.

'I'll let her know,' Jack replies, flashing a dirty look at his friend as he pops a cigarette between his lips and heads out of the games room.

'Don't console her too much!' Brandon calls after him. 'So, Jessie…' He turns back to me once Jack has gone, but I can't concentrate because my head is too full of the thought of Jack 'consoling' Susan.

I'd really better call Tom tonight.

Chapter 27

.

'Finally!' Tom exclaims down the line. 'Where have you been?'

It's Thursday morning in LA and we've been missing each other's calls all week.

'I'm sorry. I've been really busy,' I tell him.

'So I've seen from the pictures,' he replies.

'Oh, God, really?' I squirm. 'Which ones?'

'Well, first there were the ones of you going out for dinner with your dad on the back of his motorbike. You looked hot in your leather jacket, by the way.'

I smirk.

'And then you went to a club that same night?' This time there's a bit of an edge to his voice.

'Yeah, my friend's older brother was DJ'ing.'

'Which friend?' he asks.

'Agnes.' I shift on my bum.

'Aah. Was it Jack?'

'Hey? No!' I completely forgot I told him Jack was Agnes's

older brother. 'No, it was Drew. He's older again,' I quickly explain, wondering why I sound so guilty. 'But Jack was there, too.' I try to sound nonchalant. 'It's cool, we're friends now.'

'Are you?' It doesn't sound like a question.

'Actually, I've got something to tell you,' I quickly continue. 'Jack's band, All Hype, have lost their lead singer.' I pause. 'And, well, they asked me to audition.'

'Oh, right,' he says, not sounding at all excited by the prospect. 'Are you going to?'

'I already have. I've got the gig.'

The sudden silence on the other end of the line is deafening.

When he finally speaks, he sounds flat. 'I thought you didn't like singing in public.'

'Johnny has been working on me,' I explain.

'What's the name of the band again?' he asks.

'All Hype,' I reply, feeling on edge at the thought of him looking up Jack on the internet. Tom seeing pictures of my hot, indie-rock bandmate is not going to ingratiate me much. 'They're really good. I can't quite believe it, actually. But they like my voice, so—'

'I bet they do,' he interjects.

'What are you saying it like that for?'

'It's not going to hurt that your dad's famous, is it?' he says sulkily.

'Tom!' I exclaim. 'I thought you'd be proud of me! I can't believe you think that's why they want me.'

He exhales heavily. 'I *am* proud of you.' This time he sounds sorry. 'I don't know, I just really miss you.'

'I miss you, too.'

'I still remember hearing you kick arse on SingStar that time at Natalie's,' he says dully.

I smile. 'I remember that, too. I never thought I'd be able to get up in front of an audience without being drunk, but Johnny took me into the studio on Saturday and had me singing backing vocals. He might get me to sing on his album!' I relay with increasing excitement.

'You sound like you're having a really good time over there.'

He doesn't sound at all happy for me. In fact, he sounds jealous and insecure, and I can't help feeling a little pissed off about it. Surely he should be supporting me after everything that's happened?

'I haven't been having a good time at all,' I tell him crossly. 'In fact, I've been bloody miserable, thinking about you lot all carrying on as normal while I'm stuck in Limboland, but I'm feeling a bit better now, thank you for asking.'

I didn't mean to come off so sarcastic, but I can't take it back.

'I didn't mean...' He sounds frustrated. 'Oh, look, just forget it,' he continues. 'Sorry. I'm tired and you feel really far away.'

I instantly soften towards him. 'It's OK. You feel far away, too.' He *is* far away.

'Do you know when you're coming back?' he asks. 'You *are* still coming back, right?'

'Of course,' I reply, even though the thought of it doesn't fill me with the happiness it perhaps should. 'I'm not sure when, though. When things settle down, I suppose.'

And who knows how long that will be?

My singing teacher starts the next day, half an hour after my dull-as-dishwater lessons with Jan finish. When the doorbell goes, I answer it to find a cute, blond, twenty-something guy with twinkling blue eyes standing on the doorstep.

'You're not here to do the pool, are you?' I ask warily, having learnt my lesson from last time.

'No, I'm Harry,' he replies. 'Your singing teacher. That is, you *are* Jessie, aren't you?' he double-checks.

'That's me,' I grin, swinging the door open wide.

I give Meg a look as we pass her to go up to the studio. She smirks.

'Better than Jan?' she mouths.

'Just a bit,' I mouth back with a wink.

'What are you going to do when I go back to England?' I ask Jack and Brandon later. Miles is late, so we're chilling out in Jack's back garden overlooking the view.

'Skype?' Jack jokes, glancing at me sideways.

'When are you going back?' Brandon asks with a startled look.

'I don't know,' I reply honestly. 'But I won't be here forever.'

'Dude!' he exclaims, glaring at Jack.

'Chill out,' Jack replies calmly. 'We need someone for San Fran, anyway.'

'Er, hello?' They both look at me. 'You're talking about me like I'm not even here. Didn't you tell them I wasn't here permanently?' I ask Jack accusingly.

'No, he didn't,' Brandon snaps. 'Where's Miles?' he asks, getting to his feet and stalking off.

'Whoops,' I say, turning to Jack with a frown. 'Why did you keep that quiet?'

He shrugs. 'You were the best option we had. Anyway, you're not going home any time soon, are you?'

'I guess not.' Pause. 'Tom's not too happy about it.'

He leans back on his elbows, but doesn't comment and I suddenly feel weird that I confided that to him.

'We'll start without Miles if he's not here in ten.' He continues as though I haven't just brought my boyfriend into the conversation.

'Do you know where he is?' I ask, moving on.

'Er, mmm-hmm.'

I glance at him quickly, but he's staring at the view. 'That sounds ominous,' I say, but when he doesn't reply I'm concerned. 'What is it?'

'Don't tell Agnes.' He glances at me, his eyebrows pulled together. 'I think he might be seeing someone.' He looks away again.

'Oh.' I didn't know Jack knew about Agnes's feelings, but he's clearly more clued up than I gave him credit for. 'Don't you think she'd prefer to know the truth?' I ask. 'I mean, if he's got a girlfriend—'

'Unlikely,' Jack cuts me off. 'I shouldn't have said that,' he adds quickly, looking startled.

What? What's he going on about? Unlikely he'd have a girlfriend? Hang on… 'Miles is *gay*?' I ask with astonishment.

'Crap,' he mutters, getting out his cigarette packet. I think his irritation is directed at himself rather than me.

'Does Agnes know?' I ask with my mouth slightly agape, as he lights up. He shakes his head. 'Brandon?' Again, he shakes his head. 'Does *anyone* else know?'

He shrugs, looking more uncomfortable than I've ever seen him.

'Wait, how do *you* know?'

He looks past me. 'They're here,' he says, meeting my eyes. 'Don't say anything,' he warns again in a low voice.

'I won't, I promise.'

'About time!' he shouts at Miles and Brandon with a grin that I know is forced. He gets up and I follow him, my head reeling. Surely it's better that Agnes knows. Jack has to tell her the truth. Why hasn't he?

I don't get a chance to ask.

A few days later I'm still in Johnny's studio after singing practice when he comes in.

'Don't stop,' he says when I do exactly that, switching off the All Hype backing track, as well.

'Sorry, I'll get out of your way,' I say.

'No, I was just coming in to listen.' He shuts the door behind him and sits down on a chair facing the studio window. 'It's sounding good,' he adds, nodding at me to continue.

I feel self-conscious as I switch on the backing track again and start the song from the beginning. I've taken to using a mic stand, rather than the ones dangling from the ceiling, so I can practise properly.

I sneak a glance at him after the first verse: he's leaning back in his seat with his foot resting on his opposite knee, tapping along to the music. After that, I sing with a little more confidence and, when he smiles at me during an instrumental break, I smile back. He claps slowly when the song finishes.

'Was it OK?' I ask him, pressing my hands to my burning cheeks.

'Great,' he says, putting both feet on the ground and leaning forward in his seat. 'And you've done that in a matter of days?'

'I already knew their songs pretty well,' I reply with a shrug.

'I tell you what, that track would sound bloody good with

229

keyboards in the chorus. You know, like…' He starts to sing the melody and then hops up from his seat. 'Hang on, I'll show you.'

He pushes through the glass door into the studio and goes over to the keyboard. 'Play it again,' he directs me, so I start the track over. The energy in the room has ramped up several notches.

I listen without singing and, when the chorus comes in, he plays a sequence of chords on the keyboard. The sound fills the room with a whole new layer of melody. It's awesome.

'Sing!' he shouts, so I do.

I stare at him in wonder as the song finishes. 'I didn't know you could play the piano,' I squeak.

He shrugs. 'I can play anything really.'

My respect for him has just jumped to a whole new level.

'I'm not sure anyone in All Hype can play the keyboard, though,' I say.

'You could learn,' he replies, as though that's the most obvious conclusion one could come to. 'You'd look cool on the keyboards, front and centre. Not for every song, just a few,' he says casually. My head is reeling. 'You know, you should try going up on the bridge,' he says.

'I have no idea what you're talking about,' I reply.

He grins at my blank expression and then demonstrates what he means by singing a note differently to how I'd done it. I copy him, my insides expanding when I realise his advice is working.

'Ask Harry to practise it with you,' he suggests.

But I'd rather ask him. I'm getting musical guidance from one of the most successful artists in the industry. It blows my mind. I can't wait to show Jack.

And Brandon and Miles, too, of course. But in the back of my mind I know I only added them as an afterthought.

Johnny gives me a lift to rehearsals the next day, after spending two hours with me in the studio that same afternoon. Even Meg, Annie and Eddie came to listen to us in the end. I'm gradually getting more confident about singing in front of an audience. Of course, I know it'll be a whole different ball game once we're playing to a crowd of strangers, but I'm trying not to think about that.

Jack buzzes us in when we arrive. Johnny helps me down from the back of his bike and roars out of the drive before the gates can close.

Jack shakes his head with amusement as I take off my helmet. 'I'm never going to get used to you coming here on the back of Johnny Jefferson's motorcycle.'

I smile at him. 'Do you remember when you thought he was my – urgh,' I finish, not able to say the word 'boyfriend' in relation to my dad.

It was when Johnny had come with me to watch All Hype's gig back in the summer. Eve was all over Jack and I was pretty upset because I didn't even know that she and Jack had an on-off thing going – funnily enough, he hadn't mentioned it when we'd been making out on his bed. Anyway, Jack accused me of misleading him, too, and then he gave Johnny a dirty, meaningful look. When I realised he thought I was Johnny's bit on the side, I was so cross, I told him the truth, and called him a moron and a dickhead while I was at it.

He gives me a dark look at the memory. 'I said I was sorry about that.'

'I know you did.' We start walking towards the games room. 'Are the others here yet?'

'Not yet.'

So it will just be the two of us. 'There's something I want to show you,' I say.

He flashes me an inquisitive look, so I explain. 'My dad's been in the studio with me, helping me with my vocals.'

'OK,' he says slowly.

'Oh, and do any of you play the keyboards?' I double-check.

'What? No.' He gives me a wry look. 'Is Johnny messing with our arrangements?'

'He had a couple of suggestions,' I say, belatedly worrying that I've offended him. 'But he'll have to show you the chords himself as I can't play yet. I don't know, maybe I could learn…'

'Christ,' he says affectionately, wrapping his arm round my neck and giving me a playful squeeze. 'You'll be writing lyrics next.'

I already do… But it will be a while before I have the courage to show him.

Luckily he lets me go before he can see how affected I am by his touch. He still looks amused as we wander into the games room, but my next words wipe the smile from his face.

'Hey, about Miles.'

'I shouldn't have said anything,' he replies firmly.

'You have to tell Agnes.' I'm pleading with him, but he cuts me off.

'No.'

'Why not?'

'I promised Miles I'd never tell anyone. I can't actually believe I told you.'

'You didn't. I guessed,' I reply.

'Yeah, how did you do that?' He frowns at me and shakes his head.

232

'Look, I know Agnes won't be happy, but what's the big deal if he's gay?' I say.

'Shh!' he warns.

'At least it's not because of her,' I add, and then suddenly he's in front of me, his hands on my arms, staring down at me.

'Not. Another. Word.'

My heart leaps into my throat as I stare up into his blue-grey eyes.

'Please,' he adds.

I swallow, then nod and he releases me, my arms burning from his grasp. Not for the first time, I tell myself to get a grip.

He doesn't look at me as he picks up his guitar and I feel inexplicably nervous as I step up to the mic. 'What do you want to start with?' he asks, staring at his guitar strings rather than at me.

'Um, how about 'Killer'?' My voice sounds quiet and unconfident, the unease still strong between us.

'OK.' He nods and starts to play.

I'm supposed to be showing him what I've done with the vocals, so I force myself to sing to him, but it's a little while before he meets my eyes and, when he does, my head prickles.

Oh, Jack, why do I have to fancy you still?

'Nice!' I hear Brandon shout, and the tension between us shatters like glass. We look away from each other. Miles follows Brandon in. Jack stops playing.

'Her dad's been helping her with some of the vocal arrangements,' he says pointedly.

'Awesome!' Brandon exclaims. 'Let's hear it.'

They get into position and, after that, Jack barely looks at me at all.

Chapter 28

The next few weeks fly by and soon the San Francisco gig is upon us. I'm still having my daily tutoring sessions – or should that be torturing sessions – and it never fails to amaze me how long four hours takes when I'm in Jan's company compared to when I'm with Harry, All Hype, Agnes or my family.

I mention this jokily in passing on the Friday night before San Francisco. Johnny and I are in the studio.

Johnny frowns. 'What's wrong with Jan?'

'It's not that he isn't a good teacher,' I say quickly, feeling bad. 'But I'm bored out of my brains in his lessons.'

His lips turn down in sympathy and he sits down and rests his chin on the tips on his fingers, looking up at me thoughtfully.

'You miss school,' he comments.

'I know I can't go back home yet. And I don't want to go back yet—'

'Don't you?' he cuts me off, surprised.

'Well, no, not yet.' I shift on my feet. 'I like it here.'

He reaches forward and tugs another chair on wheels towards him, indicating for me to sit down.

'You like it in LA?'

'Yes.'

'You don't want to go home?'

'Well, no, not yet.' Don't I? This is the first time I've said it out loud.

'I have to say, you do seem more settled here these last few weeks.'

'It's the band,' I reply with a bashful shrug. 'And Agnes.'

'I can see.'

'That's not to say I don't miss Tom, and Stu, and my friends.' I feel a familiar sting when I think of Libby. I don't miss her *that* much and, oddly, I haven't spoken to Tom since last Sunday and I'm not pining for him in the same way as before. 'I also know that even when I do go back things won't be the same. You keep telling me I can't go to the same school.'

'Private school would be my preference.'

I sigh. 'I don't know. It will all be so different.'

'You know, you could go to school here,' he points out. 'I mean, if you stayed. Or, even if you didn't stay, you could still go to school for the foreseeable future.'

I remember something Agnes said… '*You could come to school with me!*'

'Could I… Could I go to Agnes's school?' I ask, finding it hard to believe I'm actually having this conversation.

'I'd have to check it out, make sure it's OK,' he says. 'Do you want to? Do you want to stay?'

Now Tom's words ring round my head. '*You feel really far away…*'

235

'Think about it,' he says, sensing my indecision. 'You don't have to decide now.'

I nod. 'OK.'

I speak to Tom that night, but I don't mention the possibility of staying in LA permanently.

'Good luck for tomorrow,' he says.

I'm lying in bed and we're Skyping each other so I can see his face.

'Thanks. I'm going to need it.'

'I doubt it,' he replies, a smile tugging at the edges of his lips.

'I wish you could be there,' I say, but, even as the words leave my mouth, I'm not entirely sure it's true.

'Will anyone be filming it?' he asks.

'I'm sure Agnes will get some of it on her phone.'

'Is she going?' he asks.

'Yes. I'd love you to meet her. I think you'd really like her.'

'Maybe one day I'll make it over there to visit. I spoke to my dad, by the way.'

'When?' I ask, shocked.

'Earlier in the week. He called me. He wants me to come and visit him sometime.'

'Did he? But Tom, that's brilliant!' I exclaim. 'Why didn't you tell me earlier?' I don't wait for him to make an excuse about the time difference or how far away I feel. 'Forget it, just tell me what he said!'

'He said he missed us.' His voice sounds a little hoarse. 'Becky and me,' he clarifies.

'Oh, Tom,' I say, half with sorrow, half with happiness for him. 'Is he still with that other woman?'

'Yes. But he didn't really talk about her. He said he was sorry for not being in touch before, but that he'd been so worried I'd never want to speak to him again.'

I can see tears glistening in his eyes. He sniffs. I wish I could reach through the phone and hug him.

'So, if you visit him, you could come and see me, too?' I say.

'If you're still there,' he says meaningfully and I lower my gaze so he can't see my expression. This is the problem with Skype: nowhere to hide. 'Any update on when you're coming back?' he asks.

'Actually, I have some good news,' I tell him. 'I'll be there at the end of next week in time for Christmas.'

His eyes light up and his jaw drops. 'No way!'

'Yes.' I nod, laughing as he beams at me. 'But not to stay,' I quickly correct him.

His face falls slightly. 'Oh. How long will you be here for?'

'A week. But it'll be good to catch up.'

'It's better than nothing,' he agrees with a crooked smile.

Johnny, Meg and I talked about this idea over dinner. As I'm thinking about extending my stay – perhaps permanently – I thought that I should spend Christmas with Stu. I also want to pack up some more of my things and bring them back to LA. But there's another more pressing reason, although I find it hard to think about: Mum's things. They've been left in the spare room for far too long. I feel like I'm neglecting her. They need to be sorted out. It's time to say goodbye.

I bite my lip to stop it from wobbling and smile at Tom. 'So I'll see you soon, no matter what.'

*

The next day, we all fly to San Francisco together, including, to my delight, Johnny, Meg and the boys.

Meg will stay at the hotel with Barney and Phee, but my dad has insisted on coming to watch my first-ever gig. I'm touched, even though he'll remain backstage. I'm sure it would help my nerves more if I could see him in the crowd, but Meg pointed out with a wry grin that he'd steal our limelight if he were out in the open.

I think it was the first time I'd ever seen him blush.

Agnes and Jack's dad and brother are also coming, as well as Miles's friend and Brandon's girlfriend. I found it hard to believe an ordinary girl would be able to compete with Charlotte Tremway the TV star, but when I meet Maisie I understand what Brandon sees in her. She's beautiful, with long dark hair and big brown eyes. But she seems very shy, and barely says more than two words to any of us before scooting off to their room to get ready. Brandon follows soon afterwards.

I'm sharing a room with Agnes, Jack is in with Drew, and Johnny and Meg have adjoining rooms with Barney and Phoenix.

I thought Agnes was joking when she claimed she wanted to be my stylist, but I should've known otherwise. She's brought a suitcase full of potential outfits for me.

Johnny knocks on the door when I'm trying on my third ensemble: denim cut-off shorts and a cream, midriff-baring top.

He glares at me. 'You're not wearing that.'

I tut. 'I didn't want to wear it, anyway,' I say, glancing at Agnes. She's a force to be reckoned with, but, then again, so is my dad. 'Next!'

She rolls her eyes and throws me a couple of garments. I duck into the bathroom to change.

'With your wedge heels!' she calls after me.

I can hear her chatting to Johnny as I get dressed. *Aah, my skinny black jeans*, I think with relief as I tug them on. What's this? I hold up what turns out to be a drape-neck vest top with a graphic print on the front. I like it. Finally I slip on my shoes and go back into the room.

'Nice.' Johnny nods appreciatively. 'Cool T-shirt,' he adds.

'Thanks,' Agnes murmurs, scrutinising me.

'Is it one of yours?' I ask her. I know she likes to design her own prints.

'Mmm-hmm,' she replies, distractedly hunting through her suitcase and pulling out a black belt with a chunky metal buckle. 'Try this.'

I do as I'm told. I know better than to argue.

'And this,' she adds, handing over my own leather jacket.

'Won't I be too hot?' I ask.

'Take it off after the second song,' Johnny says.

I grin at him and look down at my outfit.

'Perfect,' Agnes says, glancing at Johnny for approval.

'I'm just glad we brought Lewis,' he replies, making my shoulders slump.

'Johnny!' I cry.

'Bad joke,' he says. 'Sorry, chick.'

'It's OK,' I reply, turning to look at myself in the mirror.

'No time for that,' Agnes says, pulling me into the bathroom. 'I've gotta start backcombing your hair.'

'Sorry,' I mouth at Johnny, but he just grins and stands up.

'I'll let you know when our ride's here.'

*

The ride, as it turns out, is an enormous stretch limo.

I squeal when Agnes, Johnny and I pile out of the hotel to see it pulled up at the kerb.

'Where did you get this?' I ask him, as he chuckles at my reaction.

'It belongs to my record label. Annie sorted it,' he replies.

'Oh my God, it's amazing!' I exclaim, climbing aboard and being greeted by a chorus of male cheers. Jack, Drew, Miles and his friend, and Brandon and his girlfriend are already on board, checking out the contents of the minibar.

Johnny opens a bottle of champagne and I hold up glasses for him to pour it into. He raises a can of Coke to us.

'Here's to a great gig.'

We'll drink to that.

Later, I'm backstage and nervous as hell. My hands are shaking, my palms are sweating and I fear that, if I open my mouth, all that will come out is a squeak. I've been to the toilet three times in the last half an hour and I need to go again. I don't know what the hell I was thinking when I agreed to do this.

'Jessie!' Agnes cries, poking her head round the corner to see me sitting on a speaker, hidden in the darkness. 'What are you doing?'

'Freaking out,' I admit.

'Everyone's looking for you! We were about to have a toast.'

'Another one? I think I've had enough to drink. Or maybe I haven't had enough. No, then I'll just need to go to the loo again—'

'Jessie,' she cuts me off. 'Calm down. You're going to

be fine. You know the songs like the back of your hand.'

'I wish my mum was here.' I jolt with surprise. That sentence came out of my mouth all of its own accord.

She hesitantly comes to sit down next to me. 'You must miss her.'

Her words feel like a knife has been twisted in my gut. The truth is, recently I haven't missed her much at all. I've been too busy, too distracted with the band. Am I forgetting her? Here I am, in LA, away from Stu and our little home. Am I losing her? Am I losing myself?

Or am I finding myself?

I shake my head rapidly. I don't know. I don't know what I'm doing.

'Do you want me to get Johnny for you?' Agnes asks sympathetically.

'I'm here,' I hear him reply, and then he's in front of me, crouching down and staring at me steadily with the same shade of green eyes reflecting back at me like a mirror.

I don't even have my mother's eyes.

'You OK?' he asks.

Agnes squeezes my shoulder and leaves us to it.

'Bit shaky,' I reply, my voice wavering.

'What is it? Just the gig, or…'

I try to swallow the lump in my throat, but tears spring up in my eyes and all I can think about is Mum.

He moves to sit next to me, wrapping one arm round my shoulders and pulling me against his chest. 'I want to tell you that it's all going to be OK. Small steps and everything. But you haven't been taking small steps, have you?'

I half laugh. 'No, I guess not.'

241

'For what it's worth, I'm proud of you,' he says against the top of my head.

'It's worth a lot,' I reply quietly.

I wonder if Mum would be proud. Is she up there, looking down at me and smiling? Or is she shaking her head in horror at the thought of me on a stage?

'Your mum would be proud of you, too,' he says in a gruff voice, as though reading my mind.

'I don't know if she would,' I allow myself to say.

He looks down at me, his brow furrowed. 'Yeah, she would.'

'She kept me away from you all this time, and now here I am, trying to follow in your footsteps.'

'I hadn't seen Candy in years,' he says. 'But your mum was a rock chick, through and through. I bet that never changed.'

An image comes to me of her rummaging through my make-up bag and pulling out a deep-red shade of nail varnish.

'Aha!' she says, triumphant.

'Here we go again,' I moan jokily. 'Can't you buy your own nail varnish?'

She grins at me over her shoulder, her light-brown eyes warm and her long, wavy, dark hair cascading down her back. 'It's nice to share, Jess,' she says sweetly.

I roll my eyes at her and she giggles and arm-bumps me as she hurries back to her room with the polish in her hand.

She knew that I didn't really mind. She was always listening to my music, nicking my make-up and stealing my clothes. She was young at heart and I adored her for it, however much I might've given her stick at the time.

242

'She'd love to see you up there,' Johnny continues. 'She'd be right there at the front, smiling up at you and singing along to the music.'

He looks a little dazed as he stares off into the distance, caught in his own memory of Mum when she fell for him. 'She'd love it,' he reiterates firmly. 'Now come on, you. Go out there and make me proud.'

'You're already proud of me,' I point out with a smirk. 'You just told me.'

He chuckles. 'No need to be arrogant about it.'

I giggle and get to my feet.

'There you are!' Jack says with relief when we round a corner to the side of the stage. 'We're going on in ten minutes.'

We're the first act to play, which makes the whole thing even more nerve-wracking.

'You OK?' he checks, eyeing me with concern.

'Yes.' I nod, pleased that he seems to care. 'I didn't mean to worry you.'

Johnny goes to talk to Billy, but I'm distracted by Agnes laughing at a tall, tanned, absolutely gorgeous guy with brown hair.

'Who's that?' I ask Jack.

'Brett,' he replies with a grin. 'An old friend. Come meet him?'

'Sure.'

We wander over. Agnes's eyes are bright with excitement as she introduces me.

'Are you Australian?' I ask him, hearing the twang in his accent.

'You got me,' he replies with a lopsided grin.

243

'How do you guys know each other?' I ask, struck by how piercing his blue eyes are.

'My mum worked for the Mitchells for a few years,' Brett explains, hooking his thumbs into his jeans pockets. 'We lived on site.'

'We practically grew up together,' Agnes chips in, before elbowing him. 'Why did you stay away for so long?' she asks reproachfully.

He shrugs and grins down at her, before looking at me. 'We moved back to Australia eighteen months ago. I'm here on holiday.'

'An extended holiday,' Agnes says with a smile. Her eyes widen suddenly. 'Hey, can Jessie come, too?'

'Sure,' Brett replies with a shrug.

'Come where?' I ask with confusion.

'To the beach tomorrow, a couple of hours south of here. Brett has a kiteboard. We thought we'd go hang out for the day.'

My heart jumps at the idea, but swiftly falls. 'I doubt Johnny will let me go without Lewis in tow.'

'Ask him,' Jack suggests casually.

'Are you going, too?'

'Of course,' he replies, and there's something about the look in his eyes that makes my pulse start racing.

'You guys ready?' Miles calls to us. Jack nods and a fresh bout of nerves sweeps through me.

'That should take her mind off Miles,' Jack comments, as we make our way over to our bandmates.

'Did you ask him to come?'

'No.' He hooks his arm round my neck. 'He was coming, anyway, but I invited him to the gig.'

'Nice job.' I try to keep my voice steady at his casual contact. 'What's the deal with them?'

'First love, torn apart,' he replies with a hint of sarcasm. 'All a bit too sappy for me. Ask her.'

I give him a wry look and he stares down at me with amusement, then says in my ear: 'You look hot, by the way.'

'Hey,' Brandon warns before I can respond, and I jerk my attention away from Jack to see him glaring at the two of us. He points at Jack. 'Remember your promise.'

Is he joking? He doesn't look like he is. Out of the blue, Jack pulls me towards him, wrapping his arms round me so my chest is flush with his. He rests his chin on the top of my head and says to Brandon: 'Back off, we're friends.'

His throat vibrates against my lips with his words and it makes me shiver. Then he lets me go.

'Are we ready?' he asks no one in particular. I glance at Brandon in time to see him stare at the ceiling in a resigned sort of manner.

My head feels cloudy with confusion as I watch Jack and Brandon sling their guitar straps over their heads while a roadie hooks them up to the amps. Miles salutes us and walks out onstage. The crowd noise quietens momentarily as he takes his place at the drum kit, then he begins to play and Brandon joins him. My nerves had disappeared for a while when Jack was distracting me, but now they're back with a vengeance. Jack flashes me one last grin and runs out onstage, pounding his guitar as he goes while the crowd cheers. There must be a lot of All Hype fans here for them to make that sort of noise, I realise in a daze. But, when you love a band, you'll travel just about anywhere for them. Mum did for Johnny when he was in Fence.

I hope All Hype fans like *me*.

I peer up at the rafters and say a quick prayer to my rock-chick mother, then I glance to my left to see Johnny calmly watching me. He nods and gives a small smile. I look back at my new bandmates, watching as they work the crowd. It's almost time for me to go on. I take a deep breath and let it out slowly.

My dad has faith in me. I can do this. And so, one foot in front of the other, I walk out onstage.

Chapter 29

'That was amazing!' Agnes's high-pitched voice is the first I hear after we play our fifth and final song, but then I'm engulfed by my friends and Johnny is pushing past everyone to get to me. He swoops me up in a hug.

'Awesome!' he shouts.

'Was it OK?' I ask him, pulling away slightly, my heart racing from the unbelievable high that came with being onstage.

'You totally rocked it,' he says, looking at Miles and Brandon. 'You all did.'

Where's Jack? Johnny frowns, clearly wondering the same thing as me, and we look round to see Jack standing off to the side with a guy in his mid-twenties, nodding at something he's saying. He rakes his hand through his hair. He's so sweaty, but he still looks...

Stop it.

'Journo,' Johnny says.

At that moment, the journalist looks over at us and his eyes widen at the sight of Johnny. Jack glances towards us and then looks back at the man. He says something and the man's brow furrows, but he nods. I wonder what he's saying. A moment later he and Jack come our way. Johnny touches his hand to my arm and, without another word, makes himself scarce.

'Jessie, this is Owen from *Muso* magazine,' Jack says.

'Hi.' As I shake his hand, I don't fail to notice his look of disappointment at the disappearance of my dad.

'You were great up there. Was that really your first gig?' he asks me with an American accent. He's dressed casually and has messy brown hair.

'Couldn't you tell?' I ask with a smile.

'Actually, no,' he replies.

Jack whistles at Brandon and Miles and they both come over to be introduced.

'I'd love to do a piece on you guys,' Owen says, pulling a card out of his wallet and handing it to Jack. 'Call me next week?'

'Sure,' Jack replies, stuffing the card into his back pocket. They shake hands.

Miles and Brandon can barely contain their excitement once he's gone, but Jack just grins. 'First of many.'

Within minutes, Agnes is putting pressure on me to speak to Johnny.

'Ask him now, while he's in a good mood!' she urges.

'Are you sure there's room for me?' I check with a frown. 'You did say campervan, not bus, didn't you?'

'It's only the four of us,' she replies with a shrug.

'Wait, you, me, Jack and Brett?' I'd assumed Brandon and Miles and the others would be coming, too.

'Yeah.' She nods like this should've been obvious. 'Oh, come on, it'll be fun! Let's ask together,' she says with a giggle, leading me over to Johnny and Lewis.

Johnny raises one eyebrow at us. 'Why do I get the feeling I'm not going to like what I'm about to hear?'

Lewis chuckles.

'Mr Jefferson, we were wondering…' Agnes starts, and I can't help but snort at her referring to Johnny so formally. She shoots me a look of annoyance. 'Can Jessie please come to the beach with us tomorrow?'

He frowns. 'Which beach?'

'It's south of Pescadero. My friend has a kiteboard.'

Johnny starts shaking his head.

'I won't go kiteboarding,' I say quickly. 'I just want to hang out.'

'Who's driving?' he asks.

I point at Brett, who's talking to Drew and Billy Mitchell. Johnny follows the line of my extended digit and then looks back at me. My heart sinks at the expression on his face. Lewis folds his arms, but Agnes, who refuses to give up on anything easily, explains who Brett is and how he's a friend of the family and can be: 'totally trusted. Totally. Speak to my dad if you don't believe me.'

To my growing astonishment, Johnny doesn't give an outright 'no'.

'Please?' I find myself begging.

He meets my gaze steadily, then his attention switches to Lewis. 'You'll have to scope it out.'

My happiness is instantly stifled. I can't help but feel suffocated at the thought of Lewis watching my every move.

'Yes, sir,' Lewis says.

'If you're happy, you can leave her in peace,' Johnny continues.

'Thank you!' I gasp, jumping up on my tiptoes to press a kiss to his cheek.

He rolls his eyes at Lewis, who replies: 'Anyone would think she doesn't like me.'

Agnes runs over to tell Brett and Jack, but as I go to follow her Johnny pulls me back.

'Are you sure you know what you're doing?' he asks.

'Of course,' I reply nonchalantly.

'That boy is a bit too much of a mini-me for my liking,' he mutters, and I realise his comment is directed at Jack.

'Well, *I'm* not like you. At least not in that way. I'd never be unfaithful,' I add with a pointed look. I know a little about Johnny's history with Meg – and my mum, of course. He's a reformed man these days, but there was a time when he couldn't stay in a stable relationship without cheating on his partner.

'I hope Tom knows how lucky he is,' he says eventually.

But I hadn't planned to tell Tom I'm going to the beach tomorrow.

Or with whom.

Especially not with whom.

Maybe he's not so lucky after all, I think with a stab of guilt.

No. Jack and I are just friends. Isn't that what he said to Brandon? Even if Tom weren't my boyfriend, Jack wouldn't break his promise about keeping things professional.

I can't believe I actually feel flat at that realisation. What is wrong with me?

*

250

Despite the late night, the next morning we're all up before sunrise, keen to get on the road.

Johnny asked me to come to his room before I leave and I'm happy to see that Meg and the boys are already awake in bed, watching the songs Johnny recorded on his iPhone last night.

'You sound amazing!' Meg cries, genuinely impressed.

Johnny smiles at me proudly from his position on the end of the bed and I feel warm inside. He's already dressed.

'Lewis is downstairs with Brett,' he tells me.

I groan. Embarrassing!

'Don't look so worried,' he says. 'They're just going through a few security measures, so they're both on the same page. Are you ready to go?'

I nod. 'Agnes has already gone down.'

'I'll walk you to the lobby,' he says.

'Are you sure? Won't that draw attention to us?'

'I'll stay inside,' he promises.

Today I intend to go distinctly incognito. The sooner Lewis realises I'm in no danger, the sooner he'll leave me be.

'Be careful,' Johnny says, as we walk out of the lift.

'I will, I promise. And thanks again for coming to watch the gig last night,' I say. 'You don't really mind that I'm spending the day with my friends, do you?' We'd initially planned to do some sightseeing in San Francisco. Meg was talking about taking Barney to see a real-life submarine.

'No. I know you need a break, and Lewis won't leave you unless it's safe. If you're being tailed, he'll know about it.'

I lean up to kiss him on his cheek. 'Thank you.'

I wave goodbye and walk out of the lobby.

Agnes jumps up and down on the spot and claps her hands at

the sight of me. I smirk at her, then Jack appears from the other side of the van. He looks knackered.

'Hey,' he says, smiling sleepily. My stomach flips.

'*Are you sure you know what you're doing?*' Johnny's words ring round my head.

I ignore them and climb into the back of the campervan after Agnes. Jack gets into the front beside Brett.

'Sorry about Lewis pestering you,' I lean forward to say.

'No worries, it's cool,' Brett replies.

I'm still uncomfortable about all the fuss, so I add: 'It's a bit ridiculous that he has to follow us to the beach.'

'Your dad's just keeping you safe,' Jack says calmly. 'You should be pleased he cares.'

'I am really,' I reply quietly.

'Saying that, let's see if we can outrun the bodyguard.' Jack reaches over and slaps his pal on the leg. My mouth falls open and Jack looks over his shoulder at me as Brett laughs. 'Kidding.'

We drive through the undulating hills of San Francisco towards the Golden Gate Bridge. I saw it when we passed over it from the airport, but now it's bathed in wintry morning light, the sun turning the rust-red shade to a brilliant orange.

Jack has turned the music up and is tapping a beat out on his thighs with his hands. Agnes is on my right behind him, and I'm on the left, looking out of the window.

There's a little fridge to Agnes's right, and behind us is all of Brett's stuff. Our seats fold down to make a double bed for him, although sometimes he says he ends up in a sleeping bag on the beach.

The thought of falling asleep under the stars makes me smile. Occasionally, I turn round to check that Lewis is still following us, but, despite his presence, I feel free. Freer than I have in weeks.

Soon we're on Highway 1, driving along the coast. The road cuts through creamy orange hills, rolling down to the Pacific Ocean, which is sparkling and glittering like a billion Tinkerbells have thrown handfuls of fairy dust at it. Big birds fly over white stretches of sandy beach in a V formation, parallel to the car, and, when I ask what they are, Brett tells me they're pelicans. We pass a lighthouse and, soon afterwards, the water is peppered with fishing boats: black silhouettes against the sunlit ocean.

After a while, the rocky hills on our left become small valleys of farmed fields. We pass a lumberyard full of redwood pine tree trunks stacked precariously high and another farm with brown horses, goats and a lone alpaca wandering around.

Agnes opens a bag of candy corn and hands it around. It's so sweet it makes my gums ache, and my mouth is sore from yawning as it is.

I may be tired, but I'm deliriously happy.

We round a corner and the ocean is suddenly full of kitesurfers. Rainbow-shaped, brightly-coloured kites soar above people on surfboards, whizzing through the water.

'Is this where we're stopping?' I ask, sitting forward in my seat and peering out through the front window as Brett pulls off the road into a car park.

'Yep,' he replies, switching off the engine.

'That looks like so much fun! Damn, I want a turn!'

'Not likely with your bodyguard watching,' he replies drily.

I groan with deliberately exaggerated disappointment and slump back in my seat as Jack and Brett laugh and climb out of the car.

'Don't feel too bad,' Agnes says as they walk around to the back of the van. 'It's even more fun watching.'

'Is it?' I ask.

'Yeah, we get to see Brett in a wetsuit,' she whispers, as Brett opens the boot behind us. She fans her face and I giggle and get out of the car.

There are enormous flocks of birds – gulls, storks and pelicans – tipping and turning in a flurry of movement across the sky.

I stand and face the water, my hands in the pockets of my hoodie as I brace myself against the cold wind coming off the ocean.

Agnes is swamped in a chunky cardie. No coats necessary, at least not yet. She joins me, glancing over her shoulder at the van.

'Lord, give me strength,' she murmurs.

I look back to see what she's talking about and am greeted by the sight of two boys wrestling to pull on black wetsuits over their bare, leanly muscled chests.

I quickly face forward again and gulp.

'I'm glad you've got a boyfriend,' she jokes.

'He's all yours,' I joke back, shoving her playfully towards the sand dunes. Surely she knows that, if I didn't have a boyfriend, it would be Jack, not Brett, who I'd be interested in. 'Come on, let's go and watch from up there.'

'Take this!' Brett calls, reaching into the van and throwing us a blanket. Agnes catches it. I don't dare look at them again.

'Right, dish it,' I say, as soon as we're seated on the cool sand, huddled together underneath the blanket.

'Dish what?' she asks innocently.

254

'I haven't been able to talk to you in the car, but now I want all the dirt. What's the story with you and Brett?'

She sighs melodramatically. 'Like he said, his mum worked for my parents. She's American, but Brett's dad is Australian and, when they got divorced, she moved back over here. I was ten when they came to live with us, and Brett was twelve, the same age as Jack. They were like brothers for four years – really close – but Brett never went to school with us. He lived with us, but he wasn't like us. His mum was employed by my parents, but that didn't bother him. He didn't seem to mind that he didn't live in the house with us, either. He and his mum lived in the game room, actually. We only recently converted it. He was just totally cool, totally chilled out. He was the first person I ever fell in love with.' She looks over her shoulder. 'Oh, look, there they go.'

I follow her gaze to see them walking away from the campervan towards the beach. Brett is carrying what looks like a shorter than usual surfboard with blue and yellow fabric bunched up on top.

Agnes sighs appreciatively. 'He's so hot.'

My corresponding smile withers when I notice Lewis's car parked further up the car park. I wonder if he's watching me.

I turn back to Agnes.

'Did anything ever happen between you?' I ask.

She starts to chew on her thumbnail and nods hesitantly. 'The first time we kissed was on my twelfth birthday. No one knew, not even Jack. At least, I don't think he did. He never said anything. Brett didn't kiss me again for over a year, and I was heartbroken. He went back to acting like my big brother and I didn't think he liked me. I was miserable.' She gives a little laugh.

'Then, one night, our parents were out and Drew invited some older friends over for a party. They were all getting carried away, drinking and smoking, and I wasn't happy. Brett let me hide out at his place and we kissed again. It was way more full-on this time.'

'How old were you?' I ask with a slight frown.

'Not quite fourteen.'

'What happened after that?' I try to mask the fact that I'm shocked.

'He backed right off. I don't think he could believe he let it get that far. He was a lot older than me. Anyway, things were never the same after that, and a few months later his mom started talking about moving back to Australia.'

'Did you stay in touch?' I ask.

'No.' She shakes her head. 'But he and Jack did. I had no idea he was coming last night until he showed up.'

I look over at the beach to see Jack standing by the pale green water, white foam crashing onto the sand by his feet. Brett must already be out on the kiteboard.

'Jessie?' I start at the sound of Lewis's voice and quickly scramble to my feet.

'Everything OK?' I ask.

'It's all good,' he replies. 'I'm going to leave you to it.'

'Really?' I'm amazed. I thought he'd hang around for longer.

'No one's going to bother you here. Enjoy yourself, but Johnny expects you back by ten o'clock, latest. Brett knows.'

'OK.' I'm slightly mortified that Brett has been told to return me by a certain time or face my dad's wrath, but I'm still grateful for the respite. 'Thank you!' I call after him, as he turns away from me to head back across the sand.

I glance back at the beach to see Jack looking up at us.

'You're free!' Agnes chirps. 'Oh my God, we could run away to Santa Cruz and hide out in a motel room.'

'That's so tempting,' I say with a laugh, as I sit back down on the sand with her. And it is. But I wouldn't do that to Johnny, not after everything he's done for me.

Agnes yawns after a little while, setting me off. I barely slept last night. In fact, I've barely slept all week, I've been freaking out so much about the gig. She lies back on the sand and closes her eyes, but I stay sitting upright. Brett has just surfed onto the shore and now Jack is having a turn.

I watch, riveted, as he wades out into the surf and bends down to strap his feet to the board. The kite billows out behind him and suddenly he's off, whizzing through the water as the blue-and-yellow-striped kite soars up into the sky in the shape of an arc. A wave crashes towards him and he kicks up and over it, the kiteboard almost vertical for a split second before it crashes down into the surf and carries on zipping through the waves.

It's one of the coolest things I have ever seen.

I feel movement beside me and then Agnes is sitting up again.

'You still like him, don't you?' she says quietly.

I frown and jolt away from the sight before me, ready to brush her off.

'I know you have a boyfriend. I get it,' she says, a little wearily. 'But that doesn't mean you stop feeling. And you can confide in me, you know. You can trust me.'

I let out a small sigh, suddenly feeling desolate. 'I know I can.' I don't want to look at her, so I find myself staring at the ocean instead. At Jack. 'I'm not entirely sure I can trust myself, though.' I breathe in sharply. 'I shouldn't have said that,' I say quickly. 'It's just that I feel like I've been away from Tom for months, but it's only been weeks.' I half laugh. 'And we were only together for weeks, but it felt like months. It's all so confusing. I guess I'll feel better when I see him at Christmas.'

'You're going back to the UK?' Agnes asks with surprise. 'I thought you were going to be here for a bit longer? Lottie has the most amazing New Year's Eve party. I can't believe you're going to miss—'

'I'm coming back,' I interrupt her.

'When?'

'I'm only going home for a week,' I explain. 'Then I'm coming back and I think I'm going to be attending school here.'

'You are shitting me!' she cries. 'Which school? Please tell me it's mine!'

I laugh at her reaction. 'I hope so. Annie's going to try to get me in, but I didn't want to tell you until it was definite. Anyway, it's not like we'll be in the same class.'

'Why not?'

'You're sixteen already. I don't turn sixteen until January.'

My chest constricts painfully at the reminder that my birthday will also be the first anniversary of Mum's death.

'I got held back a year,' Agnes explains. 'I was the youngest in my year, and I didn't exactly have the most ordinary childhood with my dad getting up to the things he got up to. I fell behind, so Mom made me repeat the year.'

'No way! So we'll be in the same class?' I beam at her. That's it, then. I wasn't entirely sure I'd want to go to school here, but if I'll be with Agnes it's a done deal.

Down on the beach, Brett looks up and sees us. He's standing with his wetsuit down to his waist, a towel draped round his neck. Agnes waves at him and he points towards his van, beckoning for us to join him.

She sighs dreamily as we get to our feet.

'Over Miles, then?' I ask her, as we walk carefully down the dune, trying not to let the sand seep over the top of our shoes.

'Miles who?' she replies, and maybe it's bravado, but I don't push it. I don't want to break my promise to Jack by saying something I shouldn't. I'm just glad she's got someone to take her mind off him.

'I give up,' she says, laughing and setting off downhill at a run. I do the same, mentally cursing the billions of grains that are now cushioning my trainers.

We reach the campervan slightly out of breath but laughing. Brett has somehow managed to get more or less dressed by the time we get there and he's inside near the small fridge, boiling a kettle.

'You guys want a cuppa?' he asks.

'Yes, please!'

The doors at the back of the van are wide open, providing a ledge for Agnes and me to sit on. One after the other, we take off our shoes and shake out the pesky sand.

'What do you guys want to do for lunch?' Brett asks, passing us both steaming mugs of tea. 'We could head into town or go grab some stuff for a picnic and come back here?'

'I vote picnic,' Agnes says. 'I'm starving.'

'Me too,' I agree.

Brett stares at the water. 'Jack will be out there for a while yet. Do you want to wait here and I'll duck to the shops?'

'No way, you'll come back with a load of crap,' Agnes says. 'I know you.'

'You go with him,' I say with a smile. 'I'll wait here and let Jack know where you've gone.'

'OK, cool,' Brett says.

He gets out a collapsible chair from underneath the bed and opens it up, facing the ocean.

'Thanks,' I say, sitting down and nestling my mug of tea in my hands.

'See you in a bit,' he says.

'Hey, shouldn't I keep Jack's clothes or something?' I ask with a frown.

'Oh, yeah.' He looks a bit bashful. 'He would've killed me if I'd nicked off with his gear.'

Soon afterwards, I'm all alone. More alone physically, I realise, than I've been in a long time. No bodyguard, no family and no friends, well, apart from Jack out there in the ocean. His clothes are in a bundle on my lap and I can just make out the faint scent of his deodorant mingling with the ocean air.

There must be about twenty kitesurfers out there, but the other kites may as well be coloured black and white because Jack's is the only one I'm drawn to.

I watch as he surfs up onto the beach and looks over at me, but he's too far away for me to be able to see his expression. He's probably wondering where the van is, so I stand up and wave at him. He waves back and bends down to take his feet out of the kiteboard.

He's still wearing his wetsuit when he reaches me, his equipment tucked under his arm.

'Agnes and Brett have gone to get some food for lunch,' I call, as he approaches.

'Cool.' He nods and lays the board flat on the sand a few

260

metres away. His black hair is dripping wet, seawater trailing in rivulets down the side of his face, drawing even more attention than normal to the angles of his cheekbones. He straightens up and unzips his wetsuit, his eyes meeting mine.

What was that I was saying about enjoying my own company? I have a strong feeling that I'm going to enjoy Jack's more...

Chapter 30

Reaching behind me, I grab the towel from the back of the chair. Jack takes it from my hands and makes short work of drying himself off.

I feel nervous and jittery and I'm trying so hard not to look at his bare chest. He's more muscular than I thought he'd be. He doesn't seem like a guy who would work out. Maybe he does press-ups.

My brain chooses to show me a mental image of him doing just that, and I feel like a hot flush has overcome me, even though the wind is cold. I quickly come to my senses.

'You must be freezing,' I say, throwing him his dark-blue hoodie. He pulls it over his head, and I try to look away, really I do, but I can't help catching a glimpse of his chest again before it's covered up.

He steps out of his wetsuit and I stare steadfastly at the ocean as he dries the rest of himself off.

'Do me a favour and hold the towel up while I change out of my swimming trunks,' he says.

My eyes widen.

'Well, unless you want me to strip off with everyone watching,' he adds.

'Of course. I mean, of course not. Sure.' Flustered, I get to my feet and hold the towel up while he stands with his back to the nearest car, reaching for his boxers and his jeans from the car roof as and when he's ready for them.

He's wriggling around a lot, but I'm looking off to the side. Surely he must be done by now. Feeling his eyes on me, I turn to face him, meeting his blue-grey gaze straight on.

'Are you done yet?' I ask, discomforted by the closeness of our bodies.

'Pretty much.'

From his hand movements, he's buttoning up his jeans, but he hasn't taken his eyes from mine, so I let the towel drop and have a millisecond of panic before I see that he *is* covered up.

His wet hair is falling down across his forehead and he grins, shoving it back. It must be so obvious I'm still affected by him.

'No shoes?' he asks.

'Shit, sorry, no,' I reply.

'S'OK.' He walks towards the chair. 'Only one?'

'I'm not doing very well, am I? You sit down. You must be knackered.'

He slumps into the chair and loudly exhales. 'It's hard work,' he agrees.

I stand off to his side. 'It looks like so much fun.'

'It is.' He grins up at me. His long legs are stretched out in front of him, his feet bare and still tanned.

'Oh,' he says, patting his pocket. I assume he's going to pull out his fags, but he gets his phone out instead. 'I keep meaning to check Twitter.'

Now I'm nervous for completely different reasons.

'Stop pacing,' he says after a while.

I look at him worriedly, but he's grinning up at me.

'They loved you.'

'Did they?' I stand behind him and bend down to read his phone over his shoulder.

I like their new singer

New singer sounded awesome!

New singer is hot!

My heart is in my throat as I read comment after comment about me and the gig. The fans are raving about it.

'There are quite a few here about you being Johnny's daughter, but it's all positive,' Jack says, his thumb scrolling down the screen to show me. I lean in closer to read them and, after a moment, become aware of his proximity. His face is right beside mine and his hair smells like the ocean. I straighten up, my knees feeling a little weak.

'Phew,' I say, shifting on my feet.

'You OK?' he asks with a frown, glancing over his shoulder at me.

'Yeah, I'm fine.' I return to stand in front of him so he doesn't have to crane his neck. 'I was worried about their reaction, that's all.'

'I knew they'd love you,' he replies offhandedly.

'Eve was so... Well, she was so cool,' I say wryly, trying to concentrate.

He doesn't comment.

'What happened with you guys?' I ask him out of the blue. 'After I left? You broke up?'

He doesn't speak for a moment, but then he shrugs. 'I called it off.'

'Did you? Why?'

'It's not like she was ever my girlfriend. Like I said, we just had a thing going. But I didn't wanna get into that again with her.'

He leans forward in his seat and rests his elbows on his knees. His face is lit by the sun, his eyes lighter than normal.

'Why not?' I hardly dare to ask.

'Why didn't you tell me you had a boyfriend?' he asks suddenly, catching me off guard.

I shift on my feet again. 'You didn't even reply to my email,' I say.

'What email?'

I give him an unimpressed look.

'What email?' he persists. 'I didn't get an email from you.'

I'm confused. 'I emailed you after I got back from LA.'

'I didn't get it,' he replies with a frown. 'But I did text you. At least now I know why you never called,' he adds drily.

'You never called me, either,' I point out.

'So who is this Tom guy? You haven't told me anything about him.'

'He's someone I know from school,' I reply, wondering why he's waited until now to ask. 'He's in the year above me.'

'Did you know him before the summer?' he pries.

'Yeah,' I reply casually.

265

'Were you—'

'No,' I cut him off. 'No, we hadn't been on a date or anything.'

He doesn't comment at this, nor does he meet my eyes.

I sigh and shift the weight on my feet again.

'Do you wanna sit back down?' he asks flatly.

'No, I'm OK.'

'Come on,' he says, patting his thigh. I hesitate. 'I won't bite,' he promises, some of the spark returning to his eyes.

I don't want him to be pissed off, so I hesitantly walk over to him and sit down on his right knee. His left leg jigs up and down and neither of us says anything for a little while, but I'm completely jumpy being this close to him. I have a sudden, agonising longing to turn and snuggle into his chest. I glance at him to see him calmly staring back at me.

'Your hair's still wet,' I say on impulse, pushing the strands off his face. I allow my hand to do what it's been wanting to do for weeks: slide to the back of his head and run up and down the shorter section. 'I like your hair short like this.'

'Does Tom have short hair?' he shocks me by asking.

I quickly take my hand away and avert my gaze. 'Yeah, he does, actually.'

God, what am I doing? I tense, about to force myself to my feet, but then his arms snake round me, keeping me in place.

'Stay,' he murmurs, pulling me back against him.

I'm still tense as my back rests against his chest. He puts his chin on my shoulder. 'You're so warm,' he says sleepily.

'So are you,' I whisper. I really should get up and go, but I can't seem to make my feet move.

'Are you tired?' he asks.

'Mmm. Didn't sleep much last night.' My body does feel heavy.

'I never sleep well after a gig,' he tells me. 'Too much adrenalin.' He turns his head to look down the road. 'What's taking them so long?'

He's not trying anything on, I tell myself. He's just being friendly. Friendly and more than a little tactile. But that's OK, isn't it? We're band members. We're supposed to be close. I relax against him slightly and he breathes in deeply, exhaling slowly so my stomach follows the movement of his.

'Do you think Miles's friend was his boyfriend?' I ask suddenly.

He shrugs. 'I don't know.'

'Why won't you tell me what happened with him? Surely you know me well enough to know I wouldn't tell anyone else.'

He regards me coolly before nodding. 'True,' he concedes. 'But it's not my secret to tell.'

I narrow my eyes at him. 'Did he come onto you or something?'

His eyes widen in alarm and then he scratches the top of his head with frustration.

'That's it, isn't it?' I ask, surprised.

'What is it about you,' he says wearily, 'that has me spilling my guts out? *Every time*,' he adds, shaking his head.

I purse my lips at him, half feeling bad for getting the truth out of him because, really, it *isn't* any of my business, and half delighted because I've landed on the truth with my first guess.

'You only confided in me in the summer because you thought you'd never see me again,' I say with a knowing smile, remembering how he told me about his family and how messed up things had been between his mum and dad.

He doesn't smile back at me. 'Not true,' he says finally. 'I don't know what it is.'

'Are you going to tell me what happened?' I press.

He shifts uncomfortably. 'He was very, *very* drunk, and he tried to, you know.'

'Kiss you?'

'Yeah.' He nods. 'He was totally wasted. And completely and *utterly* mortified the next day.'

'Did you talk to him about it?' I feel bad on Miles's behalf. It's excruciating enough coming onto someone who doesn't fancy you, but when you've also been harbouring a secret like that…

'Yeah. I woke him up the next morning – he'd crashed at mine – and had it out with him. Told him it was cool.' He yawns, but I have a feeling he's playing it down. He must have handled it incredibly well for Miles and him to still be friends – and bandmates. 'Anyway, I swore to him I'd never tell a soul, so—'

'I swear, too,' I say solemnly.

As I stare into his eyes, it feels physically painful to tear myself away.

'I might go for a walk along the beach,' I say quietly. 'If I stay here, I'll fall asleep.'

'Don't go,' he says. He brushes my hair back from my face, his touch making my skin spark, before resting his chin on my shoulder and tightening his arms round my waist.

The nervy, jittery feeling inside me intensifies tenfold. If Tom could see me now, he'd go absolutely mental, but still I can't bring myself to move.

Jack begins to hum one of All Hype's songs and I relax as I listen to him.

'You should sing more,' I say eventually.

'I'm not that good,' he replies in a low voice.

'Yes, you are.'

He sighs. 'I don't know what we're going to do when you go back to England.'

'I'm only going back for a week.'

He jolts, pushing me upright. 'What? When?'

I fill him in. He looks so staggered by the news that I'll be going to school with Agnes that I can't help but laugh at his expression.

'See, there you go again, getting all comfortable and telling me things because you think I'm going home soon, when here I am, planning on staying,' I joke.

He doesn't smile. He shakes his head, confused. 'Are you OK with that? I thought you wanted to go home.'

'I'm pretty happy here at the moment,' I tell him. 'The band has helped.'

He nods, looking thoughtful.

'I miss Stu and Tom, obviously,' I clarify, 'but well, hopefully they'll come to visit soon.'

He doesn't look very happy about this revelation. 'Do you really think you can make a long-distance relationship work?'

I shrug. 'I don't know. But we can try.'

He *really* doesn't look happy.

'What are you looking like that for?' I chide, feeling bold. 'It's not like anything's ever going to happen between *us* again.'

He glares at me.

'What?' I'm taken aback by his expression. 'You promised Brandon and Miles,' I explain.

His expression instantly softens and he laughs under his breath and shakes his head. 'Oh. *That*,' he says significantly.

Out of the corner of my eye, I notice Brett's campervan returning. 'Here they are,' I say, standing up, but not before I see Agnes's look of surprise. I walk over to the van and, as soon as it's pulled to a stop, I open her door.

'About time,' I berate her jovially.

'Everything OK?' she asks meaningfully.

'Fine.' I shrug, playing it down. 'You only left us one chair,' I point out with mock annoyance, staring past her at Brett.

'Oops,' he replies flippantly, climbing out of the van.

'And how are things with you?' I whisper, my own question laced with meaning now.

She turns bright red.

'You snogged him!' I whisper.

'Shh!' she warns.

I bounce on my feet and giggle excitedly. 'We are so going for a walk on the beach after lunch,' I say. 'I want all the details.'

The day passes by in a blur. I feel so content in the company of these three people – it's going to be hard to return to normality. Whatever normality is these days.

In the late afternoon, a fog rolls in from the ocean and within seconds it turns the blue sky a murky grey colour.

'Really?' Agnes asks with a frown.

'Come on, don't be a baby,' Brett says. He'd just convinced her to go for a walk through the dunes with him. 'You can wear my jumper.'

'OK,' she concedes.

'Hey, can I put the seats down?' Jack asks him as his sister pulls another layer of clothing over her head.

'Steady on,' Brett replies, his eyes darting between us at the idea of Jack making up the bed.

'As if!' I exclaim, outraged, giving Jack a look of, 'What the hell are you thinking?'

'I'm going to take a nap,' he says firmly. 'I thought you were tired, too,' he adds for my benefit.

Brett chuckles. 'Course you can,' he says, putting his arm round Agnes and leading her away. She throws me a look over her shoulder. I can't decipher it so I don't try to.

Jack is already putting the back seats down so they lie flat. There's something about the sight of him doing that that makes me feel intensely skittish. I try not to let it show as I help him unroll a thin mattress from the boot so it lies flat across the now quite large expanse. He kicks off his scuffed Chelsea boots and falls onto his back, letting out a long sigh as he lets his left arm fall across his eyes.

I tentatively take off my own shoes and lie on my stomach beside him. I find myself scrutinising his POW! tattoo, wondering if it hurt.

'You still planning on getting one?' he asks, making me jerk my eyes up to see him regarding me from the shadow cast by his arm.

'Maybe,' I reply with a shrug. 'I bet Stu wouldn't let me,' I say wryly, 'but Johnny might.'

He reaches behind him and bunches up the pillow, resting back against it with his arm behind his head. 'It would be pretty hypocritical if he didn't,' he says. Johnny has *loads* of tattoos. 'What would you get?' he asks.

I smile shyly. 'I was thinking about noughts and crosses.'

He nods. 'That would be cool.'

271

'Mum and I used to play it when I was little,' I tell him. 'I don't know, maybe it would look crap.'

He sits up, a look of determination on his face, and then he crawls across the mattress to the front of the car, leaning over the passenger seat to open the glovebox. He returns with a black biro and a big smile.

'What are you doing?' I ask with a laugh, as he takes my hand.

'Where do you want it?' he enquires cheekily, his touch making my skin burn.

'Here,' I say, pointing to the inside of my forearm, just above my wrist.

'It really hurts there,' he warns seriously. 'How about here?' He points to the outside of my arm.

'Go on, then.'

He props himself up on his elbow and starts to draw.

'Ow,' I say, pretending to flinch.

He laughs under his breath. 'Do you wanna tell me where to put the noughts and crosses?'

'Cross in the top left.'

He draws a cross.

'Nought underneath it.'

He draws a nought.

'Cross at the top in the middle.'

My arm is tingling where he's touching me, and I can still feel where his pen has been.

'Nought top right,' I continue, as I mentally play the game in my head. There was a certain sequence Mum would allow me to play that would mean I couldn't lose. Suddenly she's looking back at me inside my mind, her caramel-coloured eyes twinkling as she pretends she doesn't know I'm about to win. My voice wavers as

I tell him where to go next. 'Cross in the middle.' He glances up at me quickly, just in time to see tears spring into my eyes.

'Hey,' he says gently, putting the pen down and sitting up.

'It's OK.' I shake my head quickly. 'I don't want to cry. Say something to cheer me up.'

'Damn. Pressure,' he jokes. 'Shall I give you a different tattoo?'

'Go on, then,' I reply with a shaky smile.

'How about…' His voice trails off as his eyes skim slowly over the length of my body. Crying is instantly the last thing on my mind. 'Here,' he says finally, dragging the end of the biro down my neck and tapping my collarbone. 'You'll have to turn over,' he says. I inadvertently shiver, but do as he says, shifting to lie on my back.

He leans in close and pulls my hoodie down.

'What are you drawing?' I ask nervously. I can feel his breath on my neck.

'You'll see,' he murmurs.

I fight the urge to squirm because the pen is tickling me.

'Stay still or it'll hurt,' he berates me like a real tattoo artist might.

'What are you doing? It's taking ages!' I exclaim after a bit.

'Patience is a virtue,' he mutters.

I stare at him furtively from beneath my lashes. He's so close to me and there's a look of concentration on his brow. I have an immediate and very pressing urge to reach up and smooth the lines away.

His eyes meet mine, and I feel like I've been given an electric shock. His pen pauses against my neck and he doesn't look away, nor can I tear my gaze from him. He moves slightly towards me and hesitates, but I'm completely frozen, our eyes locked in a stare that I have no hope of breaking. I hear him draw in a sharp breath and then he's lowering his mouth to mine.

He kisses me tantalisingly slowly, his tongue slipping between my lips and making my head spin as shivers rocket uncontrollably up and down my spine. My hands fly up to his face and I pull him passionately towards me, kissing him more fervently and without restraint. He attacks my mouth in response, shifting so his body is half covering me, his leg between mine. His hands cup my face, his fingers, calloused from playing the guitar, tangle in my hair as he clasps me to him, kissing me like I've never been kissed before. Ever.

He breaks away on a gasp and we pant into each other's mouths and then he kisses me slowly again before proceeding down to the hollow of my neck.

Somewhere, distantly, a niggling voice grows louder until it's screaming in my head: TOM!

'No!' I press my hands against his chest and shove. He goes willingly, reeling backwards into a kneeling position.

All of the blood in my body rushes to my face.

What have I done?

I've just cheated on Tom.

Lovely, kind, decent, trustworthy Tom. A boy who was there for me when I needed him.

'Oh, God, oh, God, oh, God,' I say, over and over again, covering my face with my hands. 'Oh, God…'

'Stop it,' Jack says quietly, steadily.

'No, no, no, no, no,' I groan miserably.

'Stop it,' he says again, and then his hands are on mine, drawing them down from my face.

'I can't…' I shake my head. I can't look him in the eye.

'Jessie,' he says softly. 'It's OK.'

'It's not OK!' I all but shout, glaring at him as I snatch my hands away. 'I've just cheated on my fucking boyfriend, for crying out loud!'

He looks shocked.

'And you've just broken your promise!' I add for good measure, pointing at him accusingly.

He sighs and looks away. My head is spinning. How could I have done that? I'm as bad as Isla, and Tom never forgave her. How could I have let him down so badly?

My eyes fill with tears and a lump lodges itself in my throat. I'm such a bitch. He could've been killed thanks to me and now I'm throwing this at him, too?

'Don't get upset,' Jack says, pressing his fingertips to my face.

'Don't touch me,' I snap, drawing away and sitting up. I look out of the back doors, which are still open. Anyone – Agnes, Brett – could have seen us going at it. I'm disgusted with myself. No, worse: I hate myself.

'I want to go back to the hotel,' I say to Jack in a low voice. 'Tell them I'm feeling sick or something. I'll pretend to be asleep when they come back. I don't want to talk to them.'

OK,' he says disconsolately. 'But Jessie—'

'No,' I cut him off. 'Enough, Jack. Leave me alone. I can't believe I just did that to a boy I love with someone who doesn't give a shit about me.'

'That's not true,' he says vehemently, his eyes flashing.

'Whatever,' I say. 'You've never had a serious relationship in your life, and here I am, screwing up mine for something that's never going to go anywhere.' I raise my voice and he looks away from me.

275

I flop onto my back and roll away from him, curling up on my side. After a while, I sense him moving and hear him climb out of the van, and soon the smoke from his cigarette wafts in through the still-open doors. A moment later the doors slam shut. I squeeze my eyes closed and try to forget, but I can still feel the imprint of his lips on mine, and the outline of his pen on my skin.

Chapter 31

When Agnes and Brett come back and Jack sorts out our return journey, I pretend to groggily come to, only enough to allow them to put the seats back to an upright position, before I rest my head against the window and pretend to doze off again.

But I don't sleep. Not even a wink. I hear them talking about me, about the gig and how tired I must be, and then they move on to chat about something else. My mind is completely consumed with how I'm going to tell Tom. Do I do it before I go back? Or do I keep up a pretence and lie to him until I get home so I can tell him to his face?

He's going to hate me. He's going to break it off with me.

Of course, I could *not* tell him at all… But the thought of lying and cheating is even more sickening to me than telling the truth. I don't know why, it's not like I've never lied before, but the notion of lying to Tom feels dirty and wrong, and I have never cheated, either.

*

Back at the hotel I force a smile at Brett and Agnes and try to act normally around Jack, but all I want to do is hide out in my room, which unfortunately is being shared with Agnes.

She stays with Jack and Brett while I go upstairs. I call Johnny from my room to let him know I'm back safely, and then I walk into the bathroom and face my reflection.

The green eyes staring back at me fill with tears, but I blink them away. I don't deserve to cry over this. I've got no one to blame but myself. My gaze drifts to my neck and I pull down the top of my hoodie to see the black ink stain of Jack's 'tattoo'. What is it? I frown and step closer. Cupid spearing a broken heart? You've got to be kidding me. I pull the hoodie over my head and turn on the shower, stripping off the rest of my clothes. I climb in and turn the heat up, then reach for the soap.

My tears are washed away by the water as I scrub myself raw, trying to get the ink stain – the reminder of my betrayal – off my skin. Finally I give up. There's no getting rid of it completely. And it's not like I can forget what I've done, anyway.

I exit the bathroom to find Agnes sitting on my bed.

'What happened?' she asks, and I know there's absolutely no point in lying to her.

'We kissed.' I sigh and sit down next to her.

'Is that all?' she asks.

'Yes! Isn't that bad enough?'

Her expression softens. 'Of course. Sorry. I wasn't thinking. What are you going to do?'

'I'll have to come clean to Tom. I don't know if I'll tell him now or when I get home.'

'Are you going to break up with him?'

'No!' I glare at her, but my face crumples. 'He'll break up with me.'

'Oh, Jessie, I'm sorry.' She rubs my back soothingly.

'I don't know what the hell I'm doing. You all warned me. I'm sorry, I know he's your brother, but God! What was I thinking?'

Her back-rubbing jerks to a momentary stop, but then she continues without another word.

'What about you?' I think to ask, tearing myself away from my own dilemma. 'How's it going with Brett?'

'We... I...'

I turn to look at her. She's gone bright red.

'Agnes?' I prompt. 'Did something happen in the sand dunes?'

'It got pretty heated,' she admits, and there's something odd about her expression. 'I'm going to go see him in a bit,' she whispers. I notice her hands fidgeting.

My brow furrows. Does she mean...?

'I love him, Jessie.' She answers my unspoken question. 'I've loved him for years. I want him to be my first.'

'But Agnes...' I turn to her. 'He's going back to Australia. Are you sure you want to give your virginity away to someone who's not going to be around to have a serious relationship?'

She pauses for a moment, then nods. 'I'd give it away to *him* in a heartbeat.'

I take a deep breath, concerned for her.

'There's nothing you can say to make me change my mind,' she says. 'Just... be happy for me. If you can,' she adds, 'with all of this going on.' She waves her hand around.

I smile at her sadly. 'I will be happy for you,' I promise. 'Have you got protection?' I think to ask.

'He has,' she replies.

279

Jeez, she's really going to do this.

'Are you OK?' she asks. 'I'm going to take a shower and get ready.'

I swallow and nod. 'I'll be fine. Hopefully I'll feel better in the morning.'

She heads off to the bathroom and I change into my PJs and climb under the covers, my head reeling. I've been trying to wash away my sins and now my friend is in the bathroom trying to prepare for one of the most major things that will ever happen to her.

I'm still awake when she emerges in a cloud of steam. She gets ready surprisingly quickly.

I shuffle to sit up in bed, watching her. 'Agnes, are you sure?'

'I'm sure,' she cuts me off.

A few minutes later she comes over to me and bends down to kiss me on my cheek. She smells of perfume and luxury hotel soap. 'Don't wait up,' she whispers.

'Good luck!' I call after her. A moment later I hear the door click shut.

I don't know how much time passes before I hear a knock on my door, making me sit bolt upright. I wonder if Agnes has forgotten her key or changed her mind or God, maybe she's done it and it didn't go well at all. I leap out of bed and wrench the door open and almost die of shock when I see Jack standing there. He smells of cigarettes and beer and his eyes are bloodshot.

'Can I come in?' he asks. He looks awful.

I quickly come to my senses. 'No!'

I go to shut the door on him, but his hand flies up, holding it open. He pushes it back and walks into the room. 'Sorry, that 'wasn't a question,' he says flatly, letting the door fall shut behind him.

'You're drunk,' I say.

'No, I'm not,' he snaps, and I see the clarity in his eyes. 'I've only had one beer.' He sighs and goes to sit on the edge of the desk, folding his arms and crossing his long legs. 'I've been talking to Drew.'

'You can't just come into my room like this. I was asleep.'

'Don't lie to me,' he mutters, pressing the heels of his palms to his eyes in a weary gesture. His behaviour is freaking me out.

'What are you doing here?' I ask shakily, standing in front of him.

His hands drop into his lap and he regards me with an odd expression on his face. He swallows and I've never seen him look more uncertain. 'Drew told me to come,' he says finally.

I stare back at him with confusion. 'If you've got something to say, just say it, Jack.'

'I care about you.'

I look away, upset.

'I want you to break up with him,' he continues.

I stare back at him with disbelief. 'You want me to call it off with someone who loves me for someone who doesn't?'

'How do you know that I don't love you?' he asks suddenly.

I'm stunned. 'Do you?'

'I don't know,' he admits, looking down at his hands. I let out the breath I didn't know I'd been holding. Of course he doesn't.

'When Tom finds out that I cheated on him, he'll end it with me, anyway.' My heart contracts at the thought, but hope flares in his eyes. '*If* he finds out,' I find myself adding, watching as his

281

expression turns wary. 'It's not like I *have* to tell him,' I finish, staring at him defiantly.

He holds my gaze for a long few seconds and then suddenly he's on his feet. I involuntarily step backwards, my knees hitting the foot of the bed as he walks towards me.

'Don't,' I whisper when he reaches me, his body almost flush with mine as he stares down at me. He's not touching me, but I can feel the body heat spilling from him like a radiator.

'I broke up with Eve because of you,' he says in a low voice.

Did he?

'Tell him,' he continues. 'No, don't just tell him. Break up with him.'

He's too close; it's muddling my brain.

'I want you,' he whispers, his hand coming up to almost cup my face, but he's centimetres away from touching me.

'You only want me when you can't have me—'

And then his lips are on mine, his hands in my hair. I stiffen for only a moment before my body takes over and I kiss him back, my willpower shot.

I am cheating on Tom… I am cheating on Tom… My head says this on repeat, but still I can't stop.

I've already cheated on him, anyway, the devil on my shoulder calmly points out. The damage is done, and oh… God… We fall onto the bed and my legs wrap round him. His kisses become more frenzied and hungry and I match him, kiss for kiss. I can't get enough of him. I've never been able to get enough of him. I'm completely out of control here, and I don't care. I like it.

He tears his lips away on a gasp, pressing his forehead to mine and panting slightly. 'Jessie,' he murmurs against my mouth.

282

This is the point where I should push him away, I realise. But I don't. I don't want to. I tilt my face up to his and he kisses me again, more slowly. I slide my hands up inside his top and across the toned skin of his stomach. His chest muscles ripple under my fingers as I trace the lines of his ribcage. He breathes in sharply, and then he rolls onto his back and pulls me on top of him. He places his hands on my hips, his thumbs circling my hip bones. I rock against him slightly and his lips fall open, a small murmur escaping. My PJs are flimsy and his jeans are rough and it feels dizzyingly good. A shiver ripples through me as he slides his hands up inside my top and skims them over my curves, and still I want more.

He grabs my face and draws me towards him, kissing me urgently, heatedly, and then suddenly he breaks away and, with an agonising look, he slides me off him.

He's still breathing heavily, but he doesn't make any move to touch me again.

What is he doing? Why is he stopping? What's happening?

He props himself up on his elbow and peers across at me. 'Sorry,' he whispers.

I feel instantly cold. I don't understand. I stare up at him with bewilderment that swiftly transforms into mortification. Has he gone off me because I'm too easy? A chill seeps into my bones and I feel like there's a block of ice in my stomach.

'Wait!' he says suddenly. 'No!' His hand comes down to my chest, holding me in place on the mattress. I was about to bolt. 'I only stopped because…' He looks torn. 'I didn't want to stop,' he corrects himself. 'Don't go,' he pleads.

I stare at him warily and a moment later he moves to kiss me, hesitating to check I'm OK with it before lowering his mouth to mine. This time he kisses me tenderly, surprisingly tenderly. I

283

didn't even think Jack was capable of kissing like this. To my surprise, my throat swells and my eyes sting with tears. This is all so confusing.

'I want to be with you,' he whispers.

I try to swallow the lump in my throat, but it's going nowhere.

'Break up with him,' he says. 'Please.'

I squeeze my eyes shut, but the tears spill out, anyway. A moment later I nod. He sighs heavily and draws my body against his, holding me in the darkness.

In the early hours of the morning, I'm shaken awake.

'Agnes?' I ask, putting my hand out. It lands on Jack beside me. He's completely still, but the room is moving and rumbling. I feel like I'm underwater. Am I dreaming?

Jack jerks awake under my hand. 'Earthquake!' he says urgently.

I'm frozen as the room sways and the building – thirty floors of it – rumble and shake.

It's the longest ten seconds of my life.

'Is it over?' I ask him, as the ground seems to settle.

'I think so,' he replies, drawing me to him. I rest my face against his chest, feeling terror in my gut. We're on the seventeenth floor, and if the ceiling or the floors above us collapse we're dead.

'Have you been in an earthquake before?' I ask.

'Yeah. We get them in LA a lot.'

'How can you live like that?' I demand to know. I feel so safe in England where there's barely any threat of natural disasters.

'It's OK,' he says. 'These new buildings are made to withstand earthquakes,' he tries to reassure me.

I sit up in bed and look across at Agnes's bed. She didn't come back last night. Jack notices and quietly exhales.

'Did you know she was going to see Brett?' I ask him.

'I figured,' he replies in a monotone.

'Do you think they're making a mistake?'

'It's not for me to judge,' he says. 'Agnes was heartbroken when he left.'

'She's going to be even more heartbroken now,' I point out, perhaps unhelpfully because what's done is done.

He reaches up and tucks my hair behind my ear. I manage a small smile.

'What about your promise?' I ask.

It's dark, but I can still see him rolling his eyes.

'Brandon's going to go mental,' I point out.

'He'll get over it,' he replies.

There's a knock on the door. I flash Jack a wary glance and climb out of bed to answer it. I almost jump out of my skin when I see Johnny standing in the brightly-lit corridor.

'You OK?' he asks.

ARGH! Jack is in my bed!

'I'm fine.' I try to keep my voice steady as I shield my eyes from the brightness. I really hope he doesn't want to come in.

'Listen, chick, I don't want to worry you, but Lewis is concerned about aftershocks. He wants us to make a move now.'

'Now?'

'Can you get your things together in the next ten minutes?'

'Er, yeah, sure, but—'

'Great. We're flying home by helicopter.'

'Wait, what about everyone else? Agnes? Jack?'

'It's just a precaution, I promise,' he assures me.

I nod and close the door, switching on the light. There's no sign of Jack.

'Where are you?' I ask in a loud whisper.

He comes out from behind the curtains, squinting against the light.

I smirk at him.

'That was close,' he says. 'You're leaving?'

'Yeah, gotta get packed. You'd better go.'

He rubs at his eyes sleepily. I begin to shovel things into my case.

'Will you tell Agnes I'll call her as soon as I get home?'

'Sure,' he replies groggily.

'Thanks,' I murmur, hurrying into the bathroom to pack away my cosmetics. I start with surprise when I see him at the door, leaning against the door frame.

'Will you call me, too?' he asks.

I glance at him warily. 'Let me go home first, OK? Let me sort things out with Tom.'

He sighs heavily.

'It's over,' I say quietly. 'Just let me focus on doing the right thing now, OK?'

He nods and draws me into his arms. One last hug, and then I have to let him go, at least until I speak to Tom.

His thumb comes up and traces the faded line of my 'tattoo'. He bends down and presses his lips to it. His hair still smells of the ocean.

'Come on.' I gently push him away. If he starts kissing me again now, I'll never get packed in time. 'I'll see you soon,' I say meaningfully, returning to my cosmetics.

He rakes his hands through his hair and clamps them behind

his head, staring at me regretfully. He gives a tiny shake of his head.

'Jack!' I exclaim. 'Do I have to march you to the door?'

He shrugs slightly helplessly, but doesn't move, so I decide to do just that. I put my hand on the door handle, about to pull it open, but he stops me, spinning me round so my back is against the wall. His body traps me there and I have to crane my neck to look up at him, but he doesn't kiss me this time. I can feel his heart beating strong against my chest as he stares down at me with an intensity I've never seen before. My body softens towards him, but he doesn't make a move on me.

And then he walks out without a word, leaving my head reeling and my body cold.

One thing's for certain: Jack Mitchell is a very confusing boy.

Chapter 32

The plane touches down at Heathrow on a cold and rainy day, but after the earthquake I feel a strange sort of relief at arriving on stable ground.

I smile across at Sam in our First Class passenger seats. 'Here we are again,' I say to him.

'You better not give me any trouble this time, girl,' he warns.

'I promise,' I reply with a grin. I'm so glad he's the one to return with me, that his leg has healed.

The last week has been a whirlwind – even more than usual. Our gig got a few reviews in the music press and the hype about All Hype has stepped up a level. We've even been asked to do interviews with a couple of good publications, but that will have to wait until the New Year, when I'm back. I spoke to Jack, but he kept it professional, which was a little weird, but I had to remind myself that it was the way I asked for it to be, at least until I go back.

I did speak to Agnes, and she told me that 'it' hadn't happened.

She sounded a little sad, but she said that she'd fill me in when I got back. Brett is staying in America for a few more weeks, so she wanted to spend every spare moment she has with him. There'll be plenty of time for us to catch up when he leaves. I'm guessing she'll need a shoulder to cry on.

Johnny has arranged for a chauffeur to collect us from the airport, so I told Stu not to come. A little part of me still feels disappointed not to see him at the gate, even though it's a hassle to get to Heathrow.

He's meeting me at the Jeffersons' house in Henley. Despite my pleas, I'm not allowed to spend my Christmas holiday at home. But I am allowed to spend my days there, packing up my things.

And Mum's.

When we pull through the gates of Johnny's Henley mansion, there are several cars on the driveway, but my eyes are drawn only to the blue Volvo. Tom is here?!

Oh, no. I was hoping to have a bit more time before I had to tell him. I've somehow managed to avoid his calls all week, sticking only to texts, but I can't shy away from it any longer.

Before I can ask who the other cars belong to, the front door opens and Stu comes out, closely followed by Tom, the sight of whom sends a wave of nausea coursing through me. Then out comes Lou, Natalie, Chris and... *Libby*? A lump forms in my throat at the sight of my oldest friend and, in that moment, I know that I forgive her. God knows, we all make mistakes...

Except that what happened with Jack no longer feels like a mistake.

'Not happy to see your friends?' Sam asks with a sidelong

glance as my gaze settles on Tom, who's smiling warmly at the blacked-out car.

I sigh. 'Just not ready,' I reply, as the sickness inside me spreads like a disease.

I force a smile onto my face and try to fake delight as I climb out of the car. They all come forward to hug me, Lou and Natalie making excited comments about my outfit and how even my hair looks blonder and wow, I have a tan in December!

I turn to Libby and smile shyly.

'Hey,' I say.

'Hi,' she replies quietly.

And then I grab her and pull her into my arms, giving her the biggest hug. She squeezes me back, just as hard.

'Thank you for coming,' I whisper into her ear.

'Thank you for not telling me to leave,' she whispers back.

I give her one last squeeze and let her go.

Stu next. It's not like we used to hug much, but, now that I'm in his arms, he feels so wonderfully warm and familiar. Tears prick my eyes at the thought that soon I'll be leaving him permanently. I wonder if he'd consider coming with me. I'll have to ask him, I decide, and then he pats my back with finality and lets me go.

I find myself facing Tom. Like the traitor that I am, I've more or less managed to avoid looking into his eyes as he's patiently waited his turn, but now I have nowhere to run. He's here, in front of me, smiling down at me. His tan has faded, but he still looks lovely.

'Hi,' I say.

'Hey,' he replies, taking me in his arms and clasping me tightly.

The weirdest thought goes through my mind, then: I'm being unfaithful to Jack.

But that's ridiculous. I shake my head and pull away, smiling around at all of my friends. 'Shall we go inside?'

Stu takes me aside as everyone else piles into the living room.

'Was this a bad idea?' he asks me worriedly. 'They wanted to come.'

'It's fine,' I reply. 'It's great to see them all. I'm just tired, that's all.'

'I'm sorry, Jess, I should've asked you, but they wanted it to be a surprise.'

'Honestly, it's fine,' I try to reassure him.

But it's *not* fine. I feel so on edge around Tom. I had planned to go and see him at home, so I could tell him about Jack in private. As it is, I must put up a front and pretend everything's OK so that he's not humiliated in front of our friends.

I discover that Chris also got his driving licence while I was away, and the last car belongs to Stu. He's finally given in to Johnny's insistence that he replace his Fiat with something safer, so now he drives a grey Audi.

If I stayed, I'm sure my dad would pay for us to move into a nicer home, too. The thought doesn't sit comfortably with me.

'Listen, guys,' Stu says after a while, 'Jess is exhausted after her long flight, so how about we let her get some rest now and you can all catch up this week, yes?'

Everyone agrees, but I can't meet Tom's eyes as he stands up.

He hangs back until the others have left the room.

'Are you OK?' he asks me quietly.

'Just a bit tired,' I lie.

'It's more than that,' he says, and I force myself to look at him.

291

His eyes widen at the expression on my face. I'm not denying it.

'You're worrying me,' he says warily.

'We do need to talk,' I reply quietly, glancing towards the door and the hall where everyone's milling around, waiting to say goodbye. 'But not n—'

'If you've got something to say to me, I don't want to wait to hear it,' he cuts me off. 'I'll tell Chris to take them home,' he adds decisively, going out into the hall. I follow him, feeling absolutely sick to my stomach.

'Mate, can you take the others home?' Tom asks, his voice wavering so slightly that I'm certain I'm the only one who can tell.

'Sure,' Chris replies with a grin, hooking his arm round Lou. Despite how bad I feel, I'm glad that they're still going strong.

I give Natalie and Lou brief hugs, promising to call in a day or two, then turn to face Libby, who's hanging back.

'Are you around this week?' I ask. 'It'd be good to catch up properly.'

'I'd love that,' she replies warmly, and I can see that she's fighting back tears.

We give each other another hard hug and then break away.

I really hope that we can be good friends again. We've been through too much to give up on each other now. The kidnapping stuff freaked me out, but it wasn't her fault. Life's too short to bear grudges, I've learnt. But I doubt Tom will see things like that…

I stand at the door and wave them off, then turn to Stu, horribly aware of the tension radiating from Tom as he waits for me to come clean.

'Tom's going to stay for a bit,' I say. 'We'll go up to my room.'

'Oh! OK,' he replies with surprise. I think he thought he was coming to my rescue by sending everyone home. 'Sure. We'll chat later, then.'

I flash him an apologetic smile. He'll have me for the rest of the week. It's not like Tom will want anything more to do with me after this.

I lead the way upstairs, feeling like I'm walking into court, about to be sentenced. But I haven't even made my case yet.

Maybe he'll forgive me... Maybe. But do I want him to?

We go into my bedroom, my heart beating fast as he shuts the door behind us, and then the space suddenly feels too small. I can't actually believe I'm going to do this.

I perch on the bed and stare up at him with regret. He doesn't come to sit down next to me.

'What have you done?' he asks in a low voice.

'I—' The words don't come easily.

'Is it Jack?' he asks.

Of course he knows. He's not stupid. He probably has a sixth sense about stuff like this after what his last girlfriend did to him.

But how could I? How could I do what I did to lovely, gorgeous, hottest-boy-in-school Tom? Tom who really seems to love me? Tom whom I love? Don't I?

My throat constricts, but I nod, my gaze falling to the floor. But I force myself to look at him.

'What happened?' he asks in a strangely subdued voice.

'He kissed me,' I reply quietly.

His expression doesn't change. 'He kissed you? Was that it?'

I try to swallow, but my mouth is too dry. 'I kissed him back,' I admit.

It happens so quickly that I don't know if he fell or moved on

293

purpose, but suddenly he's kneeling in front of me, his face in his hands in a gesture of absolute despair.

'I'm so sorry,' I whimper. 'I'm so sorry.'

He drags his hands away from his face and stares at me, his warm brown eyes glinting with tears, his face pale, his mouth stretched into a straight line. He looks a mess. I've done this to him.

He shakes his head at me, speechless.

'I'm so sorry,' I say again.

'Are you in love with him?' he asks.

'I—' I start to speak, but shut my mouth abruptly. I shake my head, but I can't honestly answer with a no.

Suddenly he's on his feet again, pacing the room. 'I knew it!' he says heatedly, pointing at me. 'I knew it!' He knocks his knuckles against his head, then comes to a sudden standstill, glaring down at me.

'You know this is it, don't you?' he asks angrily. 'This. Is. It.'

I nod miserably. 'I know,' I mumble. 'I know you don't go back. You don't forgive. I know.'

'You're not even asking for my forgiveness,' he says bitterly. 'What the hell is wrong with me?' he erupts. 'First Isla, now you. Don't I deserve to have a girl *not* cheat on me?'

I leap to my feet. 'Tom, of course you do! I'm so sorry! I love you, I do. I don't know how it happened. I wasn't thinking—' I realise I'm standing in front of him with my hand on his chest and he's not moving away. A distant part of me asks what I'm doing. Am I trying to win him back? Do I want to be with him? With him and not Jack?

Jack is unreliable. Tom is on the other side of the world.

Unless I stay here.

I don't have to go back to LA. I have to move out of my home, anyway, so I could stay here and live in England – even in Johnny's house, until Stu and I find a home of our own. I could get used to having Sam or another bodyguard watching over me. It's not so bad. I could still see my friends, I could probably convince Johnny to let me continue going to the same school. I don't have to go to private school, but even if I did it wouldn't be so different to going to school with Agnes. I'd still have to make new friends.

Or I could stick with my plan. Pack up my things, pack up my life. Say goodbye to my friends and see them occasionally on holidays. Go back to LA. Live with my dad and Meg, my two little brothers.

'I'll see you guys soon, OK?'

That's what I said to Barney and Phoenix.

'When will you be home?' Barney asked, his little face crumpling.

'In a week,' I said.

'You promise?' he asked.

'I promise.'

Home... Really?

I let my hand drop from Tom's chest and take a step backwards.

He stares down at me. 'So that's it?' he asks flatly. 'Are we done?'

I bite my lip until I draw blood, and then I nod.

He doesn't say another word as he walks out of the door.

295

Chapter 33

To say it's been a shit holiday is an understatement. I've been absolutely miserable for days. I've been dismal company for all of my friends. Stu is sick of seeing my moping face and I went to see Gramps yesterday and even he told me to cheer the hell up.

Now it's Christmas day and I couldn't feel worse.

It's our first Christmas without Mum, and Stu and I sit at the table together, eating a turkey cooked by Johnny's lovely part-time cook who popped by last night with instructions on how to heat it up.

We're in Johnny's large formal dining room. Expensive art hangs from the panelled, polished wooden walls and I couldn't feel further from home and the silly, small, so-called dining room that we rarely ate meals in.

The roast in front of me looks delicious, but my taste buds are dead and I can barely eat a thing. Stu seems just as glum. We couldn't even be bothered to pull our crackers earlier.

I should've let him go to see his parents. I should've

stayed in LA. I imagine he'll be glad to see the back of me.

'This is ridiculous,' he snaps finally, picking up his plate. 'Let's at least go and eat in front of the telly.'

I smile weakly and take my plate, following him into the living room. He switches on the telly and we sit there next to each other on the sofa with our dinners balancing on our knees.

'Don't be too down, Jess,' he says after a while. 'It'll all come out in the wash.'

I told him Tom and I had broken up. And we have. There's no going back. I haven't heard from him and I haven't tried contacting him, either. It's over. I just want to go back to LA again and be surrounded by warmth and family and shiny new friends.

No. I've been there before, kicking out the old and replacing it with the new because it was less painful to think about what I'd lost. I have to be stronger this time. I have to think it through, not just run away.

'Would you consider coming with me?' I ask Stu, in a tiny, tentative voice.

He gives me a startled sideways look. 'What, to LA?'

I nod hopefully, but his brow furrows with regret and he shakes his head as he speaks. 'Oh, no, Jess, no, I couldn't.'

'Why not?' I murmur.

'This is my home,' he says sadly, putting his plate down on the floor and swivelling to face me. 'I wouldn't feel right living over there, starting anew. And my parents are here. They're getting old. They need me right now. You've got a brand-new family now. You don't need me.'

'I *do*,' I state vehemently, hot tears pricking my eyes. 'I'll always need you.'

'And I'll always be here. You know that, right?'

I nod, my vision turning blurry.

'If it doesn't work out,' he says kindly, 'or if you just change your mind, you can always come back. You will always have a place with me.'

A few tears roll down my cheeks and I nod, brushing them away. 'Thank you,' I whisper.

'Come here,' he says, taking my plate away and putting his arms round me. We hug each other tightly.

'You'll be OK,' he says after a while.

I take a deep breath and pull back to look at him. 'Stu,' I say.

'Yeah?'

My bottom lip starts to wobble. 'I want to go home.'

His face falls. 'Oh, Jessie, no. Not today. Not on Christmas Day. We can deal with it later.'

'Stu, all her stuff has been sitting there for almost a whole year. I want to be with her. I want to go home. There's never going to be a good time. And, let's face it, today's been pretty shitty, anyway.'

He rubs at his eyes and sighs before glancing at me and nodding reluctantly.

Our home is dark and quiet. There are no Christmas lights on in the front window, no merry chatter coming from inside like our neighbours' houses. Stu unlocks the door. Sam is waiting in the car, having already spent most of today in the guardhouse, clearly choosing British telly over our company. Can't say I blame him.

The familiar smell overwhelms me again. The living room is dark, but there's no Christmas tree in the corner. For a moment, I can picture one, a small, spindly pine tree covered with tinsel, and my mum kneeling in front of it, her dark, wavy hair spilling down her back as she hooks another gaudy decoration onto the branches. She looks over her shoulder and smiles at me.

I choke back a sob as I run up the stairs and burst into the spare room.

Stu lets me go.

Her clothes are everywhere, still piled up exactly as I left them across all the surfaces. I go to the dressing table and open up a shoebox to discover it's full of her jewellery. I lift out a chunky gold necklace and my brain shows me a memory of her holding it against her neck in Topshop, asking my opinion. I told her to get it, knowing I'd borrow it later. I still haven't.

I open another shoebox and find her make-up. I lift out her perfume and press the nozzle to my nose, breathing it in. Tears spring up in my eyes and I can't hold back. I start to sob.

'Hey,' Stu says, appearing at the door, his own eyes red from crying. 'Come on.'

He opens up his arms to me and I crash into them. He holds me while I sob whole-body-wracking sobs, and then, unable to hold back, he begins to cry, too.

'Let's do this together,' he says in a croaky voice, once we've cried ourselves out. 'It'll be easier.'

I sniff and nod.

He goes to the bed and lifts up a red dress.

'Do you remember when she wore this to that awful school nativity the Year Eights put on? Mr Hillman couldn't stop staring at her legs.'

I laugh. The headmaster had definitely looked flustered.

I reach for another garment, a mustard-yellow dress. 'What about this one? She wore this to Marilyn's fortieth birthday.'

Marilyn is Libby's mum. 'I told her she looked like a canary.'

Stu laughs. 'She thought that was funny, you know. She never could wear yellow, but it was her favourite colour on you.'

A fresh wave of tears begins to cascade down my cheeks.

'You should keep it,' he says in a choked voice.

I nod quickly and take the dress, folding it up and putting it on the window sill.

We go on like this, laughing and crying, but eventually we get through the mountain of clothes that used to belong to Candy, a one-time rock chick and mother. Wife. Friend.

At the end of the day, the only things not in the black plastic bags for the charity shop are her wedding dress, some of her jewellery and a couple of dresses that I might want to wear someday. I'm also keeping her perfume.

I turn to give Stu a hug when it's all done. 'Thank you,' I say into his shoulder.

He holds me tightly, but this time he doesn't cry and, after a few shaky breaths, I realise I'm not going to, either.

'I love you, Stu,' I blurt out.

'I love you, too, Jessie. Always will.'

'Will you come to visit us in LA soon?' I ask, pulling away.

'Of course,' he replies. 'Hey, how about you arrange your next gig for half-term so I can come and watch it?' He looks down at me expectantly.

My thoughts dart to Jack and All Hype, and I wish I knew how everything was going to pan out. But I don't. All I can do is go with the flow and pray that there are no more natural disasters to worry about, I think with a rueful grin.

'I'll see what I can do,' I promise.

Chapter 34

'You have to come!' Agnes begs. 'It's LOTTIE'S NEW YEAR'S EVE PARTY!' she practically shouts down the phone.

'I don't feel like celebrating. I'm sorry.'

'I know you've only just got back and you're jet-lagged, but YOU CAN SLEEP TOMORROW!'

'Agnes, keep it down! You're hurting my ear!'

'Jack's going,' she says significantly.

'I know. He told me.'

'Did he call?' she asks with surprise.

'No, he texted. I said I'd see him soon. When I'm ready,' I add.

'Oh, come on!' she begs.

'I'll see you next week,' I promise, ending the call and returning to the kitchen where my family is eating dinner.

'Are you sure you don't want to go?' Meg asks carefully. 'We're finished here and the boys will be in bed soon.'

'Awww!' Barney moans. 'Can't we stay up?'

'You're already up later than normal,' she chides. 'Phee is falling asleep in his chair.'

I glance at my littlest brother in time to see his eyes close and his head jerk forward.

'Oh, God, that is so cute,' I can't help squealing and he jerks his head backwards again and looks around with confusion.

'Please, Daddy?' Barney asks, hopping down from the table.

'No, sorry, buddy. Bedtime.'

Barney moans again and grabs Johnny's leg, sliding down it to sit on his foot. Johnny kicks his leg up and Bee giggles hysterically. This wakes Phoenix up good and proper and his eyes light up.

'Da, da, da!' he says, holding his chubby little arms out.

I laugh and lift him out of his chair – he's grown so heavy! – and then Johnny takes turns with his sons on his feet while Meg rolls her eyes good-naturedly and moans about 'never getting them to sleep now'.

She reaches for the bottle of champagne in the ice bucket and pours me another glass. I sit back down and we chink glasses.

'Happy New Year,' she says. 'It's good to have you home.'

I take a sip, feeling surreal that she just said 'home'.

'What are you thinking?' she asks quietly, but still loudly enough for me to hear her over the mayhem in the background.

'About where home is,' I reply.

'I hope that this starts to feel like it,' she says gently. 'We should get your room sorted out. I can help you if you like, when all your things arrive. But we should also go shopping for a few more items of furniture, inject some colour into the White Room.'

I smile at her. 'That would be really nice.'

She reaches across and squeezes my hand. 'And of course you've got your birthday coming up.'

Her eyes are sympathetic and kind. She knows it's the anniversary of Mum's death.

'I doubt I'll feel like celebrating,' I say.

'That's exactly why you should celebrate,' she replies steadily.

'Celebrate what?' Johnny asks, pausing in his playing to look over at us.

'Jessie's sixteenth birthday,' Meg replies.

'Aah, sixteen,' he says gruffly. 'Sweet sixteen.' He grins at me. 'I suppose you'll be wanting a car?'

I sit up straight in my chair, my eyes lighting up. 'Are you kidding?'

'Here we go,' Meg jokes. 'Any excuse to go car shopping.'

'What sort would you like?' Johnny asks me.

I shake my head, totally distracted from all dark thoughts. 'I have no idea.'

'GTI? Audi A3? Both good starter cars,' he muses.

Jack has an Audi…

Both the boys are clambering around Johnny's feet, but when he tells them to cut it out they start to cry.

'Right, that's it, time for bed,' Meg says resolutely, standing up.

'I'll go,' Johnny says. 'You stay there.'

'Ooh, OK,' Meg replies, raising her eyebrows at me and reaching for her glass of fizz.

I take another sip of my drink, the bubbles going straight to my head.

'It's not too late, you know,' Meg says. 'You could still go out.'

I shrug, then shake my head.

'Come on,' she says. 'You should! Agnes is dying to see you, and now you'll be going to school here you should get to know some of her other friends a bit better, too.'

'I don't want to drag Davey out again,' I reply, shaking my head. 'It's New Year's Eve – he's with his family.'

'Johnny will take you,' she says immediately.

I hesitate, and that's all it takes for her to push herself out from the table and go out of the door. She shouts up the stairs.

'Johnny! I'll take over. Can you give Jessie a lift to the Tremways'?'

He takes me on his motorcycle, just for fun. And it *is* fun now.

'Can I get a bike?' I ask him, as I climb off.

'When hell freezes over,' he replies, deadpan. 'What time do you want collecting?'

'Can't I just grab a cab?'

He shakes his head determinedly. 'I'll come back for you. Will one o'clock be OK?' he asks.

'One a.m.?' I check with surprise. 'That late? Are you sure?'

He grins. 'That's early.' He flips his visor back down and shouts at me to have fun, before roaring off back down the driveway.

I turn and look around. This time the red lanterns and pumpkins from Lottie's Halloween party have been replaced with thousands of fairy lights dripping from the trees and icicle lights draped from the eaves of the log cabin. There are three fire pits set further away from the house, with people lounging in deckchairs around them. Music is blaring from the speakers and I nervously round the corner to see dozens of people already dancing, and others holding glasses of something red with clouds of steam rising from it. Mulled wine?

304

I texted Agnes to let her know I was coming, but she didn't reply so I'm not sure she got it.

My head, earlier fuzzy with champagne, has been cleared by the ride here, and suddenly I'm not sure I should've come.

No one has noticed me yet.

I scan the crowd, looking for someone I know. I can't see Agnes anywhere and my mind is swirling with doubt.

I catch the eye of a boy with blond hair and his face lights up. Peter, the actor from Lottie's show. He waves at me, so I go over to say hi. He gets up from his seat and kisses my cheek.

'Hey, happy New Year!' he exclaims, seeming genuinely pleased to see me.

'You too! Have you seen Agnes?'

'She's here somewhere,' he replies, looking around. 'Here with some guy. Australian, I think he said.'

'Brett?'

'That's it.'

'Is Jack here?' I ask nervously, suddenly really desperately wanting him to be.

'I think he's DJ'ing,' Peter replies. My heart flips and I touch his arm and back away, telling him I'll chat to him later.

I walk round the corner, past the speakers, until the decks appear in view, and there he is: in full concentration mode with his headphones on, his hand spinning the records.

My heart flutters as I watch him mash up Cypress Hill's '(Rock) Superstar' and Oasis's 'Live Forever'.

He is so freaking talented, I think as my heart expands.

Unable to stop myself, I nod along to the music, but don't make any move towards him. I don't want to distract him.

I'm a bit out of sight here from the rest of the party, hidden

305

by the huge speakers. My ears are going to ache tomorrow, though.

'Oh my God, *Jessie?*'

I spin on my heel to see Agnes standing in front of me, her eyes wide with surprise. 'Peter just told me you were here!' she cries, throwing her arms round me.

'I decided to come after all!' I shout into her ear.

'I'm so happy to see you!' she exclaims, and the feeling is very mutual. 'Does Jack know you're here yet?' she asks, looking past me.

'No,' I reply, glancing over my shoulder at her brother.

'He does now,' Agnes says mischievously, as Jack spots us talking. His eyes widen with shock.

I smile at him and he goes to take his headphones off, but I shake my head and point at the decks, not wanting him to get distracted. He nods and hesitantly adjusts his headphones, but he doesn't take his eyes from mine. Nor does he smile at me.

'Come get a drink,' Agnes urges, grabbing my hand and leading me towards the bar.

Lottie is there, flirting with Brandon, and, as usual, there's no sign of Maisie, his girlfriend. Some things never change.

Brandon sees me and gives me a huge hug. 'Jessie, Jessie!' he chants, clearly having had a few. I hug him back happily.

'It's our lead singer!' Miles shouts, spying us and coming over. I hug him, too, followed by Lottie.

'I hear your gig was amazing!' she exclaims. 'I'll have to come to your next one.'

'I'm lining it up at the moment,' Brandon says, as Agnes places a warm glass in my hand.

'Cheers! I'm so glad you're back!' she says.

I chink her glass and take a sip, and then two hands are touching my hips from behind and I spin round and come face to face with Jack Mitchell himself, his bluey-grey eyes staring uncertainly into mine.

'Hey,' he says, bending down to peck me on my cheek, not my lips, I notice. Nerves swirl round my stomach.

Then I remember that Brandon and Miles are here, and they don't know what's happened between us. Maybe he's being careful. Or maybe it's something else.

'I didn't know you were coming,' he says in my ear, standing closer to me than he perhaps should in front of our bandmates.

'Last-minute decision,' I reply, stepping back slightly.

I jump as his hand finds mine, and then he's pulling me with purpose across the crowded dance floor. He leads me round the back of the cabin where it's quieter and out of sight of everyone.

'Is everything OK?' he demands to know, and he's still not smiling at me.

'Everything's fine,' I reply, nodding. 'Are you OK?' I ask. 'You haven't got Susan or Eve or anyone here, have you?' Is that why he's acting strangely? Is he here with a girl? The thought makes me feel queasy.

He frowns. 'Of course not.'

A river of relief floods through me.

'What happened with Tom?' he asks.

'We broke up.'

He exhales loudly and his shoulders relax.

'You told him?' he checks, tensing again.

'Yes.' I nod and bite my lip.

'He called it off?' His eyebrows knit together.

307

'Actually, it was sort of mutual,' I reply.

He lets out a long sigh and then he gives a small smile, bringing his hand up to touch the side of my face.

'I missed you,' he murmurs.

'I was only gone a week,' I reply with amusement.

But he's done with small talk, taking my face in his rough hands and pressing his lips to mine.

My whole body tingles and my head feels like tiny little fireworks are exploding and fizzing inside it as his firm body traps me against the cabin wall.

A little voice inside my head tells me that it's not going to be smooth sailing, that we'll argue, we'll fall out, we'll piss off our bandmates and we probably won't last more than a few weeks.

But, then again, maybe we will.

Either way, at that precise moment, there's no place I'd rather be.

And so I kiss him back.

Tomorrow is a new year – and a new beginning.

TO BE CONTINUED…

Acknowledgements

Thank you first, foremost and always to my readers. Your online reviews and social media interactions mean the world to me, and I'm so grateful to all of the lovely people who took the time to post about *The Accidental Life of Jessie Jefferson*. I hope you enjoyed this sequel just as much! P.S. I can't wait to get started on writing Book 3...

If you're a new reader, I'd also love to know what *you* thought about Jessie and her adventures, so please drop me a line to say hi on Twitter **@PaigeToonAuthor, www.facebook.com/PaigeToonAuthor** or **Wattpad.com/PaigeToonAuthor**.

Thank you to my YA agent, Veronique Baxter from David Higham, my editors, Jane Griffiths and Rachel Mann, and also my adult editor Suzanne Baboneau – it is a pleasure working with all of you and indeed the entire team at Simon & Schuster. Thanks also to Jane Tait for her excellent copy editing skills and to Kat Gordon for proof reading.

Heartfelt thanks to Chris England and the English students at

Altwood School in Maidenhead, Berkshire. I spent many happy years at Altwood under the tutelage of Mr England – by far my favourite teacher, English or otherwise – and it was a pleasure to recently visit the school and see so many students still benefitting from his teaching. The students I met blew me away with their writing talent – I won't be at all surprised to see their work appearing on bookshop shelves at some point in the future.

Thanks to Mark Frith, my former boss and editor of *Heat* magazine, who I know I can always count on to answer celebrity and paparazzi-related questions!

Thanks to Jessica Hanak, Eleanor Fraser & Nicole Gross from Apple iBooks, for not only inviting me to the iTunes Festival, but letting me see behind the scenes. You helped bring Jessie's world to life! And thanks to my pal Katharine Park for coming with me and whispering ideas in my ear as we were watching the concert – what a fun night that was…

Thank you to Abbey Robertson for her help with school timetables and to Jen Hayes for letting me run some Americanisms by her, and thank you always to my friend and fellow author Ali Harris for encouraging me to write a book for young adults in the first place. Without you, Jessie might not exist!

Finally, thank you always to my parents, Vern and Jen Schuppan for always encouraging and supporting me, and my adorable little family of Toons: my husband Greg who helps me in more ways than it would ever be possible to mention, and to my children Indy and Idha who make me smile every day. I love you all so very much.

A final note from Paige

Although *I Knew You Were Trouble* is only my second book for young adults, I've been writing for a few years now and it is a pretty well-known fact that I have some of the loveliest, most passionate, loyal readers in the business.

I decided I wanted to give something back to say thank you for all of your support, so last year I launched *The Hidden Paige*, a unique new book club.

It works like this: people sign up for free at paigetoon.com, and every so often, I send out an email to all of my members. You might hear from me every couple of months or just when I have something to say that I think you might like to hear, but usually these emails will include a short story of some kind.

Many of my books are linked to each other – in fact, Meg and Johnny have already featured in their own stories: *Johnny Be Good*, *Baby Be Mine* and ebook short *Johnny's Girl*. I kind of like to think of my characters as all living in some sort of weird

311

Parallel Tooniverse and *The Hidden Paige* gives me an excuse to drop in on them from time to time!

So, recently I wrote a snippet of *Johnny's Girl* told from Johnny Jefferson's perspective, and my publisher has very kindly agreed to print it here for anyone who missed out.

This scene takes place straight after Johnny's solicitor has broken the news to Johnny about Jessie – the daughter he never knew he had. Now Johnny has to tell Meg. I hope you enjoy!

#thehiddenpaige

www.paigetoon.com

Lots of love,
Paige
Toon x

When Johnny Told Meg
About Jessie...

'I'll call you as soon as I know more,' Wendel says.

'Fine,' I reply, terminating our conversation and dropping the phone onto my desk with a clatter. I rest my elbows on the polished surface and stare in a daze at the dark computer screen in front of me. My solicitor has just told me that I have a teenage daughter. Allegedly.

How am I going to break this to Meg?

I rake my hands halfway through my hair and apply pressure to my skull with my fingers. She's going to go absolutely mental.

'Johnny?' I jolt at the sound of Annie's voice and turn to see my PA standing in the office doorway. She looks worried. 'Is everything okay? Davey's on the drive if you want him to take you to the party? Or will you go by bike?'

'What's the time?' I ask dully.

'Ten-thirty.'

313

Christ, I'm late. 'Better take the Merc,' I reply with a heavy sigh as I get to my feet.

My Ducati would be quicker, but I'll be bringing Meg home with me and the bike can stress her out. I'm going to be doing enough of that as it is.

'Is there anything I can do?' Annie asks, taking a step backwards to let me pass.

'Ring Wendel. He'll fill you in. And let Davey know I'll be outside in ten,' I say over my shoulder.

'You got it,' she calls after me.

Annie doesn't normally work this late, but she's babysitting the boys tonight. Kitty persuaded Meg to go to a film premiere and I've been in the studio all day with Mikky, my producer. I only got home a few minutes before Wendel called.

I go upstairs to our bedroom and turn on the shower in the en-suite before emptying the contents of my pockets onto the bed. I notice that a text message from Meg has come in, asking me what time I'll be there. I don't reply because she'll see me soon enough. And then she'll wish I'd stayed away.

Davey has worked for me for years, so he knows when I'm not in the mood to talk. Once I'm inside the car, he leaves the screen up and the intercom set to private. It's not far to Chateau Marmont, where the premiere after-party is taking place. I know it well – it used to be one of my regular hangouts – but I can't say I'm in any rush to face the missus. My head is all over the place as I stare out of the darkened limo windows at LA, lit up like a Christmas tree in the valley far below. I feel like there's a tiny person inside my stomach, tying my intestines into a giant ball of knots.

314

When we're nearing West Hollywood, my phone vibrates against my thigh. I dig it out of my pocket and tense at the sight of Nutmeg's name on the caller I.D.

The device carries on buzzing in the palm of my hand, but I can't bring myself to answer. I feel paralysed. Paralysed with fear. What can I say? I hope I figure it out when I see her, because I haven't got a freaking clue at the moment.

Her call goes through to voicemail, and at that moment, I totally despise myself. I'm such a coward. I suddenly have an overwhelming urge to drown my sorrows in a bottle of whisky.

No.

I've been clean for almost two and a half years and I'm not going to screw it up now. A fag wouldn't go amiss, but I've quit smoking, too, goddammit. When Meg was pregnant with Phoenix she refused to kiss me because my breath made her queasy. That was incentive enough. It killed me not to kiss her. She's the love of my life.

I wonder if she drank the champagne I arranged for her. She avoids alcohol when she's around me, but I really wanted her to indulge herself tonight. She's barely gone out since she had our little boys.

Curious more than anything, I lean forward to open the mini-fridge, and sure enough, there's a half-empty bottle of Perrier-Jouët Rosé inside. I'm happy for her, but then my demons are back and I'm fighting a fresh urge to take a swig. Steeling myself, I swing the fridge door shut and slump into my seat.

What is my brown-eyed girl going to think of me? I feel downright nauseous. I love her so much. The thought of hurting her hurts *me*. She's *got* to forgive me for this. But I know it's one of her worst nightmares come true. She's always been worried that, one day, one of my groupies will come forward and say I'm the father of their child. I've been careful over the years, but clearly not careful enough. Nowhere near freaking careful enough.

For a moment, my mind is filled with memories of Candy, the girl in question. She was only seventeen when we hooked up – and that was about seventeen years ago. I can picture her laughing, her long dark hair damp with sweat as she's bandied about in the moshpit. I remember her being at the front when we did our slow number, and I can see her looking up at me with those big, caramel-coloured eyes of hers.

I saw her at the next concert, and the next, and the next… I wanted her, but she didn't give herself to me easily, which surprised me. She certainly got my attention.

I've thought about her a little over the years. She wasn't like so many of the others. I wouldn't recognise most of them if I saw them on the street, but Candice, I remember. I liked her. I liked her a lot. So I did what I always did and dicked her around when she tried to get closer to me.

I can't believe she's dead. Out of the blue, grief hits me like a wall. She was killed a few months ago, when a loose window fell on her from a four-storey height. She was casually walking along the pavement…

What a terrible way to go. And she left behind an only child, a girl called Jessica, or Jessie, as she apparently likes to be known. Candy died on the exact day of Jessie's fifteenth birthday.

My chest feels constricted. *I have a daughter!* And she was completely clueless about me until a few days ago. Her stepdad thought it was time she knew the truth. He was the one who contacted Wendel.

How could Candy have kept this to herself all these years?

She had a baby girl – *my* baby girl – and she didn't see fit to tell me?

So many emotions are swirling around inside me. I don't know what to think.

My phone buzzes again – once – snapping me out of my thoughts. I have a voicemail – from Meg, at a guess. I put my phone up to my ear and listen.

'Where the hell are you?'

Uh-oh, she's angry with me.

'Dana is here and I could really do with your support.'

Damn, my ex-girlfriend is there? She'd better not be harassing my Nutmeg…

'I'm about to go and say hi to Joseph Strike…'

WHAT?!

'…so get your arse here ASAP.'

She ends the call.

What the…?! Jealousy swiftly snakes its way into the emotions already wreaking havoc on my gut. Joseph Strike? *Really*, Nutmeg? If I get there and see her cosying up to that actor bastard, I'll go mad.

And then I remember what I have to tell her, and my boiling blood cools to Arctic temperatures.

She might have had a fling with him once, but she's not interested in him anymore, I tell myself, as the rational part of my brain kicks in. She's just upset about Dana. I put Meg through enough shit over my drug-addict ex-girlfriend to last a lifetime. It's no wonder she's freaking out.

Needing a diversion, I press the button to bring the privacy screen down. I chat to Davey for the rest of the journey.

*

We arrive soon afterwards, and pull up right outside the venue. Davey opens the car door to clicks and flashes from the cameras of dozens of waiting paps. I can't be arsed to deal with the wolves tonight, so I ignore their shouts and head straight for the entrance. The party is in full swing and I can feel eyes on me as I make my way through the crowds, searching for my girl. A few people I know try to stop me, but I brush them off.

'I can't talk right now,' I tell them, one after the other. 'I'm looking for Meg. Have you seen her?'

When I find her, she's standing near Kitty on the other side of the terrace. She looks so beautiful tonight, even more so than usual. She's wearing a black mini-dress over skinny black jeans and her blonde hair stands out against the dark outfit. I dig black on her. She appears happy, which is weird, considering the tone of her message, but at least she doesn't seem to be angry any more. Then she spots me and her eyes widen slightly, the small smile that was on her lips freezing in place. She says something to Kitty and begins walking towards me.

I keep getting stopped on my way over to her, which is damn annoying, but finally we reach each other.

'Hey,' she says.

'Hi.'

I bend down and kiss her, sliding my hand into her hair and holding her to my chest. God, I need her so much. I can't believe I'm about to crush her with my news.

She pulls away, looking up at me with a guarded expression on her face. 'Did you get my message?'

'Just now,' I reply, frowning as I remember the crap she was spewing about Joseph Strike. Did she talk to him? Is that why she was looking so pleased with herself? 'I was already on my way when you called,' I say, scanning the room. 'Where is he?' I ask when I fail to locate him.

'I think he's gone,' she tells me. She looks guilty, which gets my back up.

'Did you speak to him?' I know I sound jealous – I freaking *am* jealous – but I'm damned if I can help it.

She blushes. Great. That's a yes, then. I feel sick to my stomach.

'I said hi, yeah,' she replies defensively, staring up at me with defiant eyes. 'Have you seen Dana?' she asks in turn.

Bollocks. Forgot about her. I scan the room again and spy her pretty quickly, pausing for a second to check her over. Jeez, she looks a state. She's been using again. You just can't help some people.

'Mmm,' I belatedly reply to Meg's question, before dragging my eyes away from my crazy ex.

'Do you want to speak to her?' Meg asks, her voice wavering.

Aw, Nutmeg! My heart goes out to her. Of course I don't, baby.

'No,' I respond firmly, wanting to ease her pain. 'I have nothing to say to her.'

I lean down again and give Meg a tender kiss, and then a fresh bout of nerves pulses through me, reminding me of what I need to do. 'Can I take you home?' I ask in her ear.

She glances over her shoulder. 'Um… Kitty.'

'She looks fine to me,' I say. She's flirting with some dark-haired dude. 'I need to talk to you,' I add quietly, nerves washing over me again.

Her eyes dart up to look at me.

'What's wrong?' she demands, knowing instantly that *something* is.

319

'I'll tell you in the car,' I reply.

'Is it the boys?'

Jesus, I didn't mean to freak her out. 'No, no,' I quickly assure her, placing my hands on her shoulders. 'Everyone's fine.'

She still looks worried, and she should be.

We say goodbye to Kitty and the bloke she's with and get the hell out of there. Davey is still pulled up out the front, so we get in the limo quickly and he closes the door behind us. I return the privacy screen to its closed position and usher Meg to the back of the car. We sit side-by-side and I shift to face her, reaching for her hands.

You've just got to say it…

Okay, okay.

Okay.

I take a deep breath, but I can't look at her.

'Wendel called me,' I start.

'Right…' she replies uneasily.

I force myself to meet her wary brown eyes, but God, it hurts.

'Just tell me,' she encourages. She wants to know, now.

I push myself to continue, but as I speak, I can see the cogs of her brain whirring, ten to the dozen. 'Wendel spoke to a man earlier today, claiming to be the stepfather of a girl who is the daughter of one of my first fans. Her mother passed away recently. She never told her daughter who her real father was.'

I experience a pang as I watch her confusion transform into horror. She knows exactly where I'm going with this. I squeeze her hands tighter.

'I'm sorry,' I whisper, feeling like I could hurl at any given moment.

'Tell me everything,' she says flatly.

320

And so I bring her up to date, breaking into a cold sweat when I realise that her hands have gone limp in mine. She's looking pale by the time I finish.

'Do you remember her?' she whispers. 'Candy?'

I glance out the window and nod. 'Yeah, I remember her.'

'So it's true?' she says.

I swallow. Nothing is definite yet. Wendel wants Jessica – Jessie – to do a paternity test. Maybe Candy lied to Stuart, Jessie's stepdad, back then. Maybe I'm not the biological father. Maybe…

But no, I have a feeling about this. I shouldn't give Meg false hope.

'There's a chance that it is,' I reply.

'But… But… What if she slept with someone else?' It hurts to watch her clutching at straws. 'What if the girl isn't yours?'

'That's possible, of course. Wendel is arranging for a paternity test.'

To my dismay, she rips her hands away from me. I reach across to try to comfort her, but she shrugs me off. 'Don't touch me!' she yells, flinching away from me.

I cover my face with my hands. I feel like the walls of the incredible life we had are crashing down around me. It's all going to shit.

'Don't you feel sorry for yourself!' she shouts suddenly, making me jolt. 'I should have known this was going to happen when I married you!'

'But you *did* marry me!' I raise my voice at her, the anger masking my fear. 'For better or for worse!'

And then her face crumples and I pull her to me and hold her against my chest, telling her I'm sorry, over and over again.

'We'll know as early as next week,' I murmur, as she sniffs. 'It might be nothing to worry about.'

But even as I say it, I know it's not true. I have a strong feeling that a teenage girl called Jessie is about to become a permanent feature in our lives.

I wonder what she's like…